TEEN Screams

TEEN Screams

VOL 1

A YA Horror Anthology

Not Suitable for Children under 13 Years Old

Curated by Maryjane Hill

Dark Moon Rising Publications | Virginia

70 Foxwood Drive
Rocky Mount, Virginia 24151
Tel: (540) 257-2861

ISBN: 978-1-972596-03-6

10 9 8 7 6 5 4 3 2 1

Printed in the United States of America

CONTENTS

FLESH

by Megan Guilliams

It was right there, just underneath the skin… Something Rowdy couldn't put his fingers on, but he sure as shit wanted to. It was a pull, a desire of some kind, that made him different from the other boys at school. Something he wanted to take out and give to someone else. He couldn't live with it anymore. He just couldn't.

Raymond, AKA Rowdy Hooser, was a fourteen-year-old menace to society, or at least that's what the local knitting circle all whispered about during their Sunday brunch circles.

"I heard he was the one who put that dead cat in Mr. O'Neal's mailbox last week," Yolanda whispered to Doris Scranton as she pulled another hook knot at the end of her bathroom cozy.

"Well, that's not all I heard," Doris whispered back. The elderly lady was much less concerned about her abandoned baby blanket and more focused on the finger sandwich pinched between a chubby finger and wrinkled thumb.

"Don't leave me in suspense, Doris! What did you hear?" Yolanda asked as she inched closer towards the woman sharing the couch with her.

Doris Scranton and Yolanda Rojas were the newest members of the Miller City knitting crew. There were four of them in total now, ever since Essie had her accident. The two newcomers spent most of their time sitting on the little white couch in Lily's living room while Lily and her sister Rose opted for the two recliners facing each other.

Oftentimes, while Doris and Yolanda were talking, Doris couldn't help but wonder if the two sisters politely ignored the gossip or were just painfully hard of hearing. Either way, neither woman cared much.

"I heard Rowdy set fire to that old garbage can out behind the comic book store."

"Did anyone see him?" Yolanda asked. Sniffing the finger sandwich, Doris took a bite and shrugged her shoulders.

"Someone must have, or they wouldn't have said Rowdy did it." Literally, nothing the woman had just said had an ounce of truth to it. Everyone in town knew that Rowdy was the scapegoat for childhood shenanigans, and it didn't matter if he had a hand in it or not. If there was an incident, his name was almost always brought up.

There was a knock on the door. Before anyone else had a chance to see who was there, Lily had gotten to her feet, shuffling towards the sound of the raps.

Lily and Rose Henderson were women in their eighties and looked every bit of it. Doris and Yolanda might have been told which one was the older sister, but they'd long since forgotten. No one could tell just by looking. Lily was the smallest of the two, with long silver hair down to the center of her back, bright eyes that matched, and a thin mouth that barely spoke a single word.

"That must be the new landscaper. Pastor Walton said this boy was the best of the bunch." Rose craned her neck as she watched her sister pull on the doorknob. It took a few tries, but finally, Lily accomplished her mission. As soon as Doris and Yolanda set their eyes on the young man standing there on the porch, they both gasped in surprise. It was none other than Rowdy Hooser.

Looking down at his feet, the boy had shoved both his hands deep into the pockets of his dirty blue jeans. His hair was cut short, but even from a distance, anyone could tell it was filthy. In fact, everything about the boy was filthy. His road cone orange shirt had a brown stain across the front and a rip under the right armpit. His shoes were caked with mud, and Lily couldn't quite tell if the speckles of freckling on his arms were actually freckles or mud.

While the other ladies in the living room clutched their pearls, whispering back and forth with wide eyes, Lily simply smiled and shuffled out onto the front porch, pushing the door shut as she went.

"I'm so sorry for my friends. They tend to gossip. Of course, it's not the Christianly thing to do, so I find myself trying to ignore them. Rose, bless her soul, is hard of hearing, so I deeply doubt she's heard any of it." Lily laughed a little to herself and then grabbed her chest a little. There was a rattle as she breathed in heavily.

"Are you alright, ma'am?" Rowdy asked as she slipped a hand under her arm to steady her.

"You're too kind," Lily said breathlessly. "Please don't tell the others. I've been keeping my condition secret for the last few months. Wouldn't you know it? Never smoked a day in my life, and I still wound up with lung cancer." Rowdy gave the woman a worried look, and then his bottom chin quivered. "Oh! Don't feel bad for me, you young buck! I've had a good run! Eighty-three years. Some people don't get half that."

Sitting down in the rocking chair by the front door, Lily pointed out to the rose bushes that had been growing in between the white picket fence, separating her yard from the neighbor's. It would have been the neighbors if the house had been inhabited.

"That's Ellie's house there. You know, I always complained about her not hiring a gardener. She was so protective of those roses. Now, it seems like a shame to pull them all up… What with her passing and all. Pastor Walton said you could do it at a fair price." Rowdy nodded as he scratched his arm. He could feel it again, just under the surface. Hiding so well, right out there in the open. How could she not see it like the others? How could she not be repulsed by who he was?

"How about I get started out here, and you can get back to your friends?" Rowdy said with a half-hearted smile.

"There's a little tool shed out back if you need anything, and I'll come back out here closer to dinner with a sandwich and some lemonade. I wish I could do more, but we're on a budget." Rowdy continued to look down at his shoes but said nothing. Disappearing around the house, Lily heard the shed door open as Rowdy began his chores.

Every day, around a quarter to four, Raymond Hooser would come back to the Henderson house. He pruned and mowed, shaped bushes, and cleaned windows. Every evening at six-thirty, right before the end of his shift, Lily would give him a sandwich and a glass of lemonade. She couldn't help but notice he was always wearing the same thing, and he was always dirty.

Finally, on the last night, as Rowdy was about to put the gardening tools away for the final time, Lily shuffled out onto the front porch. She didn't bother shutting the door this time. Ever since the boy had been coming over to do yard work, Yolanda and Doris had made themselves scarce.

"Rowdy, I'd like to talk to you for a bit," Lily said with a smile.

"Did I do something wrong?" Rowdy asked as he approached the woman who had already made herself comfortable in the rocking chair.

"No, no, nothing like that. I thought, well, I noticed that you don't have many good clothes, and I've been going through my late husband's things. There are some awful nice slacks and dress shirts just sitting there collecting dust. Would you like them?" For the first time since the boy had arrived, Lily thought she saw the hint of a smile flicker across his face, but then it was gone as quickly as it had appeared.

"You don't have to do that." He replied with a sigh. "I'd just make a mess of them, and I'm sure they mean a whole lot to you."

"Nonsense!" Lily said as she waved a hand in the boy's direction. "Hector's been gone a good fifteen years now, and his things are taking up a ton of space." Suddenly, an odd expression crossed the woman's face as she covered her mouth. She began to cough. The fit lasted a good five minutes, and by the end of it, she had blood spatter on the sleeve of her nightshirt.

"It's getting worse, isn't it?" Rowdy asked with concern. Reluctantly, Lily nodded.

"They're giving me a month, maybe less." Slipping his arm under the woman's, he helped her to stand. Walking her to the door, he finally looked up. His intense brown eyes met her gray ones.

"Maybe I could go in and take a look at the clothes you want to give me. I could help you get settled in, and maybe if I find something to my liking, you'd be so kind as to let me take a shower. Not a lot of people know this, but I've been awarded the State and spend most of my time at the church. Walton allows me to sleep outside when it's warm... I don't like the orphanage much, and they don't seem to like me either." Lily's eyes began to water a little as she silently nodded.

"Oh, it's perfect!" Lily said as she clapped her hands. Rowdy had found a red button-down shirt and a pair of black slacks. Holding them up to his slender frame, Lily just knew they would fit him like a glove. Her sister, Rose, had wandered off to bed half an hour earlier, grumbling about allowing strangers into the house. Lily wondered if her sister had even noticed the boy the last few weeks coming and going, making the yard look marvelous. "Go take a shower and then come out here so I can see how it all fits. You're welcome to more if you like."

Going to the bathroom with his new clothes, Raymond shut the door behind him and looked in the mirror. For the first time in a long time, he could actually see it, moving and sliding just under the flesh. The thing he had wanted more than anything all those years before. If only he could put his fingers on it and pull it from inside of him. It had done what the woman had promised it would, but it had done it all too well, and now everyone could see what kind of monster he was, even if they weren't aware of it.

Disrobing, Rowdy slipped into the shower and washed off all the grime, blood, and soil from his skin. He couldn't remember the last time anyone had been this nice to him. Had anyone EVER been this nice to him? The hot water steamed up the room, the girlie soaps sending vapors of wild rose and jasmine around the bath, allowing Rowdy to relax more than he had in forever. After twenty minutes, when the water was beginning to get cold, the boy got out of the shower, toweled off, and got dressed. More than anything, he hoped he hadn't overstayed his welcome. With a sigh, he slipped on his muddy shoes and pulled open the bathroom door.

"LILY!" He yelped. The woman was lying on the floor. She was breathing, but barely. Small ringlets of blood had begun to fall from the corner of her mouth. Rushing to her side, he looked down, scooping the woman's head in his hands. Tears rimmed the corners of his eyes.

"Don't worry. It won't be long now, dear. I'm sorry. I thought I had more time." A million thoughts ran through the boy's mind. Could he? Would he? No! It wouldn't be right! But he couldn't let her die like that! Not when he had just met her. Lying her head back onto the floor, he ran back into the bathroom. Retrieving an old pocketknife, he came back.

"I don't want you to say anything; just listen to me. My name isn't Raymond Hooser. I'm not fourteen; that's just when she came to see me. I don't know who 'she' was, really, but I was sick like you. She gave me a gift, and now I'm going to give it to you because, well, I don't think I deserve it anymore." Getting down on one knee, Rowdy jammed the knife into his wrist, pulling down with all his might. The flesh from his inner arm peeled back like old cellophane, exposing blood, tendon, and something else. Dropping the knife, Rowdy reached into his arm and wrapped his fingers around the worm, pulling it with all his might. Finally, it popped loose, making a sickening suckling sound. "It eats what's ailing you. That means as long as you let it stay, the cancer can't get you, but there's a catch. Isn't there always a catch?"

Lily nodded as her eyes began to glaze over. Rowdy knew he didn't have a lot of time to explain, and he could already feel himself aging.

"You must bury yourself every night. You sleep underground. That's just the way it is, and every now and again, it will talk to you and ask you to do things. No matter what, Lily, you have to do them. It may not kill you, but it can make you wish it had." Using his wounded arm, Rowdy snatched the knife. Lifting it up, he jammed it into Lily's arm and shoved the worm inside.

~~~

Rose didn't know when she woke up that morning that everything would be different. Padding in her slippers from her room, she ventured down the hall and into her sister's.

"Lily?" Rubbing the sleep from her eyes, she frowned. The bed hadn't been slept in, and there was a suspicious red stain on the carpeted floor. "Lily? Where the hell are you?" Again, there was no answer. Finally, convinced her sister wasn't in the house, Rose ran toward the kitchen, grabbed the wall phone, ready to call 911, but then she stopped. Looking out of the window, she could see the back of a little girl's head. She was filthy, her arm was cut, and she was sitting beside a hole. There was something familiar about her… Something Rose couldn't quite place.

Opening the back door, she waddled out onto the grass, watching the girl from a distance.

"Little one, do you need help?" Startled by the voice, the little girl turned around, her intense gray eyes staring intently at Rose.
~~~

"It worked. I can't believe it worked," she said with astonishment. Getting to her feet, she looked down into the hole and frowned. "I can't believe he slept down there with me. All night, he slept."

"What are you talking about?" Rose asked as she walked towards the hole.

"He wanted to make sure she came to see me. She did. I think I was eleven. Does that mean I'll be this age forever? Oh, how I've forgotten what it's like not to feel pain! What a gift he's given me!" Clapping her hands, the little girl danced and swayed as she played with the hem of her oversized pajamas.

"What happened to your arm? I think we should call..." Suddenly, Doris stopped talking as she made it to the hole and looked inside. Four feet down, lying on its side, was the skeleton of a young man wearing a red button-up shirt and black slacks.

BLOOD BOND

by Van Haney

Samantha screamed as she was rolled down the beige and white hallway. The stark greenish-white light made her squint as it ricocheted off the tile. It was an intense contrast to the darkness from seconds ago. Her eyes shut as another searing lightning bolt shot through her. Each electrical shock sucked the breath from her lungs. The noises thundering from her were beast-like. The torture subsided enough for her to realize this must be where the idea of possession came from. Childbirth. Her thoughts were again ripped from her as the pain welled up inside and burst through her abdomen.

"I found her outside on the asphalt. Her water had already broken." The nurse who pushed her down the hallway looked at a woman with a clipboard beside her.

Every few feet, the wonky wheel of the gurney squeaked. Like a rhythm, it matched her contractions. She felt like she was in her own dance club in the seventh circle of hell. A never-ending obnoxious trance beat, where the drop never came, just the pain.

Another nurse gently grabbed her arm. "Can you tell us your name? How many months are you?"

She opened her mouth to speak, but another jolt shocked the air out of her, and her mouth just opened and closed like a goldfish without water. She moaned.

"Take your time, breathe in slowly, and breathe out in spurts. Ffftt. Ffftt. Ffftt." The nurse tried to model the breathing she wanted to see.

"I can't have this baby!" Samantha gripped the nurse's arm with both hands. Her whole body spasmed toward the edge of the gurney. Eyes bloodshot.

The nurse leaned into her face, speaking in a calm, even tone. "Honey, this baby is coming whether you want it to or not."

Samantha screamed. "Then, I need a hysterectomy!"

She felt a pop from her vagina. The gooey cork shot out, followed by a tidal wave of thick fluid. Blood burst from her and trickled over the side of the bed.

"Oh shit." The nurse pushed her faster.

"Get her into room four!" The nurse who had been by her side ran to the nurses' station to page a doctor.

"No, no, no, no…" Samantha just kept repeating herself as she rocked her body back and forth. Blood covered her dress. Her G-string felt more like a wet rag than underwear. Her legs swam against the cotton sheets as another bolt hit her. She tried to gain traction in an attempt to push herself into the mattress and away from the ripping agony.

She looked off down the hall as they turned into room four, and there he was. Toby stood at the end. His hands were in his jeans' pockets. He was wearing his trademark black T-shirt that looked so neat and clean, like it had just been taken off the rack. His gaze met hers, and he smiled with his mouth, but not with his eyes. His lips said what his words didn't. He had promised he would come for her. She couldn't get rid of him forever, but ten months felt so long that he had almost seemed like a fever dream. One that had lasted her entire adolescence. One that pushed her to get pregnant at 18. One that ruined her family.

Toby had come into her life when she was thirteen. She remembered the day perfectly. During physical education, she was running 'the mile.' It happened twice a year and was the worst day of almost every middle schooler's life. You had to run, red and sweaty, like a stuck pig in front of everyone. Popular kids were always either super-fast or super-slow because they cared too much or too little, which meant they got to watch you as you ran every embarrassing lap. Samantha had been relatively invisible to the bitchy, popular crowd since starting school with them three years earlier. But today, karma pulled the rug out from under her, and her virginal floodgates opened just as she completed the first of four laps around the field. She was huffing and puffing and shuffling her feet so hard that she didn't notice as the blood trickled into her underwear and bruised her grey sweat shorts.

Finally, she finished her third lap and started to feel like she wouldn't vomit when she noticed the girls staring and snickering in the bleachers. Her already flushed face darkened further. She assumed they were laughing at how she was still running or maybe that she looked like a drowning cat as she flailed around the track. Then, she saw Toby. A kid she had never seen before. He looked a bit older, almost like high school age, and rolled his eyes as the popular girls cackled.

Seeing a cute boy watching made Samantha push harder. She passed a few kids as her legs spun in cartoon circles with little puffs of dust rising behind her. She crossed the finish line. Her breathing was ragged. She was sweaty, damp, and wet even. The girls were still staring. One pointed, and the others covered their mouths as they clucked back and forth on their little perch. Finally, a burst of laughter erupted from their clique, and one yelled out, "Hey, Sammy! You ran so hard your cooch is bleeding."

All the heat radiating from Samantha drained to a cold sweat as those words sank in. She looked down and saw the blossoming scarlet crotch of her shorts. Without even thinking, she took off running. As she reached the steps, she heard the same bitchy Barbie shout, "Better slow down before you shit yourself!"

Her legs carried her straight to the bathroom. She slammed the stall door, ripped down her shorts, and sat on the toilet to assess the damage. Tears welled in her eyes. Blood coated the inside of her shorts and soaked her underwear. She patted the fabric with toilet paper, soaking up what she could, and stuffed a wad into her underwear before sneaking out of the bathroom.

Just as she crossed the threshold, she heard a voice, "Hey, you okay?"

It was Toby. He offered her his sweatshirt to tie around her waist, but she declined. He was sweet. He seemed to like her, and he had a dark sense of humor she loved. They talked about how to get back at those brain-dead Barbies. They were going to fill the leader's locker with blood-soaked toilet paper, write "bitch" in period blood on her gym bag, or maybe hang used tampons all over her backpack. That night, Samantha filled her trash can with her ruined underwear and numerous pads and tampons from her heavy flow.

In the morning, she was in such a rush that she didn't notice the trash was empty. But she did recognize the bloody underwear hanging on the queen bee's locker and the used pads stuck like stickers all over the others. The girls were furious, but Samantha didn't remember doing it.

"Pretty good, huh?" Toby sat with her at lunch.

Samantha felt vindicated but also confused and scared of being in trouble. Toby assured her it would be fine. That the girls deserved it. However, a few days later, Toby stopped coming to school, and she had to face the repercussions alone.

Her stinging arm brought her back to the room. She saw the nurse who had been pushing her adjusting her IV. Her eyes followed the tubes up to the bags. She felt another person she had never seen before hiking her dress up. Samantha helped him get it over her head and slip on the clean gown. It smelled of astringent and was as cold as it was ugly. They were trying to strap electrodes around her belly when she saw Toby sitting in the chair opposite her bed like an expectant father.

Samantha sat up and pointed. "Get him out of here."

A nurse looked over their shoulder. "Who? Everyone here is important for the delivery. We're just here to help."

"Not the nurses. Him!" She kept pointing. Her eyes were filled with tears and fear.

The nurse looked behind her again and back to the other nurse. He shrugged in response. Another round of fury rose from Samantha's vagina, and she was reduced to gripping the bed and writhing.

Her mind wandered to the last time Toby sat in a chair opposite her. He just watched as he did now. But, that time, it was emotional pain Samantha went through, not physical. She was sitting on the couch with her dad while he explained why they were sending her away. His hair was shaved on one side, and little burns oozed moisture that crusted around the edges. She really didn't expect the dog clippers to have such bite. But he was just the newest victim of her "pranks." She had superglued her younger sister to the table, leaving her with skin ripped from the palms of her hands. She had flooded her P.E. teacher's car and given a girl she hated a dangerous dose of bleach. And… And… And… The list of crimes felt endless as her last supporter explained why she couldn't stay. She didn't remember doing any of it. But, after years of denying and trying to prove her innocence, she was out of fight. They were sending her to get her hormones regulated, to get on medication, and to do the work she needed through inpatient therapy. No one offered her birth control to stop the periods or an explanation for what they thought she was doing. They just gave up on her and made her someone else's problem.

"Push!"

In front of her was a doctor. Or at least she assumed so. His short hair was covered by a blue paper cap. His face was just plastic glasses and a white mask. His hands - blue rubber attached to a papery blue torso.

"There's something wrong. The baby is stuck. We're going to have to do a C-section."

Samantha's entire body was on fire. There was no ebb and flow. It was a constant scorching pain, like electricity, flooding her vagina and shooting out her fingers and toes. An intense pressure accompanied it. Something that told her if she bared down, it would all be over.

She remembered feeling this same sense of light at the end of the tunnel when she started dating a boy from the inpatient group she was in. He was sweet and believed her. He even gave her a book on demonology. That's where she found the path forward. Toby came every month along with her period like clockwork - He was a blood demon. There was an easy way to get rid of him. To buy her some time, she used her body to thank her boyfriend for his thoughtful gift. She thanked him over and over.

Unfortunately, Toby found the book before she was able to complete her plan. They fought. He confessed his love. He told her they could be together forever, and he would always fight for her. When persuading didn't work, he threatened her. He said she would never be without him. That he will follow her. Because of this little stunt, he said he would make her life worse than it's ever been. He said the things they had done were child's play compared to what he'll make her do in the future. The day her period stopped, she saw the cuts all up and down the inside of her thighs and her arms. Toby had never hurt her before, and she never wanted to allow him to hurt her again. Getting pregnant was the only option.

Samantha woke up. She bolted upright. "Where is she?"

Her stomach stretched uncomfortably. She pulled down the blanket and saw the long stretch of silver staples. To the left of her bed was the bassinet and the sleeping baby. Just past that was Toby. His head bent over the child.

"A girl. She's beautiful." He looked at Samantha and smiled.

"Get away from her."

Toby put his hands in his pockets. "Don't be mad. You did this, not me. You and I could have had years together, but now, after your botched birth and hysterectomy, I won't get to be with you anymore."

"Fuck you."

Toby laughed, "You sound like your mom before she bled out. I'll tell you the same thing I told her. Don't worry, because I'm not going anywhere. I'll be back in, say… thirteen years." He looked down at the baby and stroked its cheek. "I'll see you soon, sweet girl. We'll have so much fun…"

I SHOULD HAVE STAYED HOME

by Michael Errol Swaim

I hate flying. It's the one thing that scares me more than anything. I never want to get on a plane, ever. I don't want to see one or smell one, but I would do anything for my mom, and you guessed it, I'm on a plane right now, about to land in Mexico. Tulum to be exact. Out of the small window, I could see the city as we began to descend. This is my least favorite part. Landing. I'm always afraid something bad will happen. We would crash, or a landing wheel would fall off, or even a wing. My hands gripped the armrests so tightly I thought my muscles would cramp. I looked down. My knuckles were white. My heart was racing a mile a minute. I'm too young to have a heart attack. I hope we touch down soon.

I never wanted to go to Mexico, and I don't mean that because I hate flying so much. I just really don't want to go anywhere at all. I'm much happier at home, where it's safe, and nothing bad ever happens. We know everyone, and everyone we know is nice and friendly. Plus, my friends are there. Out there in the world, it's a different story. We don't know anyone. People are mean, violent creatures. Terrible things happen out there, and I've heard horror stories about Mexico. It's not like I'm afraid to go places, I mean, I like going places. The thing is, I'm afraid of dying. We all die sometime, sure, but I really don't want it to happen any time soon. I've been to enough funerals, and I'm not anxious to go to mine any time soon.

I'd much rather be at home or playing RuneScape with my friends, but my parents booked this trip for us last year and are making me go. Being seventeen sucks, sometimes. I get no say in anything. That's okay, though. Next year, I can do whatever I want. I'll be an official adult. I just wish we were going somewhere other than Mexico. Sure, it's a beautiful place, but I don't know how many times I have heard on the news about tourists disappearing or getting murdered. Mysteriously dying in their hotels. Either that or a story about how the drug cartels are killing each other and anyone else that gets in the way. Why couldn't we have just gone to England? Or Norway? I've always wanted to go there.

I closed my eyes as the plane kept going down. I felt my mom grab my left hand. She patted it.

"We're almost down," she said.

She always tried to reassure me. It never worked.

"I need a bag!" I exclaimed.

I opened my eyes. She grabbed a vomit bag from the slot on the back of the seat in front of her and handed it to me. I quickly opened it and held it up to my mouth. The wheels touched the ground, and the plane shook. I barfed. I couldn't handle it anymore. The stress was too much. As the plane slowed down, I began to calm down a little. A flight attendant came by to take my vomit bag. Mom thanked her. Finally, the plane stopped. Everyone began to disembark. My muscles began to unclench, and my insides settled down. Thank God I didn't die. Now, I'm hungry.

As we walked off the plane and into the airport, I started to feel better. I was happy we made it and didn't crash. We were here for a week, and now that we were here, and not in the sky, I could hopefully enjoy myself. I would think about the return trip when it came time and deal with it later. Right now, I'm ready to get to the hotel, get out to the beach, and hopefully meet some girls. If we make it there. Surely nothing bad could happen between the airport and the hotel. It's only like a mile away. We picked up our bags at the carousel and went out the front door to hail a cab. It was busy outside. Cabs and other vehicles came and went. Picking up and dropping off people. It was chaos.

It didn't take long for a cab to come to us, and we loaded our luggage and climbed in the back. Our driver greeted us in broken English.

"Where to, señor?" he asked my dad.

"Hilton Tulum Riviera Maya," he replied.

"Sì, sì, beautiful. You love it. Is nice," he said and started driving.

I watched as the city whizzed by while he drove. It *was* nice, but I was ready for the beach and the hotel room. I started daydreaming while we drove and finally snapped out of it. It seemed like it was taking a while for us to get to the hotel. Mom and Dad were oblivious, taking in the sights, so I opened my phone and typed in the destination on Maps. We had already passed our exit. Fuck.

I showed my dad what I had found. His smile went away quickly.

"Hey, asshole, you passed our exit!" he said to the driver.

In response, the plastic screen between him and us went up, and the speed increased. I tried the door handle. It wouldn't budge. Dad frantically tried the one on his side. Same thing. We were trapped. He banged on the barrier between us and yelled at the driver, who calmly reached into the glove box, took out a revolver, and lifted it up to show us. I looked at Mom. Her eyes were wide with fear. I reached over and grabbed her hand. I didn't know what to do. Had we been kidnapped? It seemed like it. I didn't want to stress her out. I felt like I was going to puke again.

I was really scared now. My whole body was shaking with fear. My worst nightmare was about to come true. I'm pretty sure we were about to be one of those missing people I always hear about. We rode in silence the rest of the way, holding each other's hands the whole way. Ten minutes later, we were barreling down a dirty road, and I began to fear for our lives. He pulled into the driveway of an old, run-down farmhouse with a barn nearby and stopped near the house. The driver exited the cab and walked away. I watched as he pocketed the gun.

He soon came back with a well-dressed man in a suit. They both walked around the car, looking at us all through the windows. Mom and Dad were both yelling at them to let us out. They ignored us. I heard both men laughing. They shook hands. The well-dressed man walked away, and the driver walked around to open my door. Just as I was about to open my mouth to protest, he hit me on the side of the head with the butt of the gun. Before I blacked out, I heard Mom screaming and Dad yelling. Good thing I passed out when I did because I was about to throw up all over the place.

***

A scream woke me from an uncomfortable slumber. Disorientation quickly turned to dread when I realized I was lying on a cold metal table, and it was my own scream that had awakened me. My head was throbbing. I wanted to put my hand up to touch the sore spot, but soon discovered my wrists were bound, and I couldn't move them. My head was similarly bound, as well as my chest and legs. It felt like leather. I struggled with them all briefly and quickly gave up. I was unusually tired. I didn't have the energy to fight. I needed to think. It was dark, and I could barely see. Not that it mattered. I could barely move my head around. The last thing I remember was getting knocked on the head with the gun and Mom screaming. Now I am here, strapped to this table. I struggled with the straps holding me down again, but they were tight all around. I wondered where mom and dad were, and if they were ok.

"Mom? Dad?" I called out into the darkness.

No response. It was eerie. The only things I could see were crossbeams above my head, some PVC pipes, and a long shop light.

I must be in a basement somewhere. Or a dungeon. Great, I've been abducted, and I'm about to be murdered. I panicked. I don't want to die, and I especially want my parents to be ok. The more I thought about it, the more I began to worry. I started to jerk my arms and legs as hard as possible in a failed attempt to loosen the bonds. It didn't help.

I have to get out of here. I kept working my wrists around and pulling them backward, trying to get something to loosen. I'm sure my fears about Mexico are going to come true now, and my parents and I were both about to be another news story. Another statistic. They would probably kill us and dump our bodies at the hotel. *Three Americans on vacation found dead at a resort in Tulum,* the newspaper headlines back home would say. Just like so many news stories I have read before. I tried to stop thinking about it and concentrate. I had to be smart if I was going to find a way out of this.

It seemed like the strap on my right wrist had loosened, and I concentrated on that side. I could almost get my hand through it, but not quite. I kept working. I had no idea how long I had been there. My eyes were getting used to the dark, and I tilted my head to the left, but only an unfinished wall existed. I tried to move it to the right, and suddenly, I heard a door opening and quickly shutting, followed by echoing footsteps. It sounded like someone was walking down a set of wooden stairs. I froze and ceased my work on my bonds. I closed my eyes. Maybe if I pretended to be asleep, whoever they were would disappear so I could keep working to escape. My heart began to race, and I could feel it thumping all the way up in my head. I was scared. I almost barfed. What a mess that would be, puke running down my face. Maybe I should do it anyway to make whoever this was mad. The footsteps grew closer, and suddenly, the light above me came on, instantly blinding me.

"Hola. Abre tus ojos. Open your eyes. I know you are awake." A deep masculine voice said.

A head appeared over me. He had a mask over his mouth.

"You won't be able to get those straps loose. I made sure they were tight." His voice was surprisingly soothing and muffled through the mask.

"You'd better let me go before…" I started to say.

"¿O, qué?" he interrupted, "You will call the police? Beat me up? Your threats are empty because you are on my experiment table. There is no escape."

"Experiment?"

He backed away from my view, and I heard noises like metal things clinking together.

"¡Sí, hago experimentos!" It sounded like he had lowered his mask. I could hear him more clearly.

"What do you mean, man? I don't speak Spanish! You gotta let me go, where are my parents?" I was frantic.

I pulled and jerked my body against the straps holding me down again and shook the whole table. I was really freaking out.

"Cálmate or this will only get worse."

I stopped moving. Maybe I could try to talk my way out of this.

"You do experiments? What kind?" I asked, trying to remain calm.

"Abra su boca," he replied.

"I don't know what that means!"

"Open your mouth."

"Why? What are you going to…"

He shoved something in my mouth while I was talking. It felt like a bite block that a dentist uses to keep a patient's mouth open or something similar. My eyes went wide. I couldn't close my mouth. I tried to speak, but all that came out was noise. I felt a slight pain in my neck.

"That should calm you down."

I was already feeling the effects of whatever he injected me with. I wasn't as worried as I should have been when the man's face appeared above me again. He was holding a pair of toenail clippers. I tried to laugh. Was he about to give me a pedicure? He leaned in closer, put the clippers in my mouth, and clamped one down on one of my front teeth. It was as I feared. He was going to torture me. Then I'm sure he would kill me.

"Whaya ooya!"

I had meant to say what you are doing, but that's what it sounded like when it came out.

He squeezed the toenail clippers hard, about halfway up the tooth. I screamed. He had both hands on it, trying to smash it together and cut a piece of my tooth off. He must have sharpened the toenail clippers. I cried out in pain as the tool broke through the tooth and cut it in half. The pain was indescribable. I cried out and tried to move my head away, but the strap was too tight. He raised the bottom half of the tooth up where I could see it.

"Interesante," he remarked, "I did not think that would work. I'll be right back."

I heard him walking away and up the stairs. The door shut. The relief that he had gone didn't outweigh the pain or the fear. This maniac was going to kill me. I started moving my left hand around again and pulling it toward me, trying to stretch the leather enough to slip my hand out. Hopefully, I can hold on long enough to finally work my hand free and escape.

All too soon, I heard him walking around above me. The door opened, and I heard footsteps on the stairs again. I wondered where he went. There was no telling with this guy. I heard him approaching. His masked face appeared above me again.

"Had to go get an extension cord," he explained.

I heard a noise. It was a drill. The bastard raised it up so I could see it. It was a yellow DeWalt. We have one just like it at home. He pulled the trigger and stopped. Twice, taunting me. He pressed the trigger and held it, and I watched the tiny drill bit go around and around. I knew what was coming. He leaned in close and pointed it at my mouth. I frantically tried to get away or loosen any of the straps holding me down. I still couldn't move. However, the strap on the left wrist was finally beginning to loosen. I pulled my arm back as hard as I could. The drill contacted the incisor next to the one he had already damaged.

I tried to scream. He held the drill tight against the tooth. I could feel it swirling around, eating its way through. It didn't take long. He wasn't paying attention, and the bit lightly touched the back of my throat as it broke through. I tasted the copper tang of blood. I nearly choked. I wish I would pass out. Or die. I just wanted this nightmare to end now. I was so scared I could hardly think anymore. He started to pull the bit back out. The drill was still running, and I could feel it churning against the tooth. My insides rebelled, and I finally vomited. The mixture of blood and bile and the remnants of whatever I had eaten last sat in my mouth, and I had to breathe out of my nose.

"¡Dios mío!" he exclaimed and quickly loosened the strap on my head.

He reached in to remove the bite block, and I leaned over and pushed the liquid out of my mouth. It dripped onto the table and slowly started to slide down against the side of my body. It felt disgusting. I wanted to vomit again. I could see him. He was muttering to himself in Spanish at the other side of the room. I couldn't understand it. He was changing his gloves. While he was distracted, I pulled at the loose strap again. Over and over, using all my strength. It started to give, and my hand slid through ever so slightly. I pulled it again, and it suddenly came free.

I quickly and quietly undid the strap on the opposite hand and then the strap across my chest. As I was loosening the strap on my legs, he turned around.

"¡Mierda!" he yelled and came toward me.

My legs came free just as he neared, and I lifted them up and shoved my feet as hard as I could at his chest. I was still dizzy, but I gave it all I had. He flew backward and hit the table on the far wall. He dropped to his knees and winced in pain. I panicked. What do I do now? As he began to rise, I noticed a smaller metal table right on the other side of the larger table. The drill was on it. I reached over to grab it, and his hands grabbed my waist and pulled me back toward him just as I latched onto it. I fell on top of him, and I turned over and swung the drill at his face, and he tried to block it. Too late. The drill connected with his forehead. I pressed as hard as I could. He screamed as it cut through the skin. He moved his head from side to side, and the drill slipped off, so I repositioned it and jammed it as hard as I could into an eye. I had my finger on the trigger the whole time, so it was going full speed and easily went right through and into the socket. He looked surprised for a second and then slumped over the table I had been strapped to. Must have passed out. I know I would have. I pulled the drill out. It was difficult, but I managed to get him up on the table better, flipped him over, and strapped him down as he had me.

I debated whether to run or not. I could escape right now and find Mom and Dad, but I had no idea where they were or where to look. I had a great idea on how to find out.

***

His eyes flew open and darted around. He tried to speak, but I had already put the bite block in his mouth, still dripping with my cold vomit. I watched as he struggled to move but couldn't. I was in his shoes now. I had the drill in my hand, and I smiled and lifted it up so he could see it. I repeatedly clicked the power button on the drill.

"My turn," I said.

I smiled and got to work.

LA VELUE

by Basile Lebret

For Jess

Allison had never seen skyscrapers that high. At least that's what the teenager thought. In her dreamscape, Paris was this distant town marred by shadows born from colossuses of glass and steel. Currently, Alexandre was busying himself in her mouth. She had stopped stroking him a lifetime ago. And so, he went on. All alone. At least, she had not been stupid enough to let the boy tape the whole thing. Plus, this somehow gave her time to think. She wasn't really into it.

The duet, though they weren't an item, stood on the riverside of the Huisne. A small stream which flowed lazily across the Sarthe in France. The girl, still on her knees, had found the spot through her numerous strolls, trying to avoid the hardships of young adulthood, the cold reality of a burning world, and the petty problems of inhabiting a tiny town and not owning any means of transportation. For hours on end, she would lie basking in the diaphanous light which always fell from the grey sky in her native county. More often than not, when she was certain she was alone, Allison would sing old pop tunes, mostly, but she would also loudly chant some more obscure songs like *Toutes les Femmes de ta vie.* She would dream too, fantasies of success in the capital, for her singing, for the cult acclaim her diary would get after being published, as a businesswoman helping to develop new reality TV shows. Weird scripts where there existed no sky, and she would fight worm-like monsters the size of planets.

Although Allison had never voiced it, or even consciously thought it through, she secretly wished nobody would find this place. For it was hers. Entirely.

Which changed nothing.

For the boy had found her. And they drank, they smoked, and he'd come. Well, he was almost there anyway.

Allison had gained a solid reputation for being a slut, which she could accommodate. It was… It was because of last year's incident during the last *La Fête de la Musique,* but she preferred not to think about it. *In another world, the boy growled, became stiff.* Still, there existed a really special enjoyment in knowing that at least half the town's male population jerked off while thinking about you. Sure, it had somewhat strained her relationship with fellow female inhabitants, but weighing it all, she used to hang out way more with girls from her high school anyway. All the way over there, in Le Mans, the next big city. It was like, here, in Courceboeufs, she was this other girl, living another life. Sometimes, it even made her smile.

Allison spat on the ground while the teenager thanked her. A vapid sentence along the lines of her being amazing and beautiful. Words she didn't care for.

The boy's name was Alexandre, not that it mattered. Allison got up as he adjusted his trousers, all red and blushing and visibly embarrassed. The girl watched his shame with a slight slice of pity, but showed no sign of it.

"Well, hrm, see ya?" Alexandre asked more than he asserted.

Allison watched him leave, then contemplated the river: oh-so-calm, oh-so-silvery. A small breeze crept across the wild weeds, making them twist and twirl with a gentle fury. The girl noticed the imprint her knees had left on the grass beside her, the mark of the boy's shoes surrounding them. The teenager took all this in. In a convoluted way, it was the first time she understood minuscule choices could lead to broader consequences. The high schooler sighed. This had never been a place to rest, anyway.

***

Allison had never felt this empty void, as large as the Milky Way in the back of her stomach. Nothing to do with periods. It was more ethereal. Of course, she had blown a lot of guys since… last year, but still. It was as if Alexandre had invaded her most precious garden, as if the crushed grass underneath his feet had encapsulated most of her dreams. Sure, she mostly came there after fighting with her mom, but this still *was* her place. Allison tasted the past in her chain of thoughts before looking up at the boy, and she felt it. A hate as wide as multiple stab wounds directed towards her for being a dumb fuck, towards him to have come here in the first place, towards his fucking mother, who acted all high and almighty at the local fair, towards his dad, who fucking worked at the town hall and thought he was some big shot. 'Town has a population of slightly over four hundred souls, my man, chill the fuck down!'

The boy? He had gotten over his shame real quick, now strolling along the edges of the river, which must have been three inches high above the water level. Tops. Allison stared at him intently as he grew smaller and smaller, then suddenly lost his footing and disappeared. Tall grass got in her view, yet she was surprised the boy didn't make any noise hitting the liquid. Calmly, the girl started walking towards the point she'd last seen him, rehearsing lines in her head to burn the guy for his mishaps, before settling on mindful, silent disdain. But Alexandre wasn't there.

Allison carefully stepped over the earthy edge, going as far as plunging knee high in the river when she realized there was no trace of him anywhere. She shrugged at the coldness of the water and the feeling of disgust, which always gripped her when entering natural ponds, before extending her arms in the green goo, an octopus tactilely searching for the warmth of corpses. Allison could not really see but could sense the liquid void scratching her palm, sometimes broken by a drifting piece of wood and other wastes. As fast as she could, Allison got out of the flow and began to think of drying up before she ran. Real fast.

***

She had never jogged that far in all her life. She passed by the old bakery, trying not to look at the pub and those who probably stood inside. Drinking. Allison pressed on as the asphalt crept underneath her soles. At the next intersection, to her left, was the parking lot she was aiming for. The teenage girl accelerated in a last effort, knowing they would be there, for they always were. Benji, Oumar, and Curtis, fading their youth away on their dirt bikes. The Lonesome Trinity. Motorcycles were something small, though, 125cc, tops.

The three boys stopped talking when they heard the quick succession of her footsteps hitting their territory. Benjamin was looking a little lower than her eyes, but she would have guessed so. Curtis, too. Allison didn't really mind. She once dated Benji. A lifetime ago.

"What's up?" he asked, seemingly alerted, as he leapt from his bike.

Allison bent, folded in two, trying to recoup her breath. Cigarette addiction and lack of exercise were catching up to her despite her young age; she was now trying to inhale-exhale in a somewhat decent imitation of an ever-expanding sea monster.

"A… Al," she began.

"Yeah, your name's Allison, we kinda got that," said Curtis, cutting her off.

His eyes were red, shiny, and veiny. Benjamin hit his friend's ribs with an elbow, nodded at Allison to continue, without even uttering a word.

"Alexandre fell into the Huisne." The girl finally exhaled in a single choked breath.

"Ain't no need to panic, shit's like three feet deep. At most!" Exclaimed Curtis while eyeing Oumar with a confident smile.

Benjamin had already put his helmet on while kick-starting his bike. Oumar answered:

"You dumb fuck, you really think she'd be this freaked out if the dude was just slightly wet?"

"What he said." Benjamin asserted, pointing at his black friend.

Allison had jumped behind him.

They drove on.

***

Allison had always enjoyed riding with Benji ever since his first shitty scooter, which he illegally got some four years ago. Sure, the bike was some cheap plastic thing the boy solely used in order to traverse the countryside as fast as was permitted, but the teenage girl always loved the damn thing, the tremors the motor grew in her leg, the gentle fear of riding helmet-free, as if skidding over an asphalt tightrope. The trip was short, though, even if her lungs felt as if she had run for miles on end. It got shaky when they went off the road and amongst the wild weeds. Hadn't she been so worried, Allison would have probably enjoyed it; yet she was too busy screaming and shouting over the noisy engine in order to pinpoint the exact place where Alexandre had disappeared.

Both Oumar and Benjamin instantly jumped into the water when they got there. Curtis simply dismounted, murmuring under his breath, "Dumb fucks" as if he was waiting for all of this to turn out to be nothing more than a prank.

"Wait!" Oumar suddenly yelled. "What if we do find him? Some o' y'all know CPR?"

On the slightly elevated riverside, Curtis smirked:

"Might as well call the fire department, uh? Or is your boyfriend ready to just jump out of some bushes to photograph those two imbeciles?"

He had taken out his Samsung Galaxy while asking his question.

"He fucking disappeared! The fuck you want me to say?" Answered the girl who was now waist-high in the brown current.

"I dunno, I mean, you both may have smoked or drunk or something."

"Which means dude could be swallowing water by the gallons and you still talking, my man!" Yelled Benjamin from the pond.

"FUCK YOU! Yeah, no, excuse me, sir. I'm Curtis Andrevon, residing in Courceboeufs, 14 Rue des Bleuets. It appears a friend of ours fell into the Huisne and never came back up."

***

The small town had never seen such a shit show, even when four years prior, Martine Beaumont had cut the throat of her wife-beater, asshole of a husband. Firemen asked questions, policemen asked questions, and Alexandre's mother yelled mostly. The whole village walked four kilometres in the river, which was getting colder by the minute as the dust-coloured firmament turned mostly void, partially stars.

Allison's mom, wrapped in both her happy-go-lucky attitude and the *Fête de la Musique,* which was to come on the next day, tried to appease her daughter by speaking of the dance show Allison was supposed to be a part of. Never once did she ask the teenager if she still wanted to go. This was Evelyne Beaumont for you.

Eric Beaumont, the dad, came home late as usual, talked a bit louder when he discovered what had happened, but that was all. If he ever wondered about his progeny's stress, he didn't act upon it. As was to be expected from him.

In the room exactly above her parents' kitchen, Allison pretended to sleep, wondering if it was her hatred that had killed Alexandre, if his disappearance (*murder?*) was somehow linked to her.

"Shut the fuck up, you don't know if he's dead yet," mumbled the teenager under her potty breath.

She had taken the remnants of a blunt from underneath her bed and a small bottle of Smirnoff Ice. The girl was now smoking through her open window, sipping gulps from time to time as, in the distance, the lights from the firemen's truck chased the countryside's darkness. She could see it from over the roofs of the surrounding houses. Red, black, blue, black. Red. Black. Blue. Red. Bl…

***

Allison had never woken up with such a headache. Mouth dry. The water bottles piling up in trash rubble, right next to her bed, were both dirty and empty. The girl groaned and moaned and went to the bathroom, drinking hard for a good five minutes. For some odd reason, closing her eyes, she could almost form a near-perfect mental representation of Alexandre's disappearance. The teenager didn't know why she was even surprised when all her mother could talk about was tonight's representation.

Allison was part of a modern jazz club in another village, and for the *Fête de la Musique,* they had struck a deal with a duet band from two towns over, in order to put on a little show, this very night, here, in Courceboeufs' community centre. The teenager hated this type of public event. Last year, it had led to complications. Also, she hated being stared at. There was a thin line between liking boys (*and men*) fantasizing about you and a hundred blank faces genuinely staring at you. Through this type of ordeal, she always felt weird, ashamed, and uneasy. Out of place, even more so than in her regular life. Right now, she just didn't need that.

But there was no way you could move Evelyne Beaumont. According to her daughter, both the fading beauty of the forty-something woman and her lack of any prospect had turned her into a caricature of the perfect mom, trying to stay fit and attractive for as long as possible while failing miserably at everything else. Oh, and she couldn't care less about her daughter, even though she fucking used her as a proxy to a better existence, but, hey, what can you do?

The community centre all over in Ballon, where the dance class used to train, was, to all intents, in a way better shape than Courceboeufs' one had ever been, at least according to Allison's remembrance. She wondered why the fuck somebody ever thought of making a cross-county festival be held in her native village with its decaying streets surrounded by flailing sodium lights. Even those yellow-spitting, archaic ornaments couldn't hide the mess her town was in.

The day went fast. On the side of the room they rehearsed in, her mom certainly was explaining the grandeur of her daughter to other inattentive mothers. Allison wished for some weed and a sip of vodka. Cecilia was complaining about having her period on such a special day, above all. Could you believe it? Louise would not stop talking about her pseudo-boyfriend, who was supposed to be in the Légion (*which made it illegal*) and allegedly lived in Paris (*which turned the whole story either useless or completely false*). All in all, Allison didn't care. A normal day.

***

Jean-Marie had always been this drunk. At least as far as he could remember. Outside of the pub, summer had left, painting the sky all pink and purple and blue before turning to a darker shade. The streets of Courceboeufs were empty as usual, but tonight, most of the respectable folks were in the community centre. You would have had a hard time finding a lone light shining through any windows on this very evening. Well, except for the bar. The thirty-something man, who looked both oddly beautiful and way older than his true age, knew the whole town now sat in the community centre but could not go there. At least, Virginie, the pub's owner, had not closed shop at 9 pm as she did every other day. To his right, René was on his fourth calva while a little farther away down the bar, Laurent, fat and balding, had started to fall asleep on his stool.

The crew had been banished from public events because of the fights they liked to start. If you had asked Jean-Marie, he didn't steer clear of troubles, for troubles eventually found him. That was it. Officials just didn't want to understand.

Various light sources were trying to fend off the grainy obscurity of the pub and reflected in a distorted fashion in the eyes of the drunkards. The bar was the sole commercial building able to survive in the little town, albeit entirely residing on the crumbling shoulders of those three men.

For a moment, Jean-Marie thought of *forcing* Virginie. She was decent for fifty years old, still she'd bought the establishment from a lesbian couple who would do tricks for just the right sum, which Jean-Marie always had on hand. Just in case. He wondered if the new owner was built of the same wood, but lost his train of thought. Y'see, when he didn't have money, Jean-Marie would propose booze and stuff to the young girls who liked to stay late after nocturnal celebrations such as tonight's event. Underneath sufficient shade, he was attractive enough, smiling enough, that some teenager would get tempted. He'd take them home, minors mostly, married women tended to do their own naughty stuff outside of town, he'd get them drunk, and would get down to business. More often than not, he'd invite the two crumbling fucks who followed him everywhere. Otherwise, they might never have had their dick sucked. At least once, Jean-Marie taped the whole ordeal, but he lost the computer on which the vid was burned a long time ago.

Sure, sometimes the girls would get mean, would cry, and pretend they didn't like it, but he knew. Y'see, Jean-Marie was born here and raised here by his grandpa and grandma when his mom came back home with a belly full of some stranger's semen. The old man taught him about the countryside life, how to treat women, too. When he passed away, Jean-Marie became the sixteen-year-old head of the family. Plus, the drunkard's frail mother would never have called the cops on her own blood. He'd never hit his grandma, though. Almost once, but he didn't. Sometimes, remembering this particular event, he was proud of himself.

This habit of his was why he'd drunk less than was usual. He wanted to keep his head straight enough for when they would stroll the parking lot, talking to pot-smoking teenagers, prowling.

"Can I light a fag?" He suddenly asked while already setting the tip of his cigarette on fire.

Having gotten no answer, Jean-Marie looked up, saw the terrified face of Virginie staring above his head towards the glass wall which opened to the street. Jean-Marie would never admit it, but he childishly hesitated for just a moment before diverting his gaze towards the vitrine.

What stood behind the 15-by-16-foot window largely exceeded its frame. The man gulped as cracks appeared under the pressure of the beast's body, spreading spider-web-like shatters across the translucent wall. It looked like a viper's nest. That's all it did, crashing through glass, rolling on the black-and-white floor tiles with the wet *thud* of piles of bodies being released from bulldozer buckets into mass graves. Electric impulses bit through Jean-Marie's spine as he stood, gasping for air, raising his arms to try to defend himself.

Nothing happened. The man waited four, maybe five seconds with his eyes closed, not noticing he'd pissed himself. When the warmness around his crotch got hard enough, he heard the hissing sound echoing on the dark wood which covered the walls in the establishment. The tentacles, or vines, were creeping across every surface, sometimes fighting one another as if they each possessed their own identity. Jean-Marie tried to make sense of the whole mess, dropped even the thought of it, and began contemplating the parasites slowly growing all around.

"Virginie. The door, the back exit, is unlocked, right?" He asked.

No answer.

"Bitch! Is the fucking door unlocked?!" He yelled, sounding more terrified than he wished.

There was a loud noise as Laurent, and his stool, fell, awoken and startled by the cry. After having drunkenly evaluated his environment, the balding man turned away towards the emergency exit with a howl. Reaction was instantaneous. As a single body, every creeper from the grounds to the ceiling swallowed the room whole as one gigantic heartbeat. Jean-Marie heard the screams, and didn't dare to look back.

"Cretin bastard."

From the green, veiny wall which stood in front of him, a yellow and red mass crept out, slowly closing the distance between it and the standing man. It was shaped as a bowl and covered with irregular holes in which what looked like worms were moving. Jean-Marie felt sick. The creature let out a hiss, which made every disgusting obstruction move out and back inside in an insane rhythm. The maggots dancing released a sound.

Siiiiiinn ***BLAM****

At least that's what Jean-Marie thought he heard before a blast erupted from his right. His ear hurt, then went numb, then went wet. Virginie had taken a rifle from under her counter and fired blindly.

"Stupid bitch!" Screamed the now-impaired man. Or so he thought. For the vines were already in his mouth.

***

Allison had never broken any of Mrs. Dorignet's rules. Yet, here she was, in the dressing room, which was just a bunch of curtains set up as a square, listening to Deli Girls. The singer's screams in her ears muted the world all around. Chatty female teenagers, for the most part, trying to put on their shitty attire.

It was a sure thing her dance teacher would yell if she ever came and saw one of Allison's earbuds. By simply closing her eyes, the student could summon the entire monologue. The problem was that staying in the dark long enough led her down a rabbit hole, which always ended with Alexandre's dead body.

In her blurred mind, the boy had bloated and turned all blue and violet. His eyes were swollen as if he had just woken up from a bar fight. Staying under long enough, Allison could swim through the ocean, which glittered with jellyfish and golden particles. Sometimes, the drowned boy would wake, his every move shaking what appeared to be carnivorous fish from beneath his skin. The corpse would then open its mouth, trying to warn her, but in the cavity lay even more of the maggot creatures. Stay long enough, and the worms would begin to shift back and forth to an arcane rhythm. Bubbles might start rising all around, chasing all living beings away. Those were the premises of something big coming from beneath.

Allison would try to scream, but no noise could be heard in the surrounding water.

"You hand me some water?"

"What?" Asked Allison, taking off one earbud.

"Can you hand me some water?" insisted Georges.

The tanned girl stared at her fellow dancer for quite some time before acknowledging his request. The water cooler lay underneath the table she was sitting in front of. Georges was fucking ridiculous in his black and gold body. Clothed like this, the obese boy could almost pass as some Sterdust imitator lost in the changing room.

"Sure," simply said Allison.

She had always wondered why the fuck the fat guy had gotten into the dance class in the first place. Sure, he was good at it, but did he enjoy it enough when faced with the shit he was forced to put up with? Remarks and insults stemming from the other dancers. Allison wasn't so certain. She sometimes thought the fat kid wasn't either.

"You gon' do good," she shyly mumbled while giving Georges a bottle. "You always do."

"You were with him? With Alexandre before he disappeared?" asked the sipping boy.

"Yeah."

"He was sort of a douche. Yet, with him missing, I don't have to put up with Marlène's shit."

"I did not even notice she didn't come. They... They dated?" Asked Allison, blushing.

"Yeah, don't mind it. They never were very good as an item."

"Oh."

The obese boy seemed to weigh his next sentence for just a split second. His eyes narrowed through the effort.

"Say, you saw anything special when he disappeared?"

"No... Not really. He just fell. Somehow."

"Y'know there's supposed to be a monster in the Huisne, right?" Asked Georges, his eyes glistening in the dim light.

"No."

"Civilians. They suffer from short-term memory. So, there used to be this beast that ravaged and pillaged the countryside back in the day. Like the Middle Ages stuff. La Velue, they called her. It was said the outgrowths on her body were as hard as shards of iron, though. The peasants of the time thought to fight it off, but never succeeded. That's 'til some white knight came to town, hunted the beast and drove it into the Huisne."

"T'is interesting but..."

"But wait! Two stories confront each other about the end. Some say the creature just bled to death and drowned right then and there. While other versions state it's still lying in the Huisne, waiting."

"Someone we knew has almost certainly drowned, and you're turning this into a fairy tale?"

A flash of anger passed across the boy's cornea.

"Got your mind off of shit, though," he said. "And I'm almost certain this is just some systemic myth to..."

Allison never heard the end of it. Once again, Deli Girls screamed in both her ears. After a while, more than he would care to admit, Georges left.

***

Allison had never lost the rhythm, be it in class or on stage, until now. She was attempting a side-step when a flash stabbed through her mind for a millisecond. The image was blurry, but it was the wheel of a motorbike, turning silently, while the vehicle lay on the ground. A bit of asphalt covered in blood. The young girl thought that if she concentrated enough, she would picture the whole scene in the scarlet puddle.

She tripped forward and was back in the community hall. All around, a damp darkness engulfed everything, binding the public to anonymity. That is, if you didn't take into account the emergency lights, which somehow shone a blurry redness over which the citizens were mere silhouettes. Everyone seemed to stay quiet, although you could hear someone cough when Allison had her misstep. Maybe laughter.

The song that rolled overhead, numbing the whole floor, was some perverted version of "Wuthering Heights" which turned the 80's pop track into an unrecognizable nightmare. To the right side of the stage, the jazz band was blowing in their flute and hitting like mad men upon their pianos. Louder than was needed, yet not loud enough that you could not hear the motocross speeding outside the building. The acceleration of the engine ended with a screech of torn metal and a suffering cry that ended almost immediately. In the shadowy crowd, someone had already gotten up. No dancer was able to discern the "What the fuck?" coming out of the man's voice, but they all understood.

Whoever this guy was, for it sure as shit wasn't Allison's dad since the sad fuck didn't come, traversed the alleyway which had been set up between the two hordes of chairs, with the air of someone who's going to take care of business. He was almost at the door when the whole thing bent, folded in two, and was swallowed by whatever stood on the other side.

The man disappeared before anyone in the frozen audience could do anything. Snakes, or what seemed like worm-like reptiles, slid across every wall, engulfing the whole place with the mad fury of a pest infestation. It didn't take too long before the last row of chairs got swallowed up. From Allison's viewpoint, it was as if a hole had opened up under the spectators' feet.

The teenage girl knew there existed no such hole.

Mrs. Dorignet got up on stage, yelling into a microphone that did not work as members of the audience ran on top of one another to seek refuge on the homemade structure. This made the room echo with slither and broken bones. Suffering moans. In front of Allison, Georges, who had been sweating hard, got pulled up by tendrils coming from the roof. The girl didn't care to look; she recognized her comrade's voice through his wails of pain. He sounded like a pig who had gotten his throat slit.

Blood rained down from the ceiling before what looked like an intestine hit the floor. Violently. Allison stared at the organ before noticing her mom kneeling beside her. Whether or not she accepted, the young girl let out a mental sigh. Nothing moved in the whole centre while everything shrieked.

A neon overhead suddenly came to life, spraying photons upon every matter. In the bathing light lay overturned chairs, raw meat, and a slight mist made of torn-apart flesh.

Witness enough bodies being penetrated by outside alien overgrowth, you might get accustomed to it, even though you're still puking on your mom's lap. The same goes for the cries; hear enough people dying in a short enough time, and you may be able to mute them after about ten seconds. Twelve if you don't focus on the task.

Allison's mouth now tasted like potatoes and uncooked chicken. She spat a bit more, trying not to focus on the men's corpses, for they were all men, still bound and linked to the prefabricated walls all around. There was a baby crying before this all went down, and the babe didn't cry anymore she realized suddenly as some unseen shadow spread over her body. Its very fabric was made of the same tendrils that fucked and ate and fought one another over every surface in the building.

The teenage girl stared at what would have looked like a rose bud, had it not been full of holes, in which maggots lay hidden and writhing in a dirtiness found in old men's cavities. She blinked, barfed, and the maggots began to wriggle. In and out of every orifice with the rhythm of an epileptic crisis. It made a sound.

SSsssssIIIiinNNnn, hissed the creature.

Allison looked at her mom, who was crying. Allison was also crying, touching her progenitor's head.

SSSSSSSIIIIINNNGggg!!! More violently, this time.

The young girl, she understood. Recalling, but for an instant, better days, upon the bank of the Huisne. She tried to push her mother aside, who gripped her daughter's leg more firmly. Allison had to hit her once, then twice before the woman finally let her go. With tears in her eyes, the teenager side-stepped while throwing her right hand up, drawing an invisible arc in the air.

"Toutes les femmes de ta vie, en moi réunies," she sang with tears in her eyes.

At the feet of the broken stage, among the wailing and the pain and the flat odour of decaying flesh, the monster began to hit the rhythm by pressing its tendrils on the floor. Soon, it was singing in an uneasy unison with the teenage girl.

Nobody moved.

THE LADY IN WHITE

by Bill Camp

Brent disappointedly watched the trick-or-treaters walking up and down East 37th Street in Erie, Pennsylvania. He peered out his large picture window while sitting on the sofa, unable to join the annual fun for the first time because at 15 he was deemed "too old." He could not openly admit to his friends or family that he still longed to be out there seeing all the other kids' costumes and, of course, collecting all the candy he could. This year, the only candy he'd have would be whatever was left over after he and his mom finished handing out treats to the other kids.

Brent witnessed his neighbor, Rich, a stout 17-year-old redhead, walk across the street to their friend Dean's house. Rich and Dean attended the same preparatory high school, and both planned on going to college to earn MBAs. While Dean was destined for success, his father was a local construction business owner, which Dean would inherit one day, Rich would like to follow in his father's footsteps and manage the local grocery store down the street. Meanwhile, Brent, whose father worked at the local factory, was just starting public high school instead of attending preparatory school, and was unsure about what he wanted to do with his life.

Upon seeing Rich, Brent propped up on his knees in excitement, hoping Rich would see him. Rich must have seen him pop up like a whack-a-Mole because he turned toward Brent's house and waved for Brent to come outside and join them, just as Brent had hoped. Rich was always the one to bring everyone together for any sort of group activities.

Brent ran outside, the screen door snapping closed behind him, and whizzed past a few trick-or-treaters wearing Batman and princess costumes, who were trying to find the last few treats before calling it a night. He ran up to Rich on Dean's stoop just as Dean's tall, thin frame came to his own screen door to see who was knocking, his curly blond hair shining from the streetlight through the screen door.

"Hey, do you guys want to drive around?" Rich asked both of them.

Just then, Cam, sixteen, ran up to the group to join them.

"Hey guys, I saw you through my window. What's going on?" Cam said with anticipation. Cam, whose father worked for the city, attended the same public school as Brent as a freshman but was in all self-contained special education, so they were in none of the same classes together. He had no real future plans either.

This was how the group came together most Saturday nights to decide on an activity. Sometimes it was board games on Rich's stoop, other times it was a ride around the dock to look at girls, or a trip to the movies.

"We're going for a drive," Rich told Cam, although no one else had agreed to it yet.

"I don't know, I have some homework to catch up on, and besides, I wanted to listen to this spooky radio show tonight," Dean said.

"And I'm supposed to meet up with my girlfriend, Laura, when trick-or-treating is over, in about ten minutes," Brent said, looking at his watch.

"What's the radio show about?" Rich asked Dean.

"It's supposed to be about some of the haunted legends around Erie," Dean said.

"Oh, that sounds good. Let's listen to the radio show in the car while we ride around," Rich said to Dean. "And it's Saturday, so you can do that homework tomorrow night."

Dean shrugged in agreement, apparently not really wanting to complete his homework on a Saturday night anyway.

"What about my date with Laura?" Brent asked.

"I can pick her up, so she can come with us," Rich said.

"Okay, I'll call her and let her know we're coming," Brent agreed, anticipating that would be Rich's answer.

"I'll go because my parents are pissing me off anyway," Cam agreed.

"Let's meet at my house in ten minutes," Rich said, and they all separated as though they were in a football huddle.

###

Brent approached Rich's car, an old, two-door red Toyota Camry, just as Rich came out of the side door of his house, opened the car door, and lifted the seat so Brent could climb in behind the driver's side. Then Rich climbed into the driver's seat. Cam was already sitting in the rear passenger's seat, waiting for everyone.

"Did you even go home, Cam?" Brent said.

"No, my dad is pissed off because I stepped in dog-doo in the backyard and tracked it all over the house." Cam laughed as though this might not have been an accident.

Rich started the car and put it in reverse to pull out of the driveway. Just then, Dean walked up to the front of the car, right under a streetlamp, smiled, and flipped everyone the bird. Rich laughed and flipped the bird back at him as though this was their typical salute. Then Dean climbed into the front passenger's seat, which everyone had reserved for him.

They drove a few blocks and pulled into the driveway at Laura's house. Brent squeezed out from the back seat to walk up to the rear screen door when he heard her father yelling from inside the house. Just as he was about to knock, Laura, 14 and blond, came bursting out the back door into Brent's arms. Brent felt her leather jacket as they embraced. Laura had been kicked out of preparatory school and had just started attending the public high school, where she met Brent.

"What was going on in there?" Brent asked.

"Nothing," was her exasperated answer as they approached the Rich's Camry.

"Your parents still treating you like you're ten?"

"What do you think?" she rolled her eyes.

Brent climbed in first to take the middle of the backseat and give Laura the window seat.

Rich pulled out of Laura's parents' driveway, and they began driving down Ash Street, toward 26th Street, where Rich turned toward State Street.

The night clouds prevented the moon and stars from providing any light. Streetlights provided the only light, but some roads didn't even have streetlights. A few kids in costumes were still making their way back to their homes, even though trick-or-treating had just ended a few minutes ago.

Rich turned right down State Street, apparently heading to drive around the dock, as usual.

"Hey, I have an idea," Brent said, "Why don't we drive through Ax-Murder Hollow? It's Halloween. Wouldn't that be cool?"

The excitement of driving through the scariest place in Erie County on Halloween night must have been infectious.

"Let's do it!" said Cam. "I want to get scared tonight."

Dean laughed from the front passenger's side. "Do you want to?" he asked Rich.

"I really didn't want to go that far. It's clear on the other side of town, in Millcreek Township."

"Oh, come on!" said Laura from the backseat.

Everyone began chanting at Rich, "Do it! Do it! Do it!"

"All right, all right! We're going to Ax-Murder Hollow," Rich finally relented, causing everyone else to cheer.

"Hey, that radio show about local Erie legends is coming on now," Dean said.

"Do you think they'll tell the story of how Ax-Murder Hollow got its name?" Laura asked.

"Oh, I'm sure," Brent said.

"Okay, I'll put it on," Rich said while stopping at a red light and fiddling with the radio.

"No, not that station. The other one," Dean said as a Barry Manilow song played.

"Well, which station is it on then?" Rich said, petulantly.

"Here, let me do it," Dean said.

"Fine, you do it."

"How did Ax-Murder-Hollow get its name, anyway?" Cam asked.

"I assume someone with an ax murdered someone there," Brent said, making everyone laugh.

"Oh yeah, why didn't I think of that?" Cam joked.

"Welcome to the Halloween Special, Erie Legends*,"* the voice on the radio said in a low, guttural, creepy voice. The creepiness of the announcer's voice added to the night's ambiance.

"The show that will recount many of the legends in and around Erie, Pennsylvania. Tonight, we'll first take you to the famed Ax-Murder-Hollow," it said to everyone's cheer, then continued, *"followed by the legend of Gudgeonville Bridge, a haunted swamp off Sterrettania Road, and we'll finish the night with the 'Lady in White.'"*

After a commercial for Smith's hot dogs, the show opened with a full recount of the original incident that gave Ax-Murder Hollow its name.

"Although it is not in any official police records," it began truthfully, before going into the story of a nineteenth-century farmer who found his wife at home in bed with another man and bludgeoned them both with an ax.

Everyone was silent during the broadcast and listened attentively. Cam and Dean looked out the window as they listened, while Brent and Laura leaned in toward the front seat to hear the radio, her hand on Brent's inner thigh. Rich kept watching the road in silence as he drove down 26th Street and turned onto Sterrettania Road. Their next turn would be the infamous Ax-Murder Hollow.

"The farmer's ghost is known to still haunt the area to this day, causing fright to travelers in the area, but the story does not even end there," the radio voice said before breaking for another commercial, leaving everyone in anticipation.

"I bet everyone in Erie has either heard a story or experienced something creepy at Ax-Murder-Hollow," Brent said.

"I experienced something weird at Ax-Murder Hollow," Laura said while an ad for a local haunted house called "A Nightmare on Grubb Road" played on the radio.

"Oh yeah? Let's hear about it," Brent said.

Laura removed her hand and put her legs over Brent's legs and clasped her hands around his neck playfully. "My friend Tammy was driving a bunch of other girls from school around and me, and we went through Ax-Murder-Hollow, just like we're doing tonight. It was cloudy and cold, just like tonight."

"Well, it's Erie, so it's always cloudy and cold," Brent said.

"That's true, but when we got to that part where the road dips to the bottom of that ravine, her car stalled."

"That's not unusual. Her car is a hunk of junk," Brent joked again.

"I don't see you driving anything, dear," Laura smiled.

"Whoa!" everyone said.

"Burn," Cam added.

"Anyway," Laura continued, "she couldn't get the car started, but eventually she did. We drove back to her house, and when we got out of the car, you know how Tammy's car is white?"

"You mean under all the dirt," Brent tried to fire back.

"That's just it." Laura leaned toward her boyfriend. "Tammy's car was dirty as usual, but there were two small handprints in the dirt on the back of the car, like a child's handprints. We have no idea how they got there."

"They were probably on there before you left," Rich said, concentrating on the road.

"Nobody saw them before we left, and no one got out of the car to put the handprints there," Laura said, trying to cut off any further criticism.

"Ever since that day," Laura continued, "we call her car the Tammyknocker."

"Did you just make up that story just to tell that awful joke?" Brent asked, but deep down, the story added to the night's infectious tension.

"No, it really happened," Laura said, moving her legs off Brent's lap and letting go of his neck.

"But that's not the only legend of Ax-Murder-Hollow," the voice on the radio returned from the commercials just as Rich turned off Sterrettania Road and onto Ax-Murder-Hollow. The radio voice told the more recent story of a young couple who drove through the hollow when their car stalled.

"I bet they were going to do it," Cam said, snickering.

"Get your mind out of the gutter," Rich said.

"He's been watching too many eighties slasher movies," Brent said, looking out the window past Laura. It was a dark wooded area, with no leaves on the trees since it was fall. It looked like a horror movie. Brent would not have been surprised to see Jason Voorhees jump out of the woods toward the car, holding a machete.

"They waited there for five... ten... fifteen minutes before the man got out to look around and try to find help. When he could find none, he returned to the car, and it started again as though nothing was ever wrong with it."

"I heard a creepier version of that story," Brent said, just as they passed the low ravine in the road where the car supposedly stalled years ago.

"Let's hear it," Cam said.

"The way I heard it, the guy never got back into the car. After a while, the girl got out of the car to look for him and found him hanging from a nearby tree," Brent said.

"No way," Rich said while turning the Camry around to head back toward Sterrettania Road. "If that happened, it would have been in all the papers."

"Actually, that's the way I heard the story, too," Dean said.

"Really?" Cam said.

"That he was hanging from a tree? Yeah," Dean said.

"That's weird," Laura said, "because that's about the same spot where the Tammyknocker stalled."

"So why do cars keep stalling in the same spot on this road anyway?" Brent asked just as Rich drove them to the low part of the ravine again.

Rich's Camry stopped and stalled.

A hush fell over all five people in the car, and no one moved a muscle. They barely breathed. Brent glanced at Dean, who looked sideways at the driver.

"Just kidding," Rich said, turning the ignition to restart the car.

"Whoa!" Everyone yelled simultaneously, then laughed.

Brent's heart was still pounding after the incident, and Cam was still laughing hysterically.

"All right, you got me on that one," Laura said to Rich while squeezing Brent's hand.

"Good one, Rich," Cam said, finally recovering from his hysterics. "That was awesome!"

"I'm hungry," Rich said while another commercial played and everyone simmered down. "I'm going to stop at that McDonald's on 26th and Sterrettania."

"Get me two hamburgers," Dean said.

"You got any money?" Rich asked him.

"Do you want to share a soda?" Brent asked Laura while Dean handed Rich a few dollar bills.

"Sure," she responded.

"Here, get a large soda with two straws," Brent handed a few more dollars to Rich.

Rich parked the car and took the keys with him.

"Hey!" everyone complained because they could no longer hear the Halloween radio show.

"I'll be right back," Rich said, getting out of the car.

"I'll fix him," Dean said, turning on the windshield wipers and the right turn signal. "Now, when he comes back, everything will go off."

"Hey, turn the radio up real loud, too," Brent said. "I still want to get him back for that prank."

After a few minutes, Rich came back and turned the ignition to a blaring radio, right turn signal, and wild windshield wipers. Everyone laughed. Dean looked in the backseat at the others laughing at Rich, then high-fived Cam and Brent.

"Very funny, guys," Rich said, smiling and turning off the windshield wipers and turn signal.

After the radio was returned to a normal volume, the eerie voice told the story of the Gudgeonville haunted wooden covered bridge.

"Gudgeonville Bridge is famous for being the home of the Erie area's own headless horseman," the gravelly voice said, *"almost as though it were taken right out of the pages of a Washington Irving story."*

"Hey, I know where that is. It's not too far from here," Dean said.

"Let's go there," Cam said, excitedly.

"I'll drive if you want," Dean said.

"I'll drive," Rich said.

"Yeah, let's go to all the locations on this show," Brent suggested, still thirsty to see something supernatural tonight.

"Depends on how far they are," Rich said.

"This one's back up Sterrettania Road, passed Ax-Murder-Hollow, and turn right," Dean said.

"All right, we'll go to this one," Rich said, shoveling a hamburger into his mouth while pulling out of the McDonald's parking lot toward the haunted covered bridge.

The night seemed to be getting darker, and fog was rising from the dewy grass on both sides of the road, normal weather for Erie, but creating a perfect atmosphere for the evening.

The eerie voice continued its story. *"Now, when some travelers drive over the bridge, they claim to have heard the hooves of a horse galloping louder and louder as they go, and when they look to the end of the bridge, coming right at them is the figure of a man on a horse. But it is not just an ordinary man, for he has no head, riding faster and faster, directly toward them. This headless ghost is carrying its head in its hands, racing directly toward them when they cross the infamous one-lane, wooden bridge!*

"Isn't it weird that all the Erie legends seem to be in this same area?" Brent said as the radio show worked in another commercial.

"That's because there used to be a Gypsy burial ground somewhere near here," Rich said.

"I think they call them Romani now, but yeah, I heard something like that, too," Dean said.

"I think it was right in that swamp right over there," Rich said, pointing toward the passenger's side window.

Cam turned to where Rich pointed, as though he were trying to see ghosts.

"They had a burial ground in a swamp?" Brent asked.

"It wasn't a swamp then," Dean said. "We built up around here, shifting the wetlands until their burial ground got turned into a swamp. All those houses up the road and the department stores back by the McDonald's changed the make-up of the land, you know, shifting where waterways are and stuff like that. Their burial ground eventually got drowned in a swamp." Dean's knowledge of the city's development probably came from his father's construction business, the business he would inherit one day.

Brent thought about how the urban sprawl may take the others as its victims one day, damaging the environment, siphoning tax money from the inner city, moving businesses away from their centralized location, creating longer commutes and traffic congestion, weakening the political influence, all in the name of progress. One day, even the magic of these forests, of ghosts rising from the fog, would be ruined by that urban sprawl.

"That's probably why their spirits are so pissed," Rich said.

When they reached the wooden covered bridge, Rich stopped the car. "It's only one lane and looks really old. Am I going to make it over this thing?"

"Yeah, people drive over this thing all the time," Dean said.

"Do it! Do it!" Cam said, trying to start another chant.

"Okay, but if this car falls through, you guys are pulling it out," Rich said, moving the car slowly over the bridge, shaking everyone in the vehicle.

"Well, we should make it anyway," Dean said, holding the handle on the door.

"I'll bet this bumpy bridge is what people thought was the sound of horses' hooves," Rich said, still being a skeptic.

"Anyone see any headless ghosts with their head in their hands?" Dean asked, turning toward the backseat.

"No," Cam said, disappointedly.

He stopped the car when they made it to the other side. "Okay, now how do I get out of here?"

"I think you have to turn the car around and go back over the bridge again," Dean said.

"You're kidding," Rich said. Yet, he still turned the car around on the narrow dirt road and drove it slowly and carefully over the wooden bridge again.

When the radio voice returned from yet another commercial, it told the story of a Romani burial ground, right where Rich said it was supposed to be.

"See, I told you guys," Rich said.

The radio voice told of the many ghost sightings in the area, rising up from the swamp off Sterrettania Road while everyone in the car looked out the windows, each presumably trying to catch sight of one of the ghosts. *"The ghosts would angrily rise up, float around, seeking revenge on anyone who could be blamed for the intrusion of their graves!"*

As another commercial broke through, Brent concentrated on one patch of mist rising up from the tall grass and water several yards away from the road, hoping one would form into a ghost. Although he wasn't completely sure, none appeared particularly ghostly in form.

"There really were Romanis living in this area," Dean said. "My dad once told me they actually made up a bunch of these stories to keep other people away from their village."

"Okay, guys, it's getting late, we should start heading back home," Rich said, turning off Sterrettania Road and onto 26th Street.

"We are back on this Halloween radio special presentation with one last story that may be scarier than all the others, 'The Lady in White.'" The creepy radio voice continued.

"We can't go back now," Brent complained.

"Hey, I've heard of this one," Dean said. "It's pretty good."

"Yeah, I want to hear this one," Cam said.

"We can listen to it on the way back," Rich said, stopped at a red light. "It's after eleven o'clock."

"Stories about 'Ladies in White' have littered Great Britain and the rest of Europe for centuries," the spooky radio voice continued. *"The original 'Lady in White' legend involves a nineteenth-century couple driving their horse-drawn carriage on a narrow road when they lost control and crashed into the woods. A branch is said to have lopped off the*

head of the husband. The young lady's ghost, dressed in a flowing white dress, is said to be seen walking in circles in the area where the accident occurred, still searching for her husband's remains.

"It is no wonder then that Pennsylvania has been home to numerous 'Lady in White' legends, including those in Lehigh Valley, Bedford, Franklin, and yes, even Erie County on Sterrettania Road."

"Again, with the Sterrettania Road," Brent said.

"Yeah, we have to go back there," Dean said. "We're not that far. You can still turn around."

"Do it! Do it! Do it!" Cam started the chant once again, and this time everyone else joined in. "Do it! Do it! Do it!"

"Okay, okay, we're turning back around," Rich finally relented to everyone's cheers. "But you guys are going to explain to my dad why we're so late. Remember, I only have a Cinderella license and can't drive past midnight."

"We'll still make it back in time," Dean assured him.

"On that very road, a young lady is said to have been hitchhiking, and of course she was wearing all white," said the radio voice.

"This fog is getting pretty bad," Rich said. "I hope we don't get into an accident."

As the car drove further into the wooded area of Millcreek Township, it became increasingly difficult to see very far in front of the vehicle as they drove through patches of fog. The lights of the city dimmed into the distance behind them, and the residential area in front of them was still a ways ahead. A chill from the night air could be felt even through the closed windows.

"She was picked up by a single man with a mustache wearing a gray hoodie," the radio voice said. *"The woman was never seen alive again, apparently murdered by the man who picked her up. Although a single eyewitness provided the description of the apparent killer, he was never apprehended for his crime."*

The fog came and went in patches of clearing, then thickness as the vehicle traveled along Sterrettania Road. Perhaps it was only because the time was growing late, and the group was getting tired, but everyone seemed to fall into a hush during this story, and all the bickering and joking trailed off some time ago. Very few cars were out. The Camry appeared to be the only vehicle on the road, although with the thick fog, it was hard to tell.

"Now, when traveling along Sterrittania Road, some have said to see the Lady in White still walking up Sterrettania, hitchhiking along the side of the road," the radio voice said.

Just as the story finished, the Camry drove into a particularly thick patch of fog, and there, along the side of the road, was a figure, but it was not the lady in white. The figure was distinctly masculine. He was walking with his back to the oncoming Camry. His left arm was extended with the thumb up, hitchhiking.

Startled, Rich swerved the car into the oncoming lane to avoid hitting the man as they passed him. The hitchhiker was wearing a gray hoodie, just as the killer was described in the radio show.

As they passed, they all turned around to see that he had a mustache. Everything about the hitchhiker matched the man who apparently murdered the "Lady in White."

Rich dove further up the road and turned the wheel, skidding them around 180 degrees, the tires screeching until they came to a full stop.

"Whoa!" they all screamed in unison.

Rich was still panting as the Camry came to a full stop.

"Did you see him? I saw him. Did everyone else see him?" Brent rambled.

"Holy Shit!" Cam exclaimed.

"I saw him, I saw him," Rich said.

"Was that the guy from the story?" Brent asked.

"It sure looked like him," Dean said.

"Oh my god!" Cam exclaimed.

"We should go back and see if that really was him," Rich said.

"We're not picking him up if it is," Laura said.

"I think we should get the hell out of here," Brent said.

"I don't believe it!" Cam exclaimed.

"I'm going back to see if that was really him," Rich said, hitting the gas, squealing the tires to get the car back in motion.

"What if it really was the killer?" Brent asked, his nerves shot.

"What can he do? We're in a car," Rich said.

They drove along into the fog, but no trace of anyone was seen anywhere.

"Isn't this about where he was?" Dean asked.

"I think so," Rich said.

"There were no cars behind us or in front of us," Brent said. "Where could he have gone?"

"Seriously, guys, where did he go?" Cam asked, finally coming out of his stupor.

"I don't know," Rich said. "Are you ready to go home now, Dean?" Eerily, there was no answer. "Dean?"

Rich pulled a switch to turn on the overhead light to find Dean replaced by the mustachioed man in the gray hoodie! He raised a knife, causing Rich to let out a scream.

Brent froze in shock as the killer's blade shone in the overhead car light.

Cam broke out in hysterical laughter, while Laura snatched open the car door with one hand, while grabbing Brent's hand with her other to drag him out of the car with her.

Brent instinctively followed as they ran for their lives while Rich's screams trailed off. Cam's maniacal laughter continued until Brent turned to look behind him while still running away. He saw the bloodied blade flash in the dome light once more.

"Good one, Dean," Cam said, still laughing hysterically as the blade, now dripping with Rich's blood, flashed down for another strike and another as Cam yelled, "Ow! Ooo!" Then even Cam's laughter ceased, and blood splattered across the car windows. Dean was never seen again.

MURDER AT CAMP RAVENSCAR

by Toshiya Kamei

A shrill scream shatters the silence of our cabin. Sarafina lurches out of the bathroom, a small towel barely covering her. I leap to my feet and run to her.

I cup her flushed cheeks and stroke her sun-kissed skin. Her long bangs frame her oval face, and copper freckles dot her upturned nose. Droplets of sweat bead on her upper lip, and I feel like licking them. Noticing her blood-soaked hands, however, I step back.

"Are you hurt, Sarafina?" I manage to ask after a pause.

She shakes her head, cheeks wet with tears. I step into the bathroom and pull the shower curtain back, revealing a mangled body in the bathtub. Blood, blood everywhere. The way his throat is severed seems vaguely familiar, but I can't place it. His eyes stare open and vacant.

It's Bruce, the himbo counselor. Good riddance. Alive, he repulsed me, but he's even worse now. His tongue sticks out like a reptile's, but his face reminds me of a hyena's. Fighting hard against nausea, I pull out my phone and dial 911. When I hang up, a text beeps in from Dad: "Never talk to the police without a lawyer."

"What the hell?" I mumble, confused. I've recently shared with him my murderous fantasy about Bruce over text, but how does he know about the murder already? I wipe my clammy hands on my shorts and hurry to write him back, demanding to know what's going on. I wait a few moments, staring at my screen, but my message remains unread.

Growing up, I was daddy's girl, especially after my parents split. I'm not ashamed to admit Dad was the one who bought me my first bra and sanitary napkins. Even now, I tell him everything, and he knows all my crushes by name, including Sarafina. I miss Dad, especially his bear hugs.

As the ambulance arrives, I shut myself away from everyone else, and the paramedics' footsteps recede into the background as I recall last night, which was Friday the Thirteenth.

My top bunk rattled, jolting me awake. Sarafina grumbled and moaned below me. Still foggy with sleep, I slid my hand under my shorts and touched my panties. I was wet. Sarafina consumed my thoughts, and I pretended we were entirely alone when we strolled around the camp.

As horny as any teen, I wanted to climb down and join Sarafina until I heard a man groan. It had to be Bruce. I'd texted my dad a few days ago and complained about Bruce getting in my way. I had imagined killing him myself.

Now, I have to wonder if Dad has anything to do with Bruce's gruesome demise. Knowing him the way I do, however, I know he's incapable of hurting anyone. Above all else, Dad has instilled loyalty in me. If I had to choose between him and someone else, I wouldn't hesitate to choose him. That's why I had to cut Mom out of my life. And loyalty is a two-way street. I know Dad won't let me down—unlike Sarafina.

In that top bunk, forced to listen to Bruce and Sarafina have sex below me, I pictured myself wagging a finger at Sarafina as the refrain of *Traitor! Traitor!* echoed through my heart.

Ever since camp began a week ago, Sarafina has given off bi-curious vibes. I swear her compliments were more than innocent flirting.

We hit it off from the jump and grew closer each time we spoke. A few fights here and there, but nothing serious. We soon learned we had many things in common. We were both from Ravenscar, and we were both born into a cult, although neither of us remembered much of it. It turned out our respective families belonged to the same sect at different times.

Not to mention, we kissed that night when we went skinny-dipping in the lake. She didn't exactly kiss me back, but she didn't resist either.

To block out the sounds of sex coming from below, I replayed in my head our lakeside conversation.

"Without makeup, I look like a twelve-year-old boy," I said. I hoped to pique her interest as I undressed.

"That's not true." Sarafina chuckled as she twisted her red curls into a bun.

"You should've seen me when I had my hair cut all short." I brushed my hand against her cheek. "I knew I was queer in sixth grade and came out in eighth."

"How queer are you, Gracie?" she asked. "If you don't mind my asking."

"I've never dated straight cis guys." My palms were sweaty, and I shifted my weight from foot to foot.

"That's cool."

An owl screeched overhead, causing me to jump. Sarafina laughed at me. I swatted at her, but that only made her laugh harder.

"It's not funny."

"You're such a scaredy-cat, Gracie."

I rolled my eyes, but the night felt light again. Buoyant.

"Do you listen to Girl in Red?" I asked, leaning forward.

When she nodded, I tugged her toward me and pressed my lips against hers. Her ample breasts felt good against my chest.

Afterward, she said I was the first girl she'd ever kissed, and I thought we were getting somewhere.

Sarafina waded into the lake until the water lapped her chest.

"Come on in," she said, waving me toward her. She floated on her back as the moonlight glimmered over her, illuminating her every curve.

When I dipped my toes in, something grabbed my foot, and I screamed as I wrenched away from its hold.

"Stop kidding around, Gracie! God, you're so sensitive. It's probably a clump of weeds or something." She swam toward me and splashed water in my face.

I scrubbed my eyes, unable to see if anything lurked in the darkness. "Weeds. Yeah." Heart racing, I followed her into the water.

The rustle of clothing brings me back to the present as Sarafina slips into a T-shirt and shorts.

"Let me ask you a question," I say when she sits next to me on her bunk. "What do you remember about the cult?"

"Not much." She shrugs. "Why?"

"That makes two of us," I say. "All I know is hearsay. Facts gleaned from old newspapers on file at our local library."

She nods.

"How about Lord Ravenscar?" I ask.

"The leader?"

"Yeah. He's the direct descendant of the town's founder."

"I remember an egg project. All the girls were instructed to carry mangos for a week instead of eggs. The leader said, 'Milk the fruit with care.'"

"That's creepy." I grimace.

"You can say that again. I've recovered a few more memories of the cult during therapy, but my mom says they're probably false."

Sarafina sighs. "Like I said, I was really young. Some ex-members say the leader was a cross between David Koresh and Viggo Mortensen, but who knows?"

"My mom says my dad looked like Viggo Mortensen when he was young. He's worked as a deprogrammer since he left the cult."

"Really?"

I nod and look down at my hands. "Sometimes, I think he misses the cult. I know that's strange to say, but cutting free of something like that has to leave its scars. He never talks about it, but every once in a while, he gets this odd expression on his face when we drive past the old compound."

Sarafina places her hand over mine. She doesn't try to fill the silence.

"Per the *Unsolved Murders* website," I say, needing to drag the conversation away from my dad, "Lord Ravenscar disappeared before he could be arrested. Some say he escaped to Latin America and died there."

"I had no idea," Sarafina says.

"Lord Ravenscar killed his victims by cutting their throats," I say. "He thought public mass killings would bring about a violent conflict. Possibly another civil war."

"Why are you telling me this?"

"That's how Bruce was killed." I make a slicing gesture across my throat.

"What are you saying?" Her lips twitch. "Bruce was killed by the cult? Or Lord Ravenscar is back?"

"I don't know." I shrug. "Not yet."

She remains silent.

The first officer on the scene comes over to us, holding a yellow legal pad. She wears a shiny brass nameplate that reads, "Lieutenant Shirley Rodriguez." I'm sorry, but it's hard not to stare at her busty chest. I tell myself to keep it together, forcing myself to look her in the eye.

"May I see your phone, Gracie?" Lt. Rodriguez asks. I shoot Sarafina a quick glance as if to say, "Let me handle this."

"Why? Are we suspects?" Despite my calm exterior, I tremble from head to toe inside.

"No, not for the time being. It's routine. We're asking everyone."

"Don't you need a warrant for that?" I ask. I have trouble breathing, and my face feels flushed.

Lt. Rodriguez nods, frowning.

Dad always says the police are bad guys, but I'd say good guys are even worse because they hide behind masks of respectability. The bad guys, on the other hand, are honest about who they are. I excuse myself to the bathroom and delete my entire text thread with Dad. I don't have to pee, but I noisily pull sheets of toilet paper off the roll before flushing the toilet. When I return, Lt. Rodriguez is gone.

"My family is coming for me tomorrow," I say, trying to cheer us up. Uniformed cops swarm around, but I pretend they don't exist.

"I can't get hold of mine," she says, forlorn and dejected. "They're vacationing in Europe."

"You can't stay here, Sarafina," I say. "Why don't you come with us?"

She nods.

By nightfall, a light drizzle begins to fall, and we climb into our respective bunks.

"Are you still awake, Sarafina?" I ask, but there's no reply.

I climb off my bunk and slip into hers. I cuddle against her and feel her chest move up and down. Listening to her breathing, I fall asleep as well.

At daybreak, my dad arrives, and we leave camp together.

"Dad, this is Sarafina," I say as we climb into his SUV. He shakes her hand, and his fingers linger a tad too long on hers. He meets my gaze over Sarafina's head and shoots me a conspiratorial look as if to say I'm in on something—like when we had an ice cream date behind Mom's back years ago—and I nod out of reflex.

Dad steps on the gas, gravel crunching under the tires. As row after row of cornfields blur outside the window, I doze off next to Sarafina in the backseat, my head resting on her shoulder.

After dinner, I leave Sarafina in the guest room and return to my room. There's a knock on the door, and I say, "Come in." I expect Sarafina, but my dad walks in instead.

"Gracie, you have to get rid of that girl."

"What?" I sit up in bed, taken aback. "What are you talking about, Dad?"

"Once you turn eighteen, you're an adult." His face clouds, and a dark gleam comes into his eyes. "You need to take on more responsibility."

"What are you talking about?" I stand slowly, and as I look at him—my dad, the same man who taught me how to ride a bike, who makes my school lunches and loves family movie nights—bile creeps up my throat.

I've never seen him behave this way before. My mom has warned of his dark side—his brooding solitude—since their divorce several years ago, but I've never heeded her warnings.

"Our sect has been dormant for the last fifteen years, but it's time to revive it."

I'm at a loss for words. I believed the leader had died long ago, and that his followers had dispersed across the country. I stare at my dad. He meets my gaze squarely, and I shiver at the implications. Even so, I can't bring myself to believe what's happening.

"I did you a favor by doing away with Bruce."

"Seriously?" I feel my blood drain from my face. My knees almost buckle.

"I thought you wanted him dead."

That was true, but it had only been a fantasy.

"We need more sacrifices, but I'm rusty due to lack of practice." He laughs like everything is normal. "It's time you become God's instrument."

"Excuse me?"

"You heard me," Dad says and hands me a knife. When I touch the blade, electricity jolts through my body. I want to spring away from him, but I can't move. Tears glass my eyes. This isn't real. It can't be real.

All his life was a lie. That means mine was also a lie. Confusion seizes me, and my mind goes blank.

"Leave Sarafina alone!" My scream pierces my ears. The next thing I know, my dad stumbles and collapses, and I stand over his prone body with the bloody knife in my hand.

"Gracie!" Sarafina's voice prompts me to turn around. She gasps, her mouth agape to scream.

"Wait, it's not what it looks like," I stammer. The blade feels heavy in my trembling grasp.

Dad's dying behind me. With a wet gurgle, blood pours from his mouth.

I stare at Sarafina through a mist of tears: her face, chalky white. Her hands, tucked inside her sleeves. My hands are covered in Dad's blood.

The camp, and my crush, feel so far away. I take a step toward her.

I won't loosen my grip until she promises silence.

THE PUKING MAN

by Tom Folske

Daphne Riddle sometimes wondered how she had become a part of the peer group she was involved with. It all started with her boyfriend, Frank Richards, a tall, bohemian kid, slobbish and mostly greasy, but with great genes, who rocked a fauxhawk, made with Elmer's school glue and colored with Kool-Aid packets, as well as Sid Vicious or any other punk king who rocked their mohawks.

Daphne and Frank had been going out for about three months now, and even though Frank was tall, intimidating in appearance, and boisterously vocal about his anti-government philosophies, deep down, he was the biggest teddy bear in the world.

Aside from Frank, the main group of "punks" at Chipper Valley High School, not counting all the fair-weather friends that only associated themselves sometimes, consisted of Waldo, Emery, and Frank's Sister Cheryl, but she was currently in Greece for the next two weeks. Unlike Frank, who couldn't save up two bucks, Cheryl was maybe even too frugal, but at the same time, she was able to afford the vacation all by herself; well, her friend Becky went with, but Becky's parents had paid for her portion of the trip.

It had been an evening not unlike any other; they had procured booze and had taken a couple of shots, Emery having taken a bit more than a couple, and now they were getting bored. Normally, they would have gone to the pool hall, or to the lake, or even to the park, but today, Waldo had suggested the playground behind the high school. Chipper Valley High was only about two blocks away, and the playground there was significantly bigger and better than the one at the park, but they almost never went there because they hated having the school looming over them, watching, waiting, nagging at them, making sure they knew they would have to come back.

This, however, was their last summer before senior year, the school was under construction, and the booze had helped to lower their apprehensions about such things, so after a short discussion, the group grabbed their bottle, poured half of it into an empty water bottle, in case they had to deal cops, and left the other half back at Frank's, for the very same reason. Once they all had a final swig before the journey, they tucked the bottle into the bottom of Daphne's decently spacious purse, grabbed their band-patch-covered jackets and spike-studded accessories, and then they were on their way.

While Frank sported the longer hair and fauxhawk, Emery had legitimately shaved the sides of his head for an authentic mohawk, and Waldo, also with longer hair, had molded his hairdo into that of a faux-tri-hawk. Daphne, on the other hand, had simply dyed her hair a darkened fuchsia, regularly used a great deal of eyeliner and mascara, as they all did, and had gotten several piercings. She had her left nostril pierced, her right eyebrow twice, both earlobes twice, the top part of her left ear, and her tongue. She also had a small henna tattoo of a musical note on her left cheek.

It was past dark when they left Frank's house, and full dark when they reached the park, but it was a cool night with lots of stars shining down on them and very few bugs, as was generally the case within the confines of suburbia.

They swung on the swings, took pulls off their bottle, and talked about how much they hated school and its attempt to reform them from individual thinkers into mindless automatons. They also talked about their band "Mystic Hellfire in a Unicorn's Dingleberry," and if they were really going to keep that as a band name.

"It might draw attention on a flyer or something, but even The Butthole Surfers probably didn't reach their full potential for fame, simply because people don't want to or are too embarrassed to say their name," Daphne explained.

"Bullshit," Emery argued.

"Do you really think The Sex Pistols would have gotten as big as they did if they had called themselves The Dick Pistols instead, I mean, look at The Clash and The Misfits, you need something that people aren't afraid to say," Daphne replied.

"Mystic Hellfire in a Unicorn's Dingleberry is the perfect, all-encompassing name. It has mysticism as in Mystic, Hell, and darkness with Hellfire, fantasy and love with Unicorn, and crudeness and humor with Dingleberry. Besides, dingleberry isn't even vulgar," Waldo argued.

"Maybe we should just be The Dingleberries," Emery said.

"Mystic Hellfire would be cool," Frank said. "It's too cliché, though. What about shortening it up to Hell's Unicorns?"

"That actually sounds kind of badass," Daphne replied honestly, not just supporting her boyfriend.

"Fuck it… I kinda like it too. It's all *Rainbow in the Dark*-style and shit," Waldo agreed.

"What about just *Unicorn Dingleberries*?" Emery asked.

Frank just shook his head.

Emery shrugged, then climbed up the playground and went down the slide.

Frank and Waldo were sitting opposite of Daphne, and as she watched Emery's progressively inebriated ass go down the slide. They both sat, almost motionless, staring pensively toward the school.

Daphne felt a shiver go through her, a shiver that she would later come to wonder if it had in fact been a calling, her right before Frank and Waldo both seemed to simultaneously spark with an idea.

"I bet the school doesn't have video cameras," Waldo said suddenly. "And if they do, they probably suck."

"Yeah..." Frank said uncertainly. "And it's not like they could dust for prints, not with all the kids that go there constantly touching everything."

"It really wouldn't be that hard of a place to infiltrate, I bet you half the windows on the ground floor are unlocked. All you'd have to do is pop open a screen..." Waldo proposed.

"Are you guys actually considering breaking into the school?" Daphne asked incredulously.

Emery overheard and returned to join the conversation.

"Not to do any real damage," Frank suggested. "Just to explore and say we did it."

"Yeah, we can maybe play some pranks, but we won't break anything, at least nothing valuable," Waldo added.

"Fuck yeah!" Emery replied. "I'm in."

"You guys are serious?" Daphne asked nervously.

"A feat like this would be legendary," Frank told her.

"The risk is minimal, and the reward is great..." Waldo remarked.

Daphne hesitantly inhaled. "Alright, but if you guys start committing felonies or something, I'm out."

"We'll just tell them we got lost and were looking for a phone," Emery somehow concluded the conversation as he rose and began walking toward the school. The group almost instinctively followed.

"Look Daph, we're not going to burn the school down or anything, we're just gonna stick it to the man. What better way to give the system the finger than to violate it, to get inside it where we aren't wanted and to do what we please," Frank explained reassuringly. "I mean, I hate rapists, they are loathing, disgusting creatures, but we are raping the system, not a person."

"Lady Liberty, spread your legs," Waldo added. "Hey! That would be an awesome song title."

"We're pegging Uncle Sam," Emery uttered loudly.

"Maybe you're pegging Uncle Sam," Waldo joked. "I'll stick with the hairy French chick."

"I don't know," Daphne replied. "Uncle Sam is frisky. He wants YOU! He really, really wants you… and if his legs are that long, I can only imagine."

"We aren't sperm, and the school isn't an ovum, in case you weren't paying attention, we are committed B and E or trespassing or some shit, not rape," Frank reminded them.

"I guess you're right," Waldo replied with a melodramatic sigh.

"Let's just fucking do this," Frank said as they approached the back wall of the school and began to examine the building, attempting to find a point of ingress.

"I am going to imagine I am raping the school," Emery stated awkwardly, after the conversation was over.

The small group of non-conformists didn't have to search long or far before they found an open window that Daphne, at least, could fit through, then opened it wider to let the rest of them in.

They didn't need a lookout, as the window wasn't high off the ground or highly visible, and all four of them were in the building in less than thirty seconds, with relatively no commotion at all, and nothing whatsoever that anyone else could see or hear.

Once inside, Emery immediately went to turn on a light, but both Frank and Waldo stopped him.

"No light. We don't want to push our luck."

Emery reluctantly agreed as they huddled in the darkness, assessing what room they were in, so as to plan their next course of action.

"Where the fuck are we?" Emery asked.

"The art room," Daphne replied instantly, having been the most familiar with this room as she was an art geek, an amateur artist and painter who dabbled in sculpture.

"She's right," Frank confirmed, and after a moment, Waldo also shook his head in agreement.

"What can we do in here to fuck with shit?" Emery asked. "Make a bunch of clay dicks and harden them to people's projects?"

"That's not really how it works," Daphne answered.

"We can paint dicks on stuff?" Emery asked.

"Not on other kids' projects. We are here to fight the man, not our fellow inmates," Frank replied.

"Yeah, maybe we can paint dicks on some of the lockers later, but let's see what else we can get into first," Waldo added.

Emery conceded as Frank led the small group out into the dark corridor beyond.

"This place is fucking creepy when it's empty, and the lights are all off," Daphne commented. "I feel like I'm in the Paris catacombs or something."

"The thought of school always terrifies me, light or dark, so I'm good," Waldo replied.

"It is kind of creepy," Frank agreed. "It reminds me of the mausoleum from the *Phantasm* movies, only with the dead spirits of children's childhoods behind their closed doors, instead of just bodies."

"Why the fuck would you say that?" Daphne asked, but before Frank could reply, there was a loud hissing sound as the hall suddenly began to fill up with devilishly white smoke.

Daphne could taste the disgusting flavor of chalk mixed with baby powder as she began to gag, fleeing from the smoke and coming into the clear air beyond as she realized that she could hear laughter in the thick, concealing haze.

"What the fuck is wrong with you?" Frank asked angrily.

"Yeah, you dumb, drunk bastard. That shit tastes like shit," Waldo added angrily.

The smoke had cleared just enough for them to see Emery, standing there, holding the nozzle of a fire extinguisher at them and laughter hysterically.

Daphne shook her head irately. "You're cut off for a while."

"Come on. It was just a joke. You guys can't be mad. It's just a little fire extinguisher. I made you flame-retardant. I did you a favor."

"Shut the fuck up and let's just see what else we can do?" Waldo replied.

"We can shoot basketball in the dark, just like those Nike commercials from a few years ago," Frank suggested.

"We could go to the science room and get the guinea pig drunk," Waldo suggested jokingly.

"We could steal the guinea pig," Emery commented.

"Okay, Richard Gere," Frank replied. "Maybe we can get into the principal's office and put a condom on the microphone she uses for daily announcements."

"Maybe we could change our grades," Waldo wondered aloud.

"What if we break into the cafeteria and steal all the Italian Dunkers?" Emery asked. "Not even as a stick-it-to-the-man kind of thing, but just because they are good."

"Let's go swim in the fucking pool," Daphne interjected abruptly.

They all thought about her suggestion for like half a second, then agreed wholeheartedly and started to make their way toward that corner of the school.

"We're going skinny dipping, right?" Emery asked, looking lasciviously at Daphne.

"You fucking wish," Daphne said, giving him the finger, but knowing that he was mostly kidding.

"I'm about to hang out with my wang out, and if you guys want to rock out with her cocks out, or in your case, Daphne, if you want to jam out with your clam out, then you all are more than welcome," Waldo said as he rapidly removed his shirt. They were only one turn away from the locker rooms, and the entrance to the pool was right beyond.

The other three of them were not only considering how to remove their clothes as they walked, but they were also considering how much of their clothing they wanted to remove as they approached the boy's locker room door, since it was the closest.

"I've never been in the boys' locker room before," Daphne said.

"If you had, we wouldn't be dating," Frank replied.

"It's never too late for a gang bang," Emery added.

"Give it up, man," Waldo answered. "The only pussy you're getting for the rest of your life belongs to Handgela and her five friends."

"Can I have some more booze yet?"

Before anyone could answer, they were all stopped dead in their tracks as they heard a loud cough come from the locker room. It was just one loud bark of a cough, but it was enough to unnerve every single one of them.

"What the hell was that?" Daphne asked quietly, fearfully.

"Probably just the pipes settling," Emery answered.

"Yeah, it was probably nothing," Waldo said, though he did not make a move to enter the locker room.

"It was nothing, babe," Frank consoled, putting his arm comfortingly around Daphne.

Despite their words, they all remained where they stood, still as corpses, listening intently for a sound they all hoped wouldn't come again.

Each one of them jumped in terror when another cough, closer this time, came from just behind the locker room door.

Frank moved protectively in front of Daphne.

"Let's get the fuck out of here," Waldo whispered.

They all took off down the corridor and around the corner, but not before hearing the door to the boy's locker room swing open as footsteps emerged into the hall.

"Go. Go. Go. Go. Go," Emery urged as they all ran back the way they had come.

They didn't make it far before they began to hear someone approaching behind them, only now, the encroaching person, a male from the sounds of it, was not only continuing to prominently cough and gag, they were audibly vomiting, and not only could they hear the sound of the man's stomach turning itself inside out as he wretched, they could hear the splattering of the contents of the man's stomach slapping against the ground with a chunky, watery cacophony of internal exodus.

"What in the actual fuck?" Waldo asked incredulously as they ran.

"What the fuck was that?" Frank asked.

"What do you mean what?" Emery questioned fearfully.

"Why would a teacher, or even a janitor or cop chase us, not say anything, and puke while doing it?" Frank remarked.

"This is not fucking right," Waldo stated matter-of-factly.

"Fuck this," Emery said, stopping suddenly and causing everyone else to stop as well, if only to encourage him to continue speaking. "There are three of us, and the dude is obviously sick. Let's kick his ass."

Frank and Waldo looked at each other hesitantly as Daphne continued to back away slowly, terrified beyond words at the thought of what might be making the puking sounds that had now almost made their way around the corner. She didn't know why she was so afraid, but every instinct warned her to flee. She was legitimately horrified, not like the fear of getting in trouble if a security guard found you. No, this fear was more akin to stumbling across a hungry wolf when you are lost in the woods, in the middle of the night.

"Let's just go, guys," Daphne pleaded, trying unsuccessfully to hide the dread in her voice. "Why would we hurt this guy? He is probably just a security guard doing his job."

"Puking and following us without speaking?" Waldo asked.

"Yeah, this guy is definitely fucking with us," Emery told Daphne, before turning toward the encroaching pestilent sound and yelling. "Hey, Fuckface, turn around now, or we'll fuck you up!"

The approaching footsteps stopped, but the gagging continued, and this time, when the man vomited, they glimpsed the outer rim of the chunky pool of his bile and partially digested food, signifying that the man was just around the corner.

Emery started forward.

"Hold it, man," Waldo said, starting after him, but keeping his distance.

Frank didn't move from in front of Daphne.

"Look here, you sick fuck, I am about to fuck you up," Emery said loudly, but jumped back about a foot as the man, normal in size and appearance, but with a maliciously repulsive grin, appeared from around the corner, instantly bringing his eyes to stare upon Emery with an unsettling avarice.

"Get the fuck back, man," Emery commanded. "You're spooky as fuck, and I don't want whatever the fuck you got. Get the fuck out of here, or I'm going to break your fucking legs."

The man continued to smile hungrily at Emery as he approached, seemingly weak from his illness, leaning one arm against the wall of lockers as he made his way forward, but not moving slowly in the slightest as he approached.

"Stop, man, I'm fucking warning you," Emery shouted, taking off the spiked wrist strap he was wearing and wrapping it around his fist in a mock-spiked knuckles.

The man began to laugh now, between gagging, and he puked one more time, the spatter of which splashed onto the tops of Emery's shoes as he proceeded forward.

Waldo was now right behind Emery as the boy raised his fists, ready to strike.

"I'm fucking warning you, man!" Emery said, stepping almost within striking distance.

The gagging and coughing man took two more steps, then stopped and looked intently right at Emery.

"You're fucking spooky, man," Emery said, rushing forward and swinging his spiked fist at the man.

Instead of blocking the boy's attack, or even evading it, the vomiting man just opened his mouth, then continued to open it wider, well beyond physical human limitations, horrifying the small band of onlookers, Emery most of all. The puking man's maw opened so large, Emery's fist went all the way down the man's gullet, his arm disappearing up to the shoulder, before Emery let out the loudest and most depressing scream of agony any of them had ever heard in their lives.

Waldo went to punch their terrifying aggressor, to aid his friend, when the puking man began to adjust Emery's head, pulling the poor boy's body back, as his clavicle had been previously hung up at the corner of the puking man's mouth, then he used his hands to guide the boy's torso into his mouth, like the pincers of a bug, before crutching meatily once after both shoulders had disappeared into its maw, a second time around the hips, and a third time at the knees, snapping right through Emery's patella and slurping up the last bit of the boy's legs and limp feet, just like spaghetti noodles.

Waldo halted abruptly before the macabre atrocity taking place right in front of his eyes, just as the puking man finished swallowing Emery's shoes.

"Fuck this! I'm out!" Waldo said, realizing there was nothing he could do for his friend and taking off toward Frank and Daphne, who had turned to run as soon as Waldo himself had turned.

The three remaining friends kept a relative pace with each other until they were about two corners ahead of their pursuer, judging the approaching gagging and retching.

"What the fuck is that? Why the fuck is it here? How the fuck do we get out of here?" Frank asked all three questions in one breath.

Even though they had all attended Chipper Valley High for the last three years, the school looked unbelievably different, empty and in the dark, and besides that, they were more frightened and panicked than any of them had ever been before.

"Look, an 'EXIT' sign," Waldo shouted joyfully, pointing back the way from which they had just come. It was the sign above the doors for the side parking lot, but it was across the last corridor, the hall in which, judging from the proximity of the gagging and coughing, the Puking Man was just now coming up. If they were to have any shot at freedom, they had to go now. Waldo made a run for the door.

Frank and Daphne hesitated, and then it was too late. The Puking Man was almost around the corner. Waldo, however, raced fast enough down the hall that, at his current speed, he was set to make it to the doors and outside well before The Puking Man could reach him. They felt no ill will toward their friend and wished him nothing but success. They hoped he would get away and bring back cops.

Halfway across the hall, however, the Puking Man's gagging became productive in a chunky, soupy-sounding expulsion of entrails and viscera. Daphne and Frank watched at a distance as small, chewed-up bits of Emery, his bones, scraps of organs, flaps of flesh, tattered, wet rags that were once their friend's clothes, even chunks of hairy scalp, all exploded outward from the unseen man around the corner, outward and right onto Waldo and in his path.

Waldo still might have made it; he didn't slip on the organic slop that was once his friend, but his foot did come down directly on top of one of Emery's eyeballs. His error was that he saw the eyeball, the dilated pupil, the brilliant blue iris, the bloody root and sclera, and knew, as he felt the squish and then the pop under his foot, exactly what he had stepped on. If he had just ignored it and kept going, he would have been fine, but Waldo instinctively stopped and recoiled his foot in shame and revulsion.

That moment of pause, that small hesitation, was all the Puking Man had needed. Waldo had just started to get going again when the Puking Man lunged forward, into view, and grabbed hold of Waldo's arm, pulling him close, only to take a massive bite out of his cheek, though some of the flesh that had been torn away came from his chin and lips. As he pulled away, there hung a thick flap of skin, dangling freely from the Puking Man's mouth, even more noticeable as it contained a large and distinct patch of Waldo's hair, the bit right above his ear.

Daphne, Frank, and Waldo all screamed simultaneously, though Waldo's cry was much louder, as it was a shriek of blinding pain, whereas Daphne and Frank had only been crying out in screams of pure terror.

Waldo, always one to fight against absolutely everything that tried to take any power over him, went down swinging. He hit the Puking Man in the temple with his angry right hook as he threw himself on top of his adversary, knocking him back around the corner, before beginning to pummel him wildly, at least by the sounds of it. Those sounds, however, did not last long before new sounds arrived, sounds that encouraged Frank and Daphne not to intervene. Instead of hearing the slapping of a fist against a face, the terrified teen punks began to hear the crunching and twisting of bones, as well as the rending and tearing of human flesh, before

Waldo's incoherent screaming was forever silenced by the boisterously macabre cacophony of his demise.

"Go! Go! Go!" Frank hollered in delirious alarm, urging Daphne down the hall in front of him.

"Where the fuck are we going?" Daphne asked, both fearfully, but also because she knew running around aimlessly was likely to get them killed.

"Well, fuck!" Frank shouted. "I know. I know… Let's get out the window we came through. Where the fuck is it?" He began to look around frantically.

"Follow me," Daphne told him, taking her boyfriend's bulky hand in her own and leading him down the dark, empty corridor.

As they ran, the silence of the school made their footsteps echo, and their breathing was so heavy now that they couldn't hear themselves think. Unfortunately, however, they could still hear the loud and painful sound of gagging, growing ever closer, sporadically intermixed with sharp, raspy hacking, and once or twice by the sound of pieces of their friends being regurgitated out by the atrocious fiend.

Each hack, each cough, sounded infinitely louder as they reverberated off the shadowy rows of unused lockers. It sounded like the Puking Man was gagging right in their ears, and as if the sound wasn't awful and disturbing enough, they could physically feel the Puking Man's pestilence. They felt like they were getting sick simply by hearing their noxious pursuer, as there was a definable sense of illness and malady in the air, mixed with the coppery, butcher shop smells of the blood and innards of their former friends, now the former contents of the Puking Man's stomach. Daphne started to feel so queasy that she herself began to gag.

"Come on, Daph, let's go," Frank cried, his spine going tight with terror at the encroaching menace.

Daphne only paused for a moment to regain control over her stomach, but in that small timeframe, the Puking Man seemed to gain on them a great deal. At first, they had outdistanced the morbid pursuer enough so that he was once again out of sight, but that almost made things worse, as they could still hear his harsh, dry coughing and his agonized gagging growing ever closer. Suspense and dread pervaded every facility of the young couple's beings, both physically and mentally, as they sensed, but could not see, the Puking Man approaching from around the corner.

"This way, we're here," Daphne shouted joyfully, pointing two classrooms away, at the slightly ajar door they had come through. She and Frank sprinted the rest of the way down the hall before darting into the art room and closing and locking the door behind them.

"Let's get the hell out of here," Frank said, rushing toward the window. "Here, Daphne, you go first. I'll help you out."

The classroom was dark, and Daphne slammed her hip hard against one of the desks and almost toppled over, but caught herself right at the last moment. They didn't have time for a slip-up. She could hear the Puking Man coughing and gagging a little further down the corridor. She hoped he wasn't right outside the door, being as time and sound were funny when you were utterly panicked and trying not to die, but she didn't have time to worry.

Daphne ran and jumped at the window, pulling herself out with no help at all from Frank, who had, in fact, tried to help but simply hadn't been quick enough.

Once Daphne was outside, she landed on the grass with a loud bang that sounded an awful lot like a door being kicked open. Instantly her hair stood up, and her blood went cold; she turned as she rose to help Frank, who was just now at the window and about to climb up and out himself.

Daphne went to give Frank her hand when he slipped backward and had to step back up again. He rapidly took her hand

and started to pull himself out the window when Daphne saw myriad horrendous things all occurring simultaneously. She had been staring into Frank's desperate eyes as they changed from panic to stupefied, then to absolute terror, as his mouth drooped in disbelief. Daphne watched as clammy, unhealthily white hands clasped around both of Frank's shoulders. He hadn't even had the time or coherence to gibber or scream before Daphne witnessed gargantuan, yellowed, malformed teeth appear over the top of Frank's fauxhawk, crushing the extravagant hair down against her boyfriend's skull as Frank's entire head began to disappear down into the Puking Man's gullet.

Although she had turned to look away at that point, Daphne continued to hold Frank's hand until she heard a loud crunch, right before his grip intensified to the point of pain, to where she thought he was going to break her fingers, then his hand instantly went limp as his whole body began to convulse. That was when Daphne let go of Frank's corpse and went screaming into the night.

***

Police found Daphne twenty minutes later, still screaming, and brought her straight home. As soon as she had calmed down enough to be questioned, she told the officers everything that had happened.

They immediately went to the school and found most of the remains of her friends and enough gore to corroborate with perhaps some of her story, but the Puking Man was nowhere to be found, and no one truly believed that was what they were looking for anyway, but they were all pretty certain that Daphne Riddle had nothing to do with it.

Being as it had still been fairly early in the night when they had first gone to the school, it was only about midnight when the police brought Daphne back home, and just before three o'clock in the morning before they finally left.

It was almost three thirty by the time Daphne found herself alone in her room, lying in her bed, about to try to get the sleep that her mind dreaded, but her body absolutely craved. She would have been out the moment her head hit the pillow, except she heard a noise coming from her backyard, from right below her bedroom window. It was the sound of someone gagging.

THREE'S A CROWD

by Kevin LeCompte

Walking through the woods was much easier than it had been two nights ago. This time, all they had to carry with them were shovels. And flashlights of course.

Ben rested his shovel upon his shoulder, but Mitch held his up like a baseball bat. They'd talked in detail about their plan while driving over to the woods but hadn't spoken a word to each other since they'd arrived.

Mitch broke the silence, but only in a whisper as he needed to make sure that nobody heard them out there. "Hey, you remember back in Freshman year when we went on the Boy Scout campout and snuck out into the woods in the middle of the night to drink that rum you'd taken from your parents' bar?"

Ben continued walking, staring straight ahead, not responding in any way.

"You remember that?" Mitch whispered louder this time.

Ben nodded. Said nothing.

"That was a great night," Mitch said.

They continued walking in silence for another minute or so. It was completely quiet except for the crickets, who were not being shy on this particular night. They were really making their presence known. Mitch didn't think he'd ever heard such screeching, and it would continue that way for the rest of their trip. They were getting closer to their destination now.

Mitch stared up at the sky through the trees as they walked now, thinking there must be a bright full moon staring down at him. It felt like that kind of night, felt like something must be watching him from above, accusing him, judging him, preparing some terrible punishment for him to face after he'd died someday many years down the road. But there was no bright full moon. There was barely a moon at all. A little slice of one, maybe, a sliver of light did shine down through the trees. It just wasn't the glare of a bright, full moon but rather the squinting sideways gaze of a waxing crescent moon.

"Hey," Mitch said as he backhanded Ben's arm. "You remember that time our teams both made it to the championship round of the Richton Tournament, you pitched against me in the ninth?" He laughed. "Crazy how life plays out."

Mitch, of course, had taken his friend deep, a no-doubter, to end the game. He'd spent all day long traveling down memory lane, recalling countless memories he'd made with Ben, and that one had crossed his mind a few times.

Ben stopped walking and just stood there staring at Mitch.

After a few steps, Mitch realized he was traveling alone and turned back to see what the deal was.

"Dude, why the hell would I wanna talk about any of this shit right now?" Ben asked, lifting his shovel up a bit as he did so. He teared up then, his pitch immediately squeaky high. "You fuckin kidding me? We're going to dig up my fucking girlfriend, and you wanna talk about scouts and baseball?"

"Shhh...," Mitch rushed back towards his friend. "Be quiet, bro. You can't have someone hear you saying that shit." He glanced all around, shining his little flashlight along the ground to see if there were signs of anybody nearby, grazing his friend's wrist as he turned around.

"Don't fuckin touch me," Ben whisper shouted. "Let's go get this over with." He took off walking in longer strides now, having quickened his pace. Mitch followed, staying behind a bit after the outburst.

It truly had been an accident, what happened to Ben's

girlfriend a couple of nights ago while they were partying in Mitch's basement. His parents had gone out of town for the week, and there had been some drinking going on. There was a big party on Saturday with a good thirty people or so. But on Sunday, Mitch wanted a calmer night to cure his hangover, so he only invited Ben, who just had to bring Tracey with him.

Yes, it had been an accident, a stupid accident, but still an accident. It was after eleven by then, and Mitch was drunk again. He shook his head now, recalling the moment he brought his father's gun, a revolver which was originally owned by his grandfather, downstairs, wanting to show Ben since they had just been talking about shooting BB guns in scouts back in the day. It should've been fine except that drunken Mitch had thought it would be no problem to just toss the gun to his friend, maybe thinking it probably wasn't even loaded, or that you have to pull the trigger to shoot it, and how can one possibly pull the trigger while catching it. Or maybe. Maybe he'd just tossed it because he was drunk.

Either way, it happened so fast. Fireworks went off, then Tracey was on the ground, and there was blood everywhere, and even now, Mitch felt horrible for the fact that his very first thought-sure, a million came flooding in right after-but his very first thought was just a thank god that they were in the basement and on the tile and not up in the family room where there was carpeting. Blood can be cleaned off tile, but not off carpeting.

They'd reached their destination, Tracey's unmarked grave. He was positive they had reached it because he could hear the frogs now, which meant they were by the creek. Mitch knew that she was buried close to the creek but not too close, in between two trees, each of which had moss growing along its base. It seemed memorable enough without standing out all that much. Besides, two nights ago, when they'd had to somehow navigate a way to drag two shovels, flashlights, and a body with them, they'd simply run out of strength and energy and would settle for any location.

"This is it," Mitch said to a still silent Ben. Ben had wanted to call the cops, call her parents, call 911 at first, having clearly been in shock and lost his mind as he seemed to think that somebody might still be able to help her, save her life.

But Mitch had insisted that she was gone, that they had to be smart and not let this ruin their lives as well. All he knew was what his father always said to him, had preached to him for years now, telling him to make sure he didn't screw it up, that he kept his eye on the ball and on the prize that would come with it, and more recently, to make sure he never did anything to lose his full ride baseball scholarship to Arkansas, that once he was in the majors and getting paid, his father would sell the company and they could spend a lot more time together.

So now here they were, standing over this grave, and Mitch again felt like a jerk for the thought that was running through his head, that he just wished Ben had made a smarter decision, much like he had, and he'd dumped his girlfriend before going to college.

Tracey was older, though, already a college girl, so maybe his friend just saw it all differently. The two of them had met in a tattoo parlor, as crazy as that sounds. He was getting a tattoo of the comedy and drama masks on his arm, and she was getting a butterfly on her wrist. They just happened to have been sitting close enough to small talk and got to know the basics of one another while getting their tats, and the rest was history.

Mitch felt that sick feeling starting to trickle down into his stomach as he recalled the few times he'd heard Ben call Tracey his little butterfly. He imagined he called her that often, though he didn't really know for sure.

"Let's go," Ben said. "I need to get this over with."

The two of them got to digging, and it was a lot easier than Mitch had expected, much easier than a couple of nights ago, that's for sure. He supposed it made sense. The earth was all loosened up still and was coming up rather easily.

Ben jumped and freaked the hell out of Mitch in the process. His friend had turned all the way around in an instant, jumping up, then twisting and landing facing the other direction, facing behind them. "The hell was that?" he whispered. "You hear that?"

Mitch grabbed his chest, took a deep breath, then shone his light back that way. There was, in fact, a rustling sound, and for a moment, he thought maybe that was it, that maybe a cop was about to crawl out from behind a tree and point his gun at them, screaming for them to put their hands up. Or perhaps some nice old man would step out from behind a brush back there a ways, walking his dog, becoming a witness, then needing to make a rash decision and add somebody else to the hole they were digging. Well, re-digging, technically speaking.

Instead, a little fox came sniffing around the side of a tree just a few feet away from them. It made Mitch snort a laugh, but it also helped release all that tension in his body, let his shoulders drop back down, and his chest started expanding again as he remembered to breathe. "See, it's just a little fox," he said to Ben. "A cute little guy, actually."

Ben didn't seem satisfied. Kept waving his light around, clearly still searching for something, not settling on the fox being the source of whatever he'd thought he'd heard.

Mitch put his hand on his friend's shoulder. "Seriously. Relax man. Let's get back to this."

"I can smell it," Ben whispered. "I can for sure smell it."

Mitch, who was about to get back to digging, turned back towards his friend, sniffing the air as he did so. "Smell what? I don't smell anything."

"Her perfume," Ben said, still waving his light all around, searching for something, for someone? "I heard her whisper to me, tell me she loves me, and now I can smell her."

Mitch raised his head up, took a good whiff of the air again, didn't think he really smelled anything, but it was hard to tell for sure. At this time of night, out in a forest, there were all kinds of scents in the air.

He shook his head and got back to digging, giving up on his friend for now as there was a lot of work to be done here, and Ben seemed to be lost completely. Mitch hadn't been sure, but now he was more convinced. "It's not ghosts we should be worrying about right now. It's people. Cops. Witnesses."

His friend had been making him nervous the past day or so with his texts and phone calls, what he'd claimed to have said to the cops, and Mitch had begun to realize that his friend was not going to be able to do what was necessary for them to get through this situation. Mitch did feel bad about Tracey and certainly wished that the whole thing had never happened. Hell, he'd felt truly saddened, sick to his stomach for sure, as he stared down at her still body lying in his trunk. She must've bled out almost completely by then because he could see exactly where the bullet had gone into her head, and it was no longer bleeding. It was right in front of her ear. It had made another hole just an inch or so away from the hole she'd heard sounds through her entire life, heard her parents and siblings speak to her, tell her they loved her, heard Ben call her his little butterfly, probably way too many times than Mitch even wanted to know about. Where she'd heard birds chirping and children playing, heard leaves rustling through trees just like Mitch heard now.

He'd wrapped her head in a couple of plastic bags right about then, a couple of nights ago, that is, just to make sure no blood spilled out on the drive out to the woods. He'd also glanced down at her claddagh ring, tried to take it off even, considered clipping her finger when he couldn't, but then decided against it as he didn't want to make his friend more upset. But it frustrated him because it was always some ring or necklace or some stupid little thing in the person's pocket that got the killers caught in those true crime documentaries.

Mitch stopped digging. He had hit something solid, and it seemed like they were probably at the right depth now. Ben had just recently joined back in, working hard, in fact, working quickly.

In his most recent call, just a few hours ago, Ben had told Mitch that he was going to come clean with the cops, that it was the right thing to do, and that he just couldn't lie to Tracey's parents anymore. He just couldn't.

Mitch had succeeded in calming him down, told him that he'd come up with a plan to make this right, well, as right as it could be, all things considered, that they just had to go dig the body back up and bring it out into the open and write a suicide note.

After some coercing, Ben had agreed.

Still, there was a lot of work to be done. The hardest part was still ahead of him, Mitch considered.

They were getting around to the nitty-gritty now, having found her body, working around her limbs a bit so it would be easier to reach down under her, lift her up, pull her out of her grave, then find her a new one.

Mitch smelled something sweet then, too. It may have smelled like perfume. He took another whiff, accepted that it did smell differently than it had a few minutes ago, but also accepted that it must just be coming from the grave, that the smell had been on her when she'd been buried, that the dirt must have kept the scent trapped down there, and they had released it just now. Still, he did shine his flashlight around just to be sure, feeling a speck of uncertainty clinging to his chest and the heart within it.

Something felt off, and Mitch knew that was bound to happen, so he focused on his breathing, like his coach had taught him to do right before stepping up to the plate. He stepped back a bit, stretched his neck from side to side, waved the shovel back and forth, trying to relax. He thought about what his father always told him: not to screw up his opportunities, to take advantage of the gifts he was given, and, more recently, to make sure he kept his scholarship, got good grades, and made his mother happy, whatever the cost.

He took a couple more steps back, knowing he needed more space, needed to swing big to make it a no-doubter. And then he did. He swung hard but closed his eyes, which probably wasn't good, but he just couldn't help it. His swing was already online, though, so it didn't matter. He smacked the back of his friend's head with the back of the shovel, and it sounded more like a bat hitting a ball than he would've expected. It was wet then, like he'd hit a water balloon, and it had splashed all over his face.

He wiped the blood off, along with the tears, as he recalled kneeling down next to his friend's cot at camp a few years ago, asking him if he'd brought what he said he would, the booze from his parents' bar, before the two of them snuck off into the woods to make a terrific memory.

Mitch gulped as he got to work, tossing the dirt down onto his friend. His friend, and his friend's little butterfly. That sick feeling ballooned in his stomach now, a much different sensation, growing rather than trickling down, ready to burst.

But then he thought about his parents and pictured the years to come because that's just what he had to do right now, accept that life is full of sacrifices, that hard work pays off, and that he had a bright future ahead of him as long as he didn't do anything stupid to screw it up.

He heard a rustle behind him, turned back, light in hand, shovel heading up into the air in case he needed to kill a cop or an old man walking his dog. He stood there feeling like he should laugh again as the fox played at the foot of a tree. He didn't, though. Didn't laugh. Just turned back and continued filling the hole.

He drove the shovel into the dirt, went to stomp on it to drive it down deeper, but stopped and abruptly stood still. He'd heard something scraping across the ground just behind him, then slowly raised his head up as the rest of his body froze. He couldn't imagine what could possibly be moving around behind him and thought that maybe he didn't want to know. He waited for a moment, hoping the sound would stop so he could slowly turn around and laugh at some simple, non-threatening explanation as to what the sound had been. It didn't stop, though. Mitch shivered as he turned just in time to stare in disbelief at the other shovel, which was being dragged across the dirt. It vanished into the darkness behind the tree line before he could make out who was dragging it. He clawed at his chest as confusion and anxiety boiled up from his bowels.

"Hello," he whispered, then swallowed the lump in his throat. He spoke louder then, "Who are you? What do ya want?"

There was no reply, but he could still make out the sound of the shovel dragging around somewhere out in the woods. He smelled something then, that perfume scent again, it seemed. That's when someone grabbed his ankle from behind.

He jumped away, freeing himself from the grip as his flesh tingled with a chill so deep it felt like a blast of winter had washed over him. Though nothing prepared him for what he saw peeking up at him from the hole in the ground, the source of the hand that had grabbed him, painted fingernails smeared up with dirt attached to slender fingers and mud-caked hands. But the worst was the eyes, the dark, dead eyes that just stared at him, peeking out from the hole in the ground.

His throat clapped out a scream then, fast and loud, guttural. A longer scream erupted from within him as he backed up slowly, wanting to run, needing to get away, but so taken aback by the impossible sight before him. He knew who it was, but his mind couldn't wrap around it.

She crawled up out of the hole, rhythmically but with purpose, not taking her eyes off him for a moment. Her clothes were tattered, blackened by dirt. Her hair was wild, all frizzed up around her face like gray cotton candy, a spider web blowing with the breeze. She continued her way towards him, quickening her pace.

He turned and ran, whimpering his way into the woods, which were inexplicably filled with a heavy mist now. He slowed, confused, and gradually came to a stop as he glanced all around. He heard whispers everywhere, heard the shovel dragging in circles around him. He spun, growing dizzy, nauseous, panicked. A whisper in the wind crept up close, just behind him, and he felt warm breath upon the back of his neck, felt the tingle crawling up his spine in response.

He jumped, spun around, but saw nothing, nobody. It all grew quiet then. Silence replaced the whispers, the wind, the scraping sound of the shovel dragging across the ground. He stood there breathing slowly, afraid of his own breath, glanced around again, but didn't catch sight of anybody. He turned and walked hesitantly, continuing to survey the area back from where they'd dug the hole. When he turned around, a shovel smacked him square in the face.

He lay on the ground quietly, not moving at all. Resting peacefully, it seemed.

The little fox obviously couldn't tell you what it saw happen next any more than the crickets or frogs would be able to. But if they could, they'd tell you that a young woman dragged a young man across the forest floor, then pulled him into a hole in the ground.

They'd go on to say that the woman then picked up where the young man had left off, tossing dirt over three dead bodies now. She had a ring on her finger with a heart on it, a butterfly on her wrist, and a hole on each side of her head, right in front of her ears.

SCREAM CAMPERS! I KNOW WHAT YOU DID LAST BLOODY HALLOWEEN

by Kasey Hill

"The best eighties slasher, hands down, is *Halloween,*" Eric says, tilting his beer to his mouth and taking a swig.

"You're crazy. Krueger was the best. Honestly, a man who kills you in your sleep? You never want to go to sleep! You either die sleeping or from a lack thereof," Sean retorts, knocking the red solo cup from Eric's hand.

"You just think that because that's your choice of costume. Michael Myers will always be the best. You may know the face behind the mask, but you will never know the man behind the mask. He was a genius. A silent Ted Bundy!" Eric swoons.

"You think you're top shit because your girlfriend is named after Jamie Lee Curtis' character. Fuck you, bro. You're no better than anyone here," Sean says, glaring at Eric.

The boys squared off until the girls stepped in between them.

"Okay, you two. Knock it off!" Laurie says. "My parents will kill me if we get beer stains on their fur rug!"

"All of us can't be blessed with parents like yours," Sydney chides as she walks past Laurie and flops down on the couch.

"What's that supposed to mean?" Eric asks

"Every Halloween, Laurie's parents give her the keys to their cabin on the lake for her to throw a small party with her friends. Have you ever been invited?" Sydney asks, raising her eyebrow and challenging Eric.

"Fuck you, bitch," Eric howls, stepping closer to her.

"Hey!" Chris barks. "Back off!"

"Whatever," Eric huffs as he tugs his Michael Myers mask over his face. "This is supposed to be a Halloween party. Mask it up, *bitches*!" He picks up another beer and chugs it through the mouth hole in his mask.

The guys amp up the whooping and hollering as they all slide their masks on. They had coordinated their costumes this year ingeniously. They had each chosen an '80s slasher film where one of the victims or main characters shared the same name as their girlfriend. Eric and Laurie are, of course, sporting *Halloween* gear. Eric's dad is an electrician, and the blue jumpsuit was easy to obtain. Laurie mimicked Jamie Lee Curtis' outfit down to the hairstyle. Sean and Nancy are decked out in *A Nightmare on Elm Street* costumes. Sean was burned in a small fire when he was a child, so the scars on his arms replicate the Freddy costume nicely. Nancy decided to go with a sweatpants outfit, dressing casually. Alice and Jason are coincidentally named after their same slasher flick get-up characters from *Friday the 13th*. Jason's mask hides the strawberry birthmark on his face. Alice decided to wear camping gear as her costume. Jesse and Sarah are dressed as Tom Hannigan, the psycho miner, mirroring masks from *My Bloody Valentine*. Jesse found some old mining clothes at Goodwill for both him and Sarah. However, he rolled the sleeves up so he could still show off his brand new tattoo.

"Sarah, it's only the guys wearing masks," Alice jokes.

"I know. But this mask is cool as fuck!"

Everyone laughs as Chris steps into the room wearing the infamous *Scream* outfit.

"Dude, that's not an eighties slasher. That's from the nineties!" Jessica ribs.

"It was all the damned store had left. Bite me," Chris seethes.

Jason turns the volume up on the radio system, and the party officially starts. To the average person, this is a night when all teenagers, both in high school and college, get drunk, party, and pass out until 5 pm the next day. That's what these ten eighteen-year-olds thought as well.

Boom! Thump! Boom! Thump The bass on the stereo hits hard and rattles the windows. *Boom! Thump!*

SCREAM!

They stop the music.

"What the hell was that?" Laurie asks. "All right, headcount." She looks around at the faces in the room, counting everyone. "Two short…wait…where are Jason and Alice?"

"Alice mentioned they were going for a dip, if you know what I mean," Nancy replies, winking.

Laurie tugs Eric behind her and makes her way to the back of the cabin. The sliding glass door leads onto the patio, where the in-ground pool is. She stands at the window, peering out into the dark. She reaches for the porch light switch but hesitates.

"Come on, Laurie," Eric whispers. "I'm sure they're fine!"

She looks behind her and sees everyone waiting for her. She takes a deep breath and hits the switch. A deafening scream fills the cabin as the four girls screech in unison at the sight on the deck. Blood is smeared all over the outer glass, and handprints glide their way down. Through the smudges, they can see entrails and blood leading from the door to the pool. The water is not the usual blue tint it has when lit up at night, but a deep shade of red. Their gazes come to rest on the two bodies bobbing on the surface like a sick game of ducking apples.

Jesse tears the door open and runs outside with Sean on his heels. They pull the bodies from the water; both are naked…cold…mutilated.

"They're gutted like fish!" Sean screams, dropping Jason's body to the deck floor.

"Get the fuck back in here before you get killed, dumbasses!" Nancy shouts.

The guys back away from the bodies, eyeing their surroundings, watching for any movement. They make it to the door and run in, the others slamming it shut and locking it.

"We need to call the police!" Sydney cries.

"And tell them what? Our friends were gutted like fish, but we don't have a clue who did it? Come on, are you stupid? We would all go down for murder," Sarah says.

"If we don't call them and they are reported missing, we go down for it too, you moron! Their parents know they were here. Alice fucking called her mom while sitting on the couch—I talked to her too!" Sydney screams at Sarah.

"Who would do this?" Laurie asks, rocking in her seat.

"Well, I'm sure whoever did it has gone by now. Why would they stick around? We know about them," Sarah says.

"You're such a dumb twat!" Sydney yells. "You're at an eighties-themed Halloween slasher party and don't know the rules of the movies."

"Coming from the one whose boyfriend dressed as a nineties slasher!"

"You fucking bitch," Sydney screams, running at Sarah.

Chris catches her mid-stride and stops her. "You two need to stop! We need to stick together. Who knows what that crazy person is thinking or even listening to right now? Hell, for all we know, they've found a way in."

"Don't fucking say that!" Laurie screams, crying violently.

"We need to do a perimeter check," Sean says.

"*No*! You are not leaving me to get brutally murdered while you dilly dally with the boys outside!" Nancy yells. "We'll split into groups and do checks. Start in the basement and go from there. You can all decide where you want to start," she says, grabbing Sean's arm.

"You two are the most retarded people I have ever met in my life! You don't ever split up. Jeez, don't you watch the shit you argued about earlier?" Sydney asks, shaking her head in disbelief.

"We were hoping the killer would kill you first," Nancy replies dryly.

"Fuck you, skank!" Sydney says, swinging her fist.

Once more, Chris grabs and picks her up, and then sets her on the couch. "We'll wait here until you dumb fucks return," he replies, plopping down beside her.

"I agree," Sarah says, sitting on the adjacent couch. "We're staying as well."

"Pussies," Eric replies. "Come on, Laurie - we'll check the attic and upstairs."

"No, no, no, no. I don't want to go!"

"Move your ass!" Eric says, jerking her up.

The two couples walk through the house and go their respective ways, while the remaining two stay seated.

"Who…who do you think killed them?" Sarah asks through tears.

"I have no fucking clue," Sydney replies, gripping her hands together.

"Sorry for being a bitch earlier."

"No worries," Sydney says, sitting back in her seat.

"Well, there is the one…" Chris says, trailing off.

"One what? *What*?!" Jesse asks.

"Over the summer, we got a note. Like in the movie, *I Know What You Did Last Summer*. It said, 'I Know What You Did Last Halloween.' There was a smear of blood before 'Halloween.' We showed it to Laurie, who blew it off."

"Well, what happened last Halloween?" Sarah asks.

"We've partied with Laurie here at the cabin for years. That's what Sydney's snide comment to Eric meant earlier. We've known Laurie since grade school, and he tries to make her push us aside,"

Chris replies. "Last Halloween, we had a bumping party. There were tons of students from school. Everyone was drinking, getting smashed, high—you name it, they were doing it.

"There was this girl—Amelia. She was a recent transfer student and was really quiet. We were in a couple of classes together, and she started to tutor me. She developed this insane notion that we were dating. She came to the party looking for me, and I was there with Sydney. We've dated for ages. A couple of the football players knew her weird obsession with me and rallied around her. They poured beer over her head and humiliated her in front of the entire school. They then threw her in the pool. She screamed out for help because she couldn't swim, but we all stood by and watched her drown.

"When the ambulance arrived, she wasn't in the pool. No one had touched her. We told them we found her body floating and had thought she had gotten drunk and fallen in without anyone knowing. There was an investigation into her disappearance—her foster parents were adamant about finding her. She was never found, alive or dead."

"So, you think this chick is back for revenge?" Jesse asks. "I don't buy it."

Sarah screams as she scrolls through her phone.

"What the fuck are you screaming about?" Sydney asks.

Sarah doesn't answer. She just holds her phone up for them to see. "Do you see that?" she squeals.

When they had first arrived, they had taken pictures together. Behind them in the group pictures stands a person in a fisherman's slicks and boots; their face was hidden beneath a rain hat. The person holds a hook in their right hand.

"Oh, shit. Oh, shit. Oh, shit," Jesse repeats.

"How long has everybody been gone?" Sydney asks, looking at her watch.

"It's been at least an hour, maybe longer," Chris replies.

"Well, let's all go together and look for them. Start in the basement?" Chris asks.

Jesse nods.

They each take the hand of their girlfriend and lead them through the house to the door that goes down to the basement. Chris grabs the doorknob and slowly turns it, letting it creep open on its own. The cellar is pitch black. He reaches for the string above the steps to turn on the light when Sydney stops him.

"Why would they walk into a dark basement?" she asks.

Chris pulls the chain, but nothing happens. He pulls it a few more times to no avail. "Anyone got a flashlight?"

"I think there's one in the kitchen," Sarah replies.

They make their way there and rummage through the drawers and cabinets. Jesse makes a cheerful announcement, claiming his find of the flashlight. They go back to the basement door and find it closed.

"I don't like this!" Sydney whispers.

"We need to see if they're down there or have gone outside," Chris replies.

They ease down the steps one at a time, with a slow and cautious pace. They reach the bottom and peer around the steps. They shine the light from left to right, trying to see if they can make anything out other than the old, covered furniture.

"I can't see if they're down here or not. We need to check the entire basement," Chris whispers.

He moves from the bottom step, and the others follow suit. They don't even make it halfway around the corner when Sarah screams hysterically. The bodies of Nancy and Sean are sprawled out on an old waterbed, shooting blood-tinged water from the puncture holes left in the bed. They walk closer to the bodies and find them shredded.

"It looks just like Freddy Krueger's been at them," Jesse says.

"Jason and Alice were killed at the pool. Nancy and Sean are on the waterbed with marks like Krueger. The killer is choosing how to kill everyone based on the costumes chosen for the party," Chris remarks.

"We need to get out of here and call the cops! We have proof on my phone that there was someone else here!" Sarah exclaims.

"We need to find Laurie and Eric first. No way we're leaving without them," Chris replies. "Come on. Let's go," he says, running upstairs and slamming the door behind them.

They make their way to the stairs that lead to the second floor.

"They said they were checking the attic out first, right?" Sydney asks.

"Yeah," Chris replies.

They run to the drop-down ladder and find it's still pulled out. Chris cautiously climbs up and looks around the loft with his flashlight. The beam lands on Laurie and Eric, lying naked in a pool of blood. Laurie has stab wounds everywhere, and it looks as if Eric's skull has been crushed. Chris rushes down the steps and leans against the wall, heaving and vomiting.

"They're dead, aren't they?" Sarah asks.

"The killer left the basement when we went to search for the flashlight. We gave him the opportunity to kill Laurie," Sydney murmurs.

"Hey, stay with me!" Chris says, grabbing her face after wiping his off.

"How were they killed?" Jesse asks.

"Stabbed."

"We need to get to the cars and get out of here," Sarah whispers.

The four run down the stairs to the front door and pull it open to find the killer dumping a can of gasoline onto the vehicles.

"Hey, asshole!" Jesse yells.

The person in the fisherman's slick turns towards Jesse, strikes a match, and sets one of the cars ablaze. The fire leaps from car to car. They are trapped unless they walk.

Chris and Sydney turn and run back into the cabin, screaming for Jesse and Sarah to follow. They watch as the two turn to run, but both hit the ground with axes sticking out of their backs. The killer takes a dramatic bow and walks toward the house. Chris and Sydney slam and lock the door, then back away from it, waiting for the pounding to begin.

Silence.

"The sliding glass door!" Sydney yells.

They run to the kitchen and check to make sure the door is locked. It is.

"How the fuck did he get in last time?" Sydney asks.

Chris is silent for a moment. "The basement. It has a door to the side of the house where the car park is."

They run to barricade the basement door, but it's already ajar.

"Didn't we shut it when we came through?" Sydney whispers, in tears.

"I can't remember."

They tiptoe to the basement door and peer down the empty steps. They slam the door shut, and Sydney holds it while Chris pushes a table in front of it. They both sit on it to gather their thoughts.

"What are we going to do? There's no cell reception. We can't drive for help, and Laurie's mom took the phone out the year the guys called all of those porno lines," Sydney says.

"We could try to make a run for it. The bluff isn't even a mile away, and they have an emergency phone there."

"Do you think we can make it? I mean, he threw two axes at once and nailed Jesse and Sarah."

"It would have to be a stabbing for us if he follows his own game. Ghostface's weapon was a knife. But the difference between our movie and his is that Sydney lived in the end. Somewhere along with those franchises, the girl was killed. Aside from Sarah…I just don't get that one…"

"All right, let's make a run for it!"

They jump up and make their way to the front door. They peer through the peephole and see nothing but the blazing cars.

Chris opens the door and finds the coast is clear. He grabs Sydney's hand. "Whatever you do, don't let go."

She nods, and they run. He has always been faster than her, so in reality, he is nearly dragging her behind him. They run through the trees, straying from the trail, following the riverbank uphill. By the time they reach the bluff's clearing, they are panting and scraped up from branches and weeds that had lashed out at them as they ran.

They catch their breath for a moment and then continue up to the light pole with the emergency phone on it. They catch the shadow of someone already standing there. Relief washes over them.

"Hey! We need help!" Chris screams.

They pick up their pace and reach the pole faster. As soon as they get within ten feet of it, the person, dressed in the fisherman's slicks, steps into the light. And this time, they can see the face hidden beneath the hat.

"Amelia! You're alive! You're the killer?!" Chris gasps.

Amelia giggles. "Oh, Chris. If you had only told everyone the truth, none of this would have ever happened. There's a lot of innocent blood on your hands. All you had to do was admit to having a relationship with me. But, *aww*, you didn't want Sydney finding out. So you told everyone I was obsessed with you. I nearly died that night. But I had a friend there with me who saved me. Too bad I had to kill her. I didn't want Sarah giving me away once she saw Jesse dead. See, Sarah knew my plot behind tonight. I just didn't expect the bitch to turn into a big baby whiner. She thought I was just going to scare you all. So, she had to learn a lesson."

Amelia looks from Chris to Sydney and says, "In truth, Sydney, you really are innocent. It was all his fault, and we both got played. He told me he was breaking up with you for me; he told everyone I was psycho. I had a case of this once before, and the guy ended up dead. That's why I had to transfer." Amelia gazes at Chris. "Tell her the truth. Tell her how you kissed me, how we went out for dinner on multiple occasions, and how we went on dates to the movies. *Tell* her!" she screams, pointing a knife at him.

Chris looks over at Sydney, who is shaking her head in disbelief. "No, no, no, it's not true," he defends.

"I can't believe you! I think Amelia is telling the truth. I called one night, and your mom said you took her out to dinner for helping you with tutoring. When I asked the next day, you said it wasn't exactly that and changed the subject. I am an idiot!"

"Now you have to pay, Chris," Amelia says, stepping closer to him.

"Yes, you do!" Sydney says, joining Amelia.

Chris looks at them, confused. "What are you doing, Sydney?"

"Getting rid of a problem that should have been dealt with years ago," she replies, smiling.

They back Chris up against the railing of the cliff. "Sydney, please—I love you, and *only* you!"

Amelia steps closer, and Sydney gets in behind her, slipping something from the back of her pants. As Amelia raises her knife, Sydney jabs a blade into her side.

"Cheater or not, no one deserves to die like this. All those people weren't at that party!" Sydney says, stabbing her again, driving the blade deeper.

Chris moves as Amelia leans up against the railing, blood trickling from her mouth.

"Your one mistake, Amelia," Sydney huffs as she drives the blade into her again, "is that this isn't the eighties anymore. Movies play by different rules now."

Sydney and Chris pick her up and toss her over the railing. They walk over to the emergency phone and place the call, then sit and wait for the police to show up. When they arrive, they give their statement and direct them to the cabin where all the bodies are. It takes a couple of hours for the cops to sift through all the mess. Chris and Sydney remain outside at the cruisers for a few hours until a cop tells them they can return to their dorm. They give them their information to be contacted and begin to walk away from the cabin. They realize that Laurie's car hadn't caught on fire and decide to drive it back to the dorms.

Chris and Sydney drive back to town quietly, taking turns heading to the university.

"Everything will be okay. She's gone," Chris says, kissing Sydney's hand.

"We are going to have a talk later on this week, Chris. Not tonight—I'm too tired—but we are really having a talk."

As Sydney looks out the window, a loud groan escapes her mouth and turns into a gasp. Chris glances over and sees blood trailing from her mouth and pooling on her stomach.

Amelia pops up in the backseat and grabs Chris by the throat, holding a switchblade to his jugular. "Sydney was so naïve. Just like you, Chris. You actually thought I was dead and you were going to get away with everything. Your mistake!" she says, slicing into his skin. "I chose a nineties killer to match you, my darling. Remember, they always come back for one last scare."

She digs the blade deeper into his neck as he struggles to breathe through the blood filling his lungs. She reaches forward, braces herself by wrapping a seat belt around her arm, and flips the gear shift into park. Both Chris and Sydney fly through the windshield.

Although her arm is broken, she'll live. She climbs into the front seat and glances into the rearview mirror, smiling as she puts the car back into drive.

THE GOLDEN GIRL

by H.L. Dowless

The winking twinkling of multicolored lights cast a brilliant cascade of intense colored designs upon the plain white walls of a certain cabin's interior. Inside this humble dwelling were only two rooms; one large, in order that a few guests might be entertained, and one small, so that a single occupant might have a tidy place to retire after the daily labors.

On the western wall opposite the door, rested a mahogany Grandfather clock that dutifully announced the measurement of time with an outstanding consistency. The clock's endless TICK TOCK seemed to thunder as forcefully as any shotgun blast on this Christmas fortnight, for in the dead silence, a vivid imagination harbored only the small elf and the tiny baby reindeer, allowing them to play about the few furnishings of this humble abode.

In the corner, formed when the western wall met the northern, stood a bright green fir tree. Tall and erect it stood, for it was chosen among thousands to show one's love for that most gentle babe of Bethlehem. Throughout its entire stand, not even one time did a single needle wilt or droop. It was almost as if the lifeblood that had sustained it rejoiced in its final destination. About the tree's foot was spread a snow-white cloth of pure cotton, sprinkled with the dust of ruby, emerald, and glittering sapphire. On the outstretched limbs of the fir rested lengthy strings of winking lights joyfully singing the good news message in their own voice of winks in time to well-known songs of the season.

Against the southern wall was carefully placed a withered couch that seemingly had seen more than its share of visitors. The intent was to replace it, but its owner had long since abandoned the possibility of accomplishing such a demanding task. On this couch, with its tattered covering of cloth and its well-worn cloth buttons, sat a young lady who was the sole survivor of a terrible disaster that had cruelly removed the only ones from her life who truly offered genuine love in a world of hate. Her heart was pure, in the traditional sense of the word, and her mind firmly fixed on God – like desires. In this respect, she was enjoined with all that is positive; in a world of forlorn negative darkness, she was doomed to walk alone on the dusty roads of life.

During her life in this warm, cozy shelter of love offered by her parents, her cheeks were rosy, her body full of vibrant energy, and her golden locks appeared to be encased in an aura of moonlight, as though a halo had been placed upon her head by the holy angels in heaven above. In those days, when the cold world pushed her aside in rejection, some cruel ones even violently attempting to shatter her qualities of passionate beauty, she would race into this shelter of love spread before her by those who had given her life.

Unfortunately, those days had forever passed, and now fate itself had delivered a horrible blow in a single attempt to crush her vitality. Those once rosy cheeks were now pale as hazed moonbeams; her bouncing hair of flaxen had wilted upon her head, and her once glittering eyes of sapphire had dulled into a pasty, near-blue film. The ability to sleep had long since fled from her grasp, and as she sat gazing blankly at the floor in front of this Christmas fir, the small, energized girl that she once was again sat in the midst of the cabin floor, cuddling a doll clothed in a long satin dress. The small girl would gingerly nudge the doll's mouth with her tender hands, then quickly snap her radiant, smiling face in the direction of her parents for their approval.

Today, as every day, that small girl had remained in her company, allowing her to find relief from personal stress through the power of fantasy. As that small girl played with numerous dolls on the floor of the cabin, during those times of trouble, *she* would sit upon the floor, conversing with the girl in child-like phrases, becoming totally absorbed in a delightful world of time lost to eternity. Inert dolls constructed of wood and plastic would suddenly breathe and assume a fleshly consistency. The world inside the cabin would provide new hiding places for a disobedient child to hide, and the tree provided new situations in which a reigning mother could exercise discipline and authority.

In this world, Carol would reign supreme, dominant over all situations, and would likewise find love and respect in return. As she rolled about upon the red carpeted cabin floor, lovingly taunting her imaginary child, she would lose all sense of time and space. Hours would seem only as minutes, even days would whisk into the somber blackness of midnight. Tonight, as always, the play that had inspired such overwhelming joy would suddenly deliver a blow of jolting depression, and she would awaken only to find her room empty, her playmates only inert plastic images. All of life's blood now drained, she would fade off somewhere into the night, enveloped in heaving surges of self-sympathetic tears. Tomorrow would bring a new day that was only destined to end like the one before it... But somewhere in the darkest recesses of her mental voice, a gentle whisper reassured her that a new time would one day arrive, and all would be eternally well for her in the end.

An orange sun seared away the thick blanket of mist that had enveloped the countryside during the coolness of nightfall. Soon, the orange transformed into the yellow brilliance of a fully arrived day. Though the young lady was supported by a grand bank account left in the wake of her father's demise, she used it only to complete necessary repairs in her house that she could not make herself.

In the quest for food, she had acquired an extreme resourcefulness. Directly behind her cabin, in the woods, was a well-beaten trail that shone brilliantly in the rust-colored clay of the foothills. The trail wound through small bushes and towering grasses for a few feet ahead, then disappeared into the timber stand behind. The trail meandered between towering oaks and birch trees, many times frequented by leaping bunnies and bounding deer filled with strength acquired from a life deep in the bush. These beasts traveled the trail because for them it was ready-made and led to areas that spawned green grass to quench their burning appetites.

Frequently, these animals traveled behind Carol, who arose early in the eve of the morning while the gray mist still hung in the air, so that she might follow the trail to the rippling creek that gave life to the rainbow trout that she found so much to her liking. In the center of the creek was a funnel-shaped trap woven from the springy vines and limbs of the elm trees that stood nearby. Every morning, it was as though the angels themselves had supplied her with all the food that she needed the night before, for the traps were always teaming with twisting rainbow-sided fish.

Upon removal of the traps, the young lady would slide round twigs of oak across the opening in a manner that would weave the mouth shut, then place them back into the creek. With this task complete, she would gather small dry twigs to construct a fire, and with the aid of twig skewers, the fish were in the flame, fresh from the traps.

This was the way that she loved to live; to breathe the fresh morning air, savor the new sunshine, to eat the fruits that Mother Earth provided, living life stress-free and easy. As she finished her meal, releasing all those fish unused, she would ease back upon a grassy knoll overlooking the crystal water where it suddenly transformed into thrashing foam upon obscure rocks below. In her mind's eye, she would once again transform the world about her into a scene where a spring girl with dancing locks of golden hair would leap with joy at the sight of her new conquest.

"Mother, mother," the small girl would yell in her direction. "Look, I caught a fish!"

"Oh, John, look, she did catch one! I've never seen her this happy before in my entire life!" said a voice from behind, coming from an unseen person.

The small girl would tug on an old cane pole, many times banking a fish that seemed half her own size. Her method of banking fish was truly unique, for she would lift to set the hook, then walk backward with the pole in hand until the struggling trout leaped furiously onto the grass before her small feet.

"Mother, mother, come quick, I've caught another one! Mama, Daddy, come here and look at what I've done!"

Over and over, the small, piercing voice would rehearse itself in fading tones until only the monotonous chirping of the insects could be heard throughout the contours of the timber stand.

Once again, Carol was alone, deserted by the comforting ghost of her now dead past. With every visit that the ghost made, ecstatic excitement consumed Carol, but this time, as with every past visit, its exit produced a backlash of tears, as did every reason for living that she had so desperately attempted to cling to.

To prevent her depression from causing her to regurgitate the contents of her morning meal, Carol arose from her place of rest and proceeded to walk the foot-worn trail back toward the cabin door. As she walked along the beaten trail, her mind drifted back to a young boy whom she once knew back in school, who had taken an interest in her company, graciously offering courtship on numerous occasions. The boy was nearing manhood, as evident by the progressive muscular swelling of his chest and the presence of fine hair inside the crevice of his chest. His voice had already deepened into a distinctly manly tone, but it was only at that time that she had come to notice his body justifying the deep pitch of his voice tone. She could recall how, when she spoke in phrases concealing loving overtones, she would begin to recognize him as being more than *just a boy* but as an object that was destined to develop her into more than *just a girl.*

She recalled being afraid of that thought but remembered how intensely she desired development... that reason to become more than just a child. She had long since recognized that all people who call themselves *women,* and were universally recognized as such, only acquired such recognition in the presence of a man, upon whom they had laid a solid claim. More and more, she had come to desire this object in her life, and from within the midst of that desire arose a form of attachment that had expressed itself in numerous passionate hugs and kisses, of which she generously gave on a single motivating whim.

Even amid that surging joy lurked a horror with devastating potential. Though she had refused to admit to the fact over and over again, the closer that she became in mind, the farther that he had departed from the grasp of her aching heart. She lunged forth in desperation, tenaciously attempting to seize upon her last chance for acquiring womanhood. Suddenly, as the hurt from that tragedy was dying, she awoke one dark, dreary, rainy morning only to find herself alone, and she had remained alone from that moment forward ...to brave the savage elements of life all on her own. Many times, the endless loneliness proved overwhelming, and she concluded that she could no longer live in the company of such hopelessness. She deeply longed for the company of one who really cared, and her mouth parched for the taste of manly lips.

Ahead, the trail meandered around the bulk of a massive tulip poplar tree that had long since been gutted by fire, and as a result, was hollow. The prospective volume of its hollowed area was enough to house four men comfortably, and on many occasions she had envisioned herself as the sole occupant therein, dwelling in complete harmony with nature. She envisioned, as she awoke, that scores of cotton-tailed bunnies and small fluffy fawns would be there to accompany her on the bank of the frothy gurgling stream as she made her morning bid for bath and refreshment.

The young lady paused before that massive poplar, caressing its coarse texture, worn ragged by centuries of pelting moisture pellets. The pasty, leathery composition of the towering tree's bark caused her to be reminded of flesh, blackened in places and wrinkled by the weight of the ages. Suddenly, in the wake of it all, she came to acknowledge that the tree was not an inanimate object at her disposal, but a living, breathing organism of life. She became humbled as a small child does on the eve of a new discovery in the new surrounding environment. On its side, the great tree possessed a massive gap that had been formed by the actions of past wood fires and the years.

"This is now the door of my new house," she said out loud to herself.

Usually, the tree was void of any surrounding elements, both organic and inorganic, but on this day, a truly unique phenomenon had made itself known only to Carol. Within the trees' interior, the floor dropped approximately two feet below that of the ground level as a direct result of the huge expanding roots decaying in their uppermost extremities. By some inexplicable means during the course of the past month, this area had become flooded, and now a small cesspool filled the cavity to the lower edge of the side gap. The sap from within the veins of the tree, which continuously rises upon the tree's interior in droplet-like tears, had combined with the crystal-clear water inside, producing a sweet aroma highly pleasurable to the sense of smell. The mist of a medicine-like aroma was so intense that its effect was that of i*ntoxication,* and the young lady gazed forth into the crystal clearness of the pool as though she were hypnotized by the power of some enchanting spirit within.

There, as she gazed forth into the smooth, crystal-clear surface of the cesspool, her mind once again began to race. She envisioned a small house sitting snugly in the distant richness of a hardwood timber stand, where peace and eternal tranquility could be found to abide within. No longer would she be forced to flee from daily existence, but she could live and enjoy conquest over all unmerciful confrontations. She saw a boundless meadow full of lush grass and forever shaded by the arms of towering sycamore and wild pear. Upon a small knoll in the meadow's midst sat the young golden girl that she once was, dressed elegantly in an ankle-length cotton gown of pink muslin. In the child's arms was a small male doll, upon which she tossed her unrestrained love and affection.

"Now mommy says you are going to grow up and become a great man someday. Yes, how would you like that? Well, I think that it would be great! Then, oh then, I could be ever so proud of you, Michael. Why don't you smile for me, Michael? Now that's right!"

The golden girl attempted to stretch the contours of the doll's mouth with her tender right index finger.

"You're being bad, Michael. Mommy says smile! NOW!"

The girl raised the doll high above her head, then dashed its head to bits upon a granite slab nearby. She did not mean to destroy the doll, only to punish it. As she gazed down upon the shattered fragments of the doll's head, she began to long for the comfort of its completeness and company. Helplessly, she gazed down at the injured doll, covering her face with both hands as torrents of tears obliterated the world surrounding her.

"I broke Michael's head! I killed him! Oh, what will I do now? Help me, help me, somebody!"

The small child uncovered her face, turning in the direction of Carol. Suddenly, her tears dried, and she sat staring into the face of Carol as if she were fully aware of her presence.

"Can you help me? Mommy? Momma! Please come here, I love you, Momma! Will you bring Michael back to life?"

Carol gasped for air in utter shock, muttering aloud to herself with trembling lips.

"This is not real, this cannot be happening, but it is! I see it before me now!"

"Mommy, please come here. I love you! Mommy!" cried the golden girl.

Carol muttered again to herself.

"Oh, how can this be? How could it be possible for a vision to become living flesh and blood?"

"I love you," cried the golden girl, as Carol attempted to analyze the distorted information that she perceived!

"I am coming, sweetheart," said Carol aloud, without realizing it.

The young lady's bare feet came to rest in the lushness of the meadow. She paused, gasping for breath as her tender feet tingled with the freshness of new life that the meadow now hauntingly afforded her. No longer did her limbs tire with the weight of stress. No longer did she worry about the way that she would find her daily bread. She now, at least, had discovered peace, perfect peace with herself and total harmony with her environment. High energy now coursed through her veins as though she had consumed some new form of drug that truly resurrected the lost souls of the eternally damned.

There sat the young girl, her voice was clearly audible, and the light rustle of her cotton gown created a clear impression upon her ear. Her golden hair radiantly danced about in bursts of gentle breeze that only shaded meadows afford. The clearness of her flesh glistened in the gleaming sunlight; surely this child was no mere figment of any vision!

"What is your name, child?" inquired Carol, attempting to induce the child to speak by offering a soothing smile.

"My name is Carol."

"My name is Carol, too, but friends call me Goldie. They call me that because my hair is so blond that it turns into golden strands in the sunlight, they say."

"That's nice, you have beautiful hair, Goldie. Have you heard the story of Goldilocks and the three bears?" asked Carol in a loving tone of voice.

"Oh yes, bunches of times! I guess that's where they got my name."

"Where are your parents?" asked Carol.

"They're over there," said the child, pointing toward the hill in the near distance.

Carol turned in the direction of the hill, squinting to allow her eyes to adjust to the distance. The hill crest was shaded by huge drooping oaks that had given shade for hundreds of years. The birds zipped to and fro as though they had found true paradise.

"Where are they, honey? I don't see them."

"They're over there," said Carol, once again pointing toward the hill crest.

Once again, a quick glance in that direction revealed only the singing dance of the songbirds amid the boughs of huge drooping sycamores and oaks. Two by two they appeared to sit, filling the air to overflowing with the song of their courtship.

"Here, honey, let's take your doll to Daddy. Maybe he can fix it. I am not good at repairs."

"Won't you please try? I can't take it to Daddy," replied the child.

"Why not? I am sure that he will not mind the trouble of helping you."

"No," replied the child with a harsh, scornful, angry face. "No! No! No!"

"O.K. Then, we will not take the doll, but I would like to have the pleasure of meeting your Daddy."

"Only if you promise not to mention the doll," snapped the child with a slightly, relaxing face.

" Sure, just take me to him. I just want to meet him."

The child seized Carol's left hand, guiding her down a trail of bent grass where heavy feet had trodden earlier. As they traveled, the child sang a happy ditty to the tune of *Pop Goes the Weasel.*

"My father went into the woods to hunt,

Thought he had a bear,

But oh....it was a beaver!"

"Where on earth did you learn that silly song?" laughed Carol.

"Oh, I like making up rhymes. I got an A in poetry the other week. Ain't I good?" asked the small child.

"Why yes, and a bit unusual, I might add as well," laughed Carol.

By now, they had reached the hill crest that was delightfully shaded by numerous oaks and sycamore trees. So sparsely positioned were they that the shaded area from one intersected the other along the area's edge. A chilly breeze hissed through the leaves in such a manner that it finally filtered through to cool the inhabitants below. The songbirds chirped joyful, melodious hymns to the tune of their quest for mates with obscure words that tend to soothe the human mind, inducing sleep and overall relaxation.

"Where are your parents?" inquired Carol to the child.

"Oh, there is a pool on the other side of the hill, that's where they are."

"They sure are awfully quiet if they are down there," said Carol in a muffled tone of voice.

"Oh, they are down there all right. Come follow me, I'll show you!"

The hillside below jutted out into a granite overhang that tended to stick out like some sort of huge fingernail. From above, one could only view the surrounding area at that point, but indeed a new world did lie below. Centuries of sand and leaves accumulated, cushioning any penetration of sound vibrations, and in this manner, the voices of the child's parents remained obscured from the ear. A foot-worn trail led the couple around the overhang, so that they entered into a depression in which the basin was filled with murky water. Upon flat rocks that aligned the water's edge next to the overhang, sat the two parents of the child.

Her father was a man chiseled stern in appearance, his face hardened by years of toil and strife. So heavy was the years' weight upon his face that his very skin was ruddy with sun and stress, and it appeared to be well-tanned boot leather rather than flesh. His chest was exposed by the release of the uppermost shirt button, was of the same texture, but covered by a thick mat of wiry gray hair. He never offered speech unless spoken to, as if he had distrusted any conversation that was offered to him.

Her mother was glowing with light, so it appeared to all who met her. She appeared to catch the glory of the golden sunlight, releasing it to anyone that passed her by. Her complexion was extremely fair, as though she had been freshly taken from some distant land covered year-round by snow and ice. Her eyes glittered like two sapphire jewels centered with black onyx. The ruby smile radiated forth as though it were produced by some fairy that dwelt in those cheer filled rhymes of Carol's lost childhood. Her countenance, in all of its beauty, was completed with hair that transformed the yellow beams of sunlight into gold, like that of the small child. Clearly this lady was the child's mother.

"Mother, mother, I've found a new friend!"

"Let me see her child, let me gaze upon her," replied the mother, flashing a glittering smile that appeared to betray the immense warmth and compassion deep inside her soul.

As Carol stood gazing into the woman's eyes, she came to feel as though she had stood before her many times in days now long since passed. As she allowed her eyes to roam the ladies' delicate features, abrupt flashes betrayed the fact that with certainty, she had indeed known this lady somewhere deep in the murky past. In her mind's eye she witnessed the lady playing on the floor with the child who now stood beside her. The lady was not an adult who was indifferent to the child's imagination, but as a mother who delighted in a chance to share in the secret story of a child and the small doll.

"Mother!" Carol screamed at the top of her lungs toward an image that was transmitting a sensation of being more a bizarre mirage than reality.

The lady never answered, only continued to speak to the golden girl, but Carol could not discern the words that issued forth from her moving lips. The lady would only glance in Carol's direction, then turn toward the child, while continually speaking to her in inaudible tones.

"Mother! Please answer me! Do you hear me? Please... Mother!"

Still the lady continued to speak to the golden girl as though Carol never even existed.

Oh, how impolite these people are, she said in the silence of mental voice. She abruptly burst into tears, covering her face with her hands and asking herself if she was still sane.

"What's the matter," inquired the child, tugging hard on Carol's loose shirt tail. "Why are you crying?"

"Oh, I don't know. I just don't know! Where are we?"

"We're at the Emerald Horizon, or at least, that's what I've always heard it called," replied the child.

"Emerald Horizon?" Carol gazed into space for a short span. "Sounds so familiar..."

"You've probably heard of it before, that is, if you've ever been on a date! My brother used to come here all the time with his girlfriend. I bet you'll never guess what happened to him."

Carol gazed into space for a brief moment, then replied on a sudden whim. "He was chased off by old man Hamrick, who lived from where we just came, just on the other side of the timber stand."

"How did you know? I suppose that you heard all about it too. Everybody else sure has!"

"I don't know… oh yes, ...I heard it from a friend."

Carol glanced before them toward the flat rocks where the child's parents were just sitting, which were now empty.

"Where are your parents?"

"Oh, they've already left. They headed toward the house. They usually don't mind me playing alone, just as long as I am home by supper time. I really do enjoy this meadow with the songbirds and animals. I come up here lots! Want me to show you the rest of the meadow?"

"Sure!" Carol snapped in reply."

Once again, they retraced the foot-worn trail from whence they had come. The route uphill produced a great struggle, causing Carol's mind to drift back toward the days of her carefree youth, in which she played amid the trees and shrubs of the woodland. The aromas of savory meals simmering in the obscure distance caused her mind to reflect on the walnut table upon which she had helped herself to many meals during the course of her traumatic and cheerful childhood. A smile jerked across her face as she completed the uphill climb; not that she had triumphed in the physical feat, but that the memories themselves had inspired such an everlasting scene deep in her mind's eye.

"Do you see that thick timber that stands next to the horizon, right where the trees are the greenest? That's where I live!"

A column of smoke arose from what appeared to be a short distance above a chimney obscured by the greenery of the distant trees. This column of smoke billowed upward in an endless flow to such an extent that it puddled against the skyline of the distant horizon. Within the puddle's center, Carol imagined, was a hole that sucked the column upward so that the puddle would not expand.

"I'll race you!" said the child with a sharp smile and a quick dash.

The child's body zipped and bounded through the waist-high grass that flourished in the meadow. For a short distance, Carol followed right at her heels, but the age difference between them began to weigh heavily on her. Soon the child was ahead by a hundred yards or more, consistently gaining speed with a newfound energy that propelled her forward in sharp, brisk bursts. Carol panted heavily; she never was an athlete at heart, her wind simply never sustained her body through the race. Ahead, Goldie disappeared into the distant timber stand across the meadow from where she now stood. The leaps and bounds of the young girl were almost animal-like, and the weight difference between them... the weight difference... oh!

Carol paused in the tall grass, gasping for breath while gazing toward the woodland where the child had disappeared. The wind about her moved in sharp bursts, tossing and licking the golden locks as though they were being fondled by some ghostly lover. This meadow was strangely void of all life signs, not even the birds chirped as they usually did. A well-worn trail betrayed the fact that the area had been used on a regular basis. Carol gazed forward in the direction of the smoke column, noting that the trail headed forward in that direction. Maybe this trail will carry me to the house, she thought to herself.

The light of day had already begun to dim into orange as nightfall became more imminent. She picked up the tempo of her pace. As she jogged along, a small branch that lay across the beaten trail snatched her leg with a sudden jolt. Her entire body was suddenly thrown violently upon the cool, damp earth, her head striking a very solid object that felt just like a rock, causing a veil of pitch-black darkness to settle before her eyes. The thickness of the dark was so boundless that she lost all account of time and space.

Time had passed, she did not know just how much, and as her eyes gingerly opened, they revealed a world of light blurred by a conglomeration of tears. She rubbed her eyes with her index fingers, causing the blurred light to clear. Now she lay beside the vaporous cesspool contained inside the massive tulip poplar tree.

A certain tense, dull sensation suddenly gripped the pit of her stomach, and she realized that the terror of her impending loneliness was once again upon her. She picked herself up, feeling as though she had not touched a single morsel of food in days.

"Why did I have to return?" she kept saying aloud to herself.

In that world, she felt secure, warm with the sensation that only true love has the power to bestow on individuals in want. Over and over again, that sensation kept recurring, hinting that she had trodden down that dusty road before. Deep in the darkest recesses of her past, she had rambled through that lush meadow with her bare feet, allowing them to tingle with the sensation of fresh dew that sprinkles the morning grass in the cool of a new summer's day. She had known the girl before as well, much more than she had ever realized, but she somehow could not recollect the meeting place. Repeatedly, her subconscious mind continued to whisper these words into her ear, but simultaneously, she had told herself that she and the golden girl were two separate individuals, unbound by any personal knowledge of each other.

As her eyes beheld the well-worn trail glowing with the red clay of the hillside, and she stood gazing through the crisscrossed trees standing tall on the hill crest, once again coming to grips with the cabin that housed that enemy of sanity called *loneliness, she* then turned, falling upon her stomach only to bury her flaxen head in crossed arms, crying. Tears poured from her eyes in a manner not previously experienced since her long, lost childhood.

Why must I live like this? she repeated to herself in the silence of her mental voice. Is there anything that I can do to end the pain of this despair? Pray, replied her subconscious mind! She then began to unravel a prayer that had been bottled up inside her breast for a period that seemed like years. She began to pray aloud.

"Dear God," she said with a sob and a sigh. "Please deliver me from the grips of this insanity. Give me warmth and strength, that I might find a new life. Please whisper the instruction into my wanting ear. Allow me to enter that promised land of eternity, to live and truly savor happiness once more. Show me the way, Lord, show me the way, please, Lord."

She gazed upward into the heavens with its lights that twinkled in winks in such a way that it caused one to believe that the skies were like one body. She thought of the words that she had spoken and wondered if God really paid any attention to their seriousness… if he even cared that she hurt so inside.

The grip of despair tightened around her very throat in such a manner that she had difficulty breathing. In the past, the only remedy that she had made use of that had truly released this tightening despair was the soothing burn of alcohol, but since she did not possess any at the moment, she would now be forced to endure her suffering, to seek another means of escape.

There comes a time when one must arise to face the real world about them, she told herself in silence. This was to be a time when daydreams proved to be worthless, and dreams in unison are only attributable to childish minds. Why must this be so? Why couldn't God have allowed adults the means to escape reality from time to time?

"This is not fair," she mumbled aloud to herself. "It isn't fair, Lord!" she screamed, as if she intended to seek vengeance upon the Almighty himself.

She rose and began to plod along in the direction of the cabin on the hilltop, *that dungeon of loneliness,* as she called it in silence. The sweet song of the night bug, the blue sparks of the firefly, all were music that soothed her troubled mind. Her tension began to ease like she had taken medicine as she ambled along the beaten trail. As the pressure began to release, even a warm smile discovered its solace in the evening.

"What's the matter? Did you tire of the race?" said the voice of the golden girl from behind.

Carol snapped around as if she felt massive hands grip her about the tender nerve of her neckline,

"Oh, I'm more cunning than to allow you to catch me simply by turning around, dear."

Carol snapped in the direction of her cabin, then glanced both before her and behind her.

"Child, why do you wish to fool around with my mind like this?"

"I am all alone since you left me, just me and my doll. Come and play with us," asked the voice of the golden girl.

Carol's breast heightened its thumping pace. The night bug's call grew more intense, and her pace quickened into a brisk walk. She glanced over her shoulder and before her as well.

"I can't now. I have things that I am obligated to do, child. Maybe some other time."

"Now you wouldn't want to disappoint me... PLEASE!"

"Child, I told you!"

She glanced toward that great tulip poplar tree, which now glowed with the strange sapphire aura. A low-pitched voice spoke as a voice of whispering wind rustling amid the new leaves of spring, constantly repeating her name with each burst. She raced toward the cabin door, enveloped with the fear that some dreaded ghost from Christmas past might ascend upon her to drain all spiritual vapors from within her fleshly existence. A beckoning sensation gripped her, for she had come to feel that turning from the call might sever her from the eternal bliss that she had just experienced in the child's company. Her mad dash abruptly.

"Oh, that's right," said the voice of the golden girl. "Come to the enchanted cesspool now, or lose me forever! To gaze into it is only to find eternal peace and happiness within. If you should leave now, you shall regret it for the duration of your natural life. Come to me, mother! I love you."

Carol turned to gaze upon that great tulip poplar tree. There by its side, materialized a small flaxen-haired girl adorned in a pink muslin dress, motioning with open arms for Carol to walk in her direction.

"Child, what's the matter?" asked Carol in a distressed tone of voice.

Suddenly, the child burst into tears, covering her face as if to shield it from harm's way.

Carol raced toward the child, seizing her fragile arms, then embracing her with the free arm in order that she might comfort the child's troubled soul. The small, tender, tear-stained face of the child gazed upward through glittering eyes of crystal sapphire, then her mouth poured forth a potion of words that thoroughly bewitched Carol's already despairing heart.

"I have been a very troubled person. My grades at school were not very good at all, and my mother deserted me yesterday, saying that I could not contribute to the positive image of the family, so I was of no worth. I have been considering running away! Would you come with us?"

"Who has been advising you to run, child, who? You know that to run from your problems is not the proper thing to do!" said Carol, seizing the child by her shoulders, shaking her as she spoke.

"Christopher Nichols. He's the best friend that I have."

"Who?"

"Christopher Nichols, the Christmas charity leader. Don't you remember him from your childhood?" said the child through a steady stream of tears.

Carol paused; the very words that the girl had spoken sent jolts of electrical passionate sensations pouring into her breast. She could still stand back and admire that tall statue of a man. She could still see the moonbeams glitter from the gloss of his jet black hair. She could still see the splendor of his fine body in a tuxedo. She could still recall, as a young lady of sixteen, her gazing forth upon the man with an idyllic gaze of total admiration. Carol had always felt that deep inside, Chris had always held the same desire for her, but because of their age difference, he inhibited all expression of this forbidden pleasure.

"One day I will be as old as you, and I will come back to marry you," she blushingly recalled saying as a small child of five.

By the age of sixteen, she had come to realize that such desires were only for fantasy alone and for fools to pursue. Even so, his ghost still inhabited the darkest recesses of her mind.

"Introduce me to this man," said Carol, gazing into space as though entranced by some magical potion.

"What's the matter?" asked the dear child.

"Nothing, oh nothing, just take me to him!"

The child seized Carol's trembling hand. "Come with me then. He will enjoy seeing a new face."

The pair raced down a small trail that branched off from the tulip poplar tree to its left. The trail was seldom traveled, but the bending of the grass betrayed excursions that had been made at some time during the recent past.

"Where are we headed, Goldie?" demanded Carol. "I have never seen this trail."

"This is the way to where he lives, Carol. Don't you remember?"

The trail wound in and out through the thick entanglement of the surrounding woodland. Periodically, Carol would demand time for a rest, which was usually cut short by the girl's prodding phrase.

"Better hurry, Chris does not wait forever, he has work to do, you know."

Hours passed, Carol did not know how many. The sun still shone from its lofty perch high in the sky, but Carol knew that things were strangely not as they appeared lately.

"Are we there yet?" she would ask.

"Yes, it's just around the bend ahead."

The couple raced around the curve of the trail, and suddenly the entanglement opened without warning, exposing the lush meadow where she and the girl first met. Carol took a seat upon a small mound of dirt that encased an oaken root that branched from some unknown source in the timber stand.

"So, this is it, huh? I thought that I would never get here. Where is Chris at?"

The reverberating slap of an ax against hardwood sent sharp shocks across an expanse of openness.

"He should be just over that knoll, behind the hickory stand on the other side. I believe that he is preparing to heat his stove for Christmas dinner tomorrow."

Carol stood, brushing the sand from the seat of her faded jeans.

"I have to meet him."

She seized the hand of the child, and the two briskly strode toward the grass-covered knoll ahead.

"Mama! Mama! Don't go there, he has work to do! He will get very angry at our rude intrusion!" screamed the child through more tears.

Carol clenched her teeth at the thought of the elements that were attempting to lead her away from this chance of a lifetime. She was predestined to have this gentleman of the range, she thought. Why else was she here?

"Hush up now. We're going to visit him, and you had better just like it!" Carol huffed at the child.

As the couple reached the summit of the knoll, Carol's pace quickened into a jog, then a hungry gallop. She released her hold on the golden girl, racing forward as though she had taken some strange pill that gave new strength to her weary limbs. The child turned, then disappeared into the timber stand, which swallowed her up like a hungry demon from the underworld.

"Hey there! Hey!" Carol waved her arms frantically as though she were attempting to cause her body to lift from the ground beneath her feet. "Hey, do you remember me? I told you that one day I would grow up and be old enough for you to marry!"

"Carol!"

The man tossed aside his ax and raced forward to offer a wide, open-armed greeting.

"Where have you been, dear? It's been so long!"

"I've often thought of you in my dreams," she said. "I've always had a special kind of love and adoration for you, Chris."

"Mine is for you, likewise," he said, gazing into her glistening eyes, as he simultaneously brushed her hair with his free right hand.

"You know, I have spent my entire life waiting for this moment," he said. "I hope that we can spend eternity here together, in this very meadow."

She tenderly allowed her warm, moist lips to embrace his.

"I want to be with you."

"We can do it, child," he said, placing the palms of his hands against the rosy cheeks of her tender face. "We live in two worlds, but you can make the difference. You were not meant to be mortal forever, but in spirit, you can be flesh again in the realm of the metaphysical world. Only a dramatic transformation can make your mind forget the secular world."

"I never said that I wished to remain in the mortal world," she replied as she gazed upward into the man's enrapturing face.

A small bulge remained noticeably protruding from the midst of his velvet vest pocket. His vein-streaked sun-browned hands eased into the pocket of his vest, producing a shiny black, pocket-sized .38 caliber revolver.

Her mind abruptly flashed back, revealing a small cozy cabin on the hillside, above the winding creek from whence she had gathered her breakfast of fish each morning. Inside the cabin, a small girl who was consistently thrown into depression over the negligence of family and friends, crawled for solace under a decorated fir tree. Her tender hand eased underneath the cotton cloth that draped the foot of the tree, producing a shiny black pocket-sized .38 caliber revolver.

"Only you can make the difference," the man said to her with a warm, beckoning smile. "Come be with me for eternity."

The tender hands raised the revolver upward, causing the cold, hard barrel to sink deep into her soft, plush temple. The hammer clicked backward, seemingly moving all by itself, as if done so by an unseen phantom hand. A great noise issued, greater than any produced in the history of the entire world, echoing vibrantly throughout the contours of the entire universe. A heavy, vaporous cloud of smoke suddenly choked all vision from the eyes and breath from the nostrils.

Into the slightly opened door of the cabin, a small burst of evening wind abruptly poured forth, clearing the heavy blue smoke from the room, exposing a now completely opened door to a lush meadow extending as far as the eye can see. An orange sun gingerly crept downward nearer the horizon... and in the shimmering horizon distance, two figures amble forward, arm lovingly entangled in arm, into the berth of eternal bliss.

A GIRL AND HER MIRROR

by Mark Mackey

The night was dark, the wind cold. Despite his having a sinking feeling that he would die within an hour, he did it. Being a now-fired former employee working out of the house, doubling as an antique shop, he expected it would be easy to get in without the alarm going off. This was his mistake. Setting foot into the shop, she was there. The woman he had seen countless times in the mirror, his boss informed him, was cursed. She had burning red eyes like dots, her brilliant radiance causing him to squint. In his mind, she was a demon, a creature.

And then he screamed.

***

In Mary Catherine Yearson's mind, he had given her little choice but to kill him. With the woman, her latest descendant, running the store asleep up in the bedroom, she was afraid he might harm her. She couldn't have that.

In her panicked state, she emerged from her mirror to send him to one of the worst, most nightmarish places ever. The below zero icy cold demon world that was present inside her mirror.

***

"It's not like I'm about to depart off the face of the Earth, Sharon," my cousin Julie Argyles, and practically best friend, said to me. The two of us were standing on the porch of the enormous mansion I called home, embracing each other. I am Sharon Elsters, eighteen. Like my two seventeen-year-old sisters, Angela and

Bridget, I'm a natural witch. The two of them stood on either side of me in observance of this whole heartfelt goodbye taking place. As is Julie, she just hasn't come into her full powers yet. Thanks to her mom wanting to take things slow with that. Now you may find yourself asking, why don't I have a stronger relationship with my two sisters as I do with Julie? It's simple, Angela and Bridget have taken to bonding together just like my cousin and me.

"Yeah, but it just won't be the same without you, Aunt Katharine, and Uncle Fred continuing to reside here in Darkwood," I said. Feeling the first tears starting to develop in my eyes.

"Well, my parents are probably getting impatient waiting for me. You think you're going to be all right, Sharon?" Julie asked.

"Yeah, I'll be fine."

"Don't worry, Julie," Angela and I will make sure she's okay," said Bridget.

Watching Julie turn and start heading toward the waiting vehicle, the sadness already within me grew significantly.

"I have to get the heck out of here," I said, watching my cousin, Aunt and Uncle starting to drive off.

"Uh-uh, you're upset. There's no telling what you might do, being the most powerful witch among the three of us, Sharon," Angela replied.

"She's right, Sharon, Angela, and I will go with you," Bridget said.

***

Downtown Darkwood was so close that there wasn't a need to drive. Angela, Bridget, and I slowly headed on foot down Sotens Street. Heavily dominated by businesses and stores, I couldn't help but feel there was something in one of these stores just waiting for me to find and buy.

No, you're just upset Julie's gone on her way to live in Blue Winter, and want to appease it by buying yourself some materialistic object. I had pushed this from my mind by having it invaded by an eerie, hollow-sounding voice.

"Buy me," it whispered into my mind.

"What's wrong, Sharon?" Bridget asked, seeing the slight, nervous look I had on my face.

"You're not going to believe this, Angela and Bridget, but I could have sworn I just heard a voice enter my mind telling me to go buy it."

"Now that's strange," Bridget said. "Hey, you don't think another witch may now be living here?"

"I'm not a witch," it answered in the same, hollow voice.

"Tell me who you are, and where can I find you?"

"I'm in the antique shop just up ahead, Sharon."

"Whoever it is knows my name and says he or she is in the old antique shop up ahead," I said, feeling curiosity start to build over wanting to know who or what this was. "Come on, let's go see who it is."

As the three of us made our way into what was named Bev's Antiques, my nostrils were immediately filled with a strong smell. It was a combination of musty furniture and Swiffer Dust and Shine cleaner.

"Is there something I can help you three young ladies with?" the woman behind the counter, in her late twenties or early thirties, from my estimation, didn't hesitate in asking.

"You're not going to believe this, but I just had a voice enter my mind. It told me to come in here and buy it. It's kind of strange, huh?"

"Not necessarily. My family and I, going back generations, have been waiting for you to finally show up."

The next thing I knew, I watched her come from around the counter and approach the entrance. She locked it and turned the hour sign from open to close.

"Come on in back, there's something I want to show you."

This led me to start following the woman, Angela, and Bridget close behind, watching her stop in front of a life-size mirror.

"This mirror was what called out for you to come buy it."

"What is it, like magic?"

"No, it's so much more than that. This mirror holds the spirit of my ancestor, Mary Catherine Yearson. She was cursed into it by a witch, made a demon creature so she could save her younger sister from suffering the same fate."

"So, if this Mary Catherine is related to you and your family, how come she didn't fill your mind with the buy me message?"

"Because a true witch was the one who placed the curse on her, and only another one can use Mary Catherine and the power she has. And so far, you're the first one ever since she was stuck in the mirror that Mary Catherine has contacted. So, are you interested in her? I'll give it to you for just twenty-five dollars, since, well, you're the only one who can use it."

Heading to the mirror and standing in front of it, I didn't expect to see the most beautiful, radiant woman in my life appear. She wasn't much older than me and dressed in a stunning white gown. Her hair was a perfect shade of navy blue, and her eyes were icy blue. The only thing bothering me was the sadness on her face. She looked so unhappy and alone, just like I felt now with Julie gone. I understood then it was my destiny to take ownership of this mirror.

"That look tells me you're interested in it," the woman said.

"Yeah, sure, I'll take it."

***

"Thanks for bringing the van on such short notice mom," I said as Angela, Bridget, and I loaded the mirror into it. In our family, Diane, that's her name, is the most powerful witch of all. She's even stronger than Julie's mom and her younger sister Katharine.

"I'm just happy you were able to find something that will take away your misery of Julie being gone," she replied.

***

"I just bet you're glad you now have a mirror with a spirit held in it, Sharon," Bridget said as she and Angela helped me get it into my bedroom. We placed it against a wall to allow me to face it from my bed.

"Yeah, I sure am." Sitting down on my bed, I draped my legs against the side.

"So, Bridget and I will let you spend some quality time with your new mirror," Angela said, taking her sister by the hand and leading her toward the door.

"Just be sure to be ready to help us run the fortune teller table at the fair tonight," Bridget said.

Once Angela and Bridget were gone, I found myself wondering just how I was supposed to interact with Mary Catherine. Surprisingly, the answer to this came almost immediately, as she appeared in the mirror.

"Hey, is this how we're supposed to communicate, through mirror glass?"

"No, there's also this way," Mary Catherine said, stepping from the mirror and into my bedroom. With her joining me on the bed, I was amazed, and at the same time relieved by this. Mary Catherine and I would be able to communicate face to face, and without glass stuck between us.

"So, I can sense you're sad about something," Mary Catherine said. "What's wrong?"

"Oh, it's just my cousin Julie. "She just moved to a town called Blue Winter, so her mom and my aunt could take the job of running a branch of her job."

"Now that is sad," Mary Catherine said. "I could take your cousin's appearance if you want."

"You could do that?"

"Yes."

"Okay, since you said you're not a witch, and you're clearly not human, what are you defined as?"

"Sharon, I was born in the tenth century. What you just bought, and where I live, it's no ordinary mirror. It's a portal to one of the most horrifying, most brutally cold demon dimensions ever. I just pray you, or anyone else, never suffer the fate of seeing what it's really like in there."

"Is there anything else I should know?"

"Just a couple days ago, I had no choice but to send a former employee of the antique store into the demon dimension held in my mirror."

"Why was that?"

"He was fired for robbing money from it. I didn't want to do it, but didn't know what else to do. Now I feel like nothing more than one of those sadistic, murdering demon creatures inhabiting my mirror."

"But you're not Mary Catherine, I'm sure there wasn't anything else you could have done."

"So, give me your opinion about what you think about me?"

"Honestly, I kind of enjoy having someone around to replace Julie. The only thing I don't like about you is your name. You don't mind if I change it, do you?"

"No, I have no problem with you doing that. What do you have in mind?"

Staring at Mary Catherine, for some unknown reason, the first thing to pop into my mind was Pixie Sticks. Now, why would I think of that? I wondered. Taking the word and starting to play around with different variations of it, Dixie, Mixie, Bixie, Trixie…Trixie. Trixie. Yes, that would be the name I would call Mary Catherine from now on!

"So, have you come up with something yet?"

"I have, from now on, I'm calling you Trixie."

"Hmm, Trixie, that has a nice sound to it."

"I'm glad you approve of it. But now, if you'll excuse me, Angela, Bridget, and I have to get over to a fair taking place in town. We have to go set up the fortune teller booth."

"Okay, I guess I'll see you when you get back."

Standing up, Trixie returned to the mirror.

***

"So, are you enjoying your mirror so far, Sharon?" Angela asked as the three of us were sitting behind the fortunate teller's booth.

"I am. As a matter of fact, I've renamed the spirit slash demon creature, Trixie."

"Trixie, it sounds pretty catchy," Bridget said.

"Yeah, you got that right," Angela added.

Just as I started to say something else, I saw her. The girl Angela, Bridget, and I hated the most, Tracy Sanders. Her boyfriend, Jason Timbers, was standing to the right of her.

"Why, if it isn't the three weird Elster's sisters!"

"What the heck do you want, Tracy?"

"What else, to have my fortune read?"

An idea instantly came to me with Tracy saying this. Given that Tracy had delighted in humiliating us countless times in the past, I thought I would return the favor.

"Give me your right hand."

Without delay, Tracy did as I requested. Allowing me to turn it palm side up, putting my plan into action.

"So, what's in my future, Sharon?"

"Oh, this isn't good," I said, trying my best to keep from bursting out laughing. "What I see in your future is, in fact, you headed for a great, big downfall."

As was not unexpected, this sent both Angela and Bridget bursting into laughter.

"She told you, Tracy," Bridget said.

"Stupid liar! Tomorrow morning, I'm going to destroy you and your sisters' reputations, Sharon, pathetic witch!" Tracy spat out.

"Okay, now you've crossed the line with that, Tracy," I said, the anger starting to build over her insulting my heritage as a true witch.

"What's that supposed to do, scare me or something?" Tracy asked.

"You'll find out," Bridget replied. "And when you do, you'll wish you had kept your damn mouth shut."

"You think I crossed the line now? Just wait until tomorrow. Jason, let's get the hell out of here. I can't stand the sight of these three bitches right now."

"But we just got here," Jason whined.

"Damn it, Jason, I'm not about to take your whiny crap! You've been given the opportunity to date the most popular girl at Darkwood High and bring her to the annual springtime festival! You'd better do as I've ordered!"

"Fine, all right, we'll get the heck out of here!"

***

"Can you believe the way Sharon and her two freak sisters treated me?" Tracy raged, once she and Jason were safely within his shiny black new pick-up truck. "I have half a mind to demand you run them over one by one!"

"Now just calm down, Tracy, let me take you home so you can get a good night's sleep."

"Fine, whatever," Tracy grumbled, turning her head to stare out the passenger 's-side window.

"You know, Sharon," Angela said as she was behind the wheel of her car, driving the three of them back home. "We should, well, not hurt Tracy for her evil comments, but scare her just a little."

An overwhelming feeling of wanting to do this started growing in me with Angela's suggestion. The way Tracy had treated my sisters and me, insulting witches as she did, she deserved to be taught a lesson so that she would not do it again.

"So, what do you say, Sharon?" Angela asked. "Are you up for it?"

"Yeah, it's what she deserves, with how she insulted us."

***

"Welcome home, Sharon," Trixie, present in the mirror, said to me the moment I set foot back into my bedroom, and sat down on the bed.

"Come on out, Trixie, I need your help with something."

"What's wrong?" she asked, emerging from the mirror glass and joining me on the bed.

"Some girl named Tracy Sanders insulted Angela, Bridget, and me at the fair tonight, and threatened to humiliate us in some way at school tomorrow. If it's no trouble, I'd like you to well, scare her a bit, to show her what a mistake it was for her to do such a cruel thing."

"Sure, I have no problem doing that, Sharon." A genuine look of concern was on her face. Her eyes turned a piercing shade of red.

***

Sitting in the passenger's seat of Jason's truck, Tracy happened to glance into the rearview mirror. What she caught sight of was something that caused her one heck of a bone-chilling fright.

What it was that came to fill Tracy's sparkling hazel eyes was her reflection. It was horribly distorted and out of focus. Even worse, her eyes were a piercing red. This caused Tracy's face to grow with horror. This didn't escape Jason's notice. Were Sharon and her two sisters using their witch powers to try to strike back at her?

"Hey, what's wrong?" Jason asked.

Immediately, Tracy was filled with a deep-rooted sensation of pure dread. Should she reveal to him that she had just seen her own reflection, horribly distorted and out of focus? *Oh yeah, sure, that'll come off as me being totally sane,* she quickly realized.

"It's nothing," Tracy said. "I'm just pissed at how Sharon, Angela, and Bridget treated me, that's all."

"Well, I wouldn't continue to get yourself all worked up about it," Jason replied in an amazingly calm, sure-of-himself tone of voice. "We're no longer at the fair, and chances are extremely good we won't be making a return trip there."

"Yeah, you sure as hell got that right. Still, those three freak sisters aren't going to get away with what they did. At school tomorrow, I'm going to humiliate them so bad they won't ever want to come back."

***

Returning home and into the safe, warm confines of her bed, it didn't take Tracy long to fall into an uneasy slumber and dream. In it, she was standing in front of the booth, with Sharon, Angela, and Bridget across from her. Instantly, she felt a combination of fear and anger start swirling up within her, striking her with unrelenting nausea.

"I see you've come back for a second round, you smart-mouthed, witch-hating bitch," Sharon sneered, sounding as if she was suffering from blocked, snot-filled nostrils.

"Go ahead, Sharon, insult me all you want," Tracy countered. "It's not going to change my mind about humiliating you and your two freak sisters tomorrow."

"Okay, look, I'll tell you what, to show you there are no hard feelings between us, I'll give you a free palm reading," Sharon replied in an easy-going, calm voice.

"I'll pass thanks," Tracy said. She wanted nothing from this witch and her two pathetic siblings.

"But it's on the house," Sharon replied, sounding more and more like the antagonist of Tracy's favorite movie the Wizard of Oz, as each moment passed.

"Look, I said no!" Tracy yelled. Her mind became filled with the thought of asking Sharon about what she had seen in the rearview mirror of Jason's truck.

"I know what you're thinking, Tracy. You think what you saw in your date's mirror was a figment of your imagination. Well, guess again, you smart-mouthed, witch-hating bitch! Your life is going to reach all new levels of pain and torment!"

And then just like that, Tracy awoke with an abrupt start. Immense sweat lubricated her face, her mouth incredibly parched and cotton dry. Quickly leaping from her bed, she rushed from her bedroom into the nearby bathroom. Tracy used her right hand with its fingernails covered with day-old, cracked red nail polish to spin the cold-water faucet far to the right so it was hitting the white porcelain sink full blast. Seconds later, sheer nervousness struck away at her heart. The light present above her head, burning with full illumination, now seemed to take on a life of its own. It started to flicker wildly, drilling Tracy with nervousness. *Just what the heck did those wannabe fortune tellers, Sharon and her siblings, do to me?* Tracy wondered as she made herself scarce from the bathroom.

After getting a few more hours of sleep, she once again awoke from sleep to have bright September morning sun strike her face. As she lay there in bed, she hoped what she had experienced during the past few hours was now at an end. That things would be all right.

Setting foot back into the bathroom, Tracy saw her face starting to show signs of aging. "Damn you, Sharon, this is all you're doing, witch!"

***

"What happened to you, Tracy?" Her best friend, Becca Coldman, said as she pulled her car up to the front of the Sandlers' house, and Tracy climbed in. "You look like you're thirty!"

"Don't ask," Tracy grumbled.

"Whatever," Becca said.

By the time she and Becca arrived at school, Tracy noticed, glancing into the rearview mirror, that the age on her face had now advanced to the point she now looked well into her forties.

"Oh crap, you look worse than ever!" Becca exclaimed.

"I can see that perfectly well," Tracy said.

"Okay, what the heck is going on?"

"I insulted Sharon Elsters and threatened to humiliate her sisters and here last night at the fair."

"What don't tell me, the rumors of the Elsters sisters are true, and Sharon or all of them have put an aging curse on you?" Becca asked.

"It looks that way."

"Oh, come on, Tracy, that witch curse crap is only the stuff of movies and books!"

"Then how do you explain what's happening to me?"

"You're right. Come on, let's go talk to them," Becca said.

***

As I stood in front of my open locker, Angela and Bridget close by, in front of theirs, I happened to glance down the hallway. What I saw was Tracy, and she looked fifty. She was approaching us with her best friend, Becca Coldman. I knew then what Trixie had done, hastened her aging process.

"You sure have a lot of nerve coming near my sisters and me, with the way you treated us last night."

"I'm sorry, Sharon, but you can't leave me like this!" Tracy pleaded. "If you do, by the time school ends, I'll be so old, death won't be far behind!"

"But you insulted us, Tracy. Not only that, but you threatened to humiliate us sometime today."

"Please, Sharon, I'm sorry and begging you, don't leave me this way!"

"No, I'm sorry, Tracy, I can't. You need to suffer for how you treated my sisters and me."

"Oh, come on, Sharon, that's not fair!" Becca yelled.

"No, just forget it, Becca. It's my fault I'm this way, and I'm just going to have to suffer for it," Tracy said. "Now come on, let's go."

Standing there watching the pair depart, out of nowhere, I felt a sudden change of heart. Should I take pity and not let her suffer anymore?

"Trixie, I know you can hear me, undo what you've done."

"*As you wish, Sharon,*" I heard fill my mind.

***

Stepping into the bathroom, the first thing Tracy did was rush to one of the bathroom mirrors over the sink to check her reflection.

She felt relieved that her face was back to normal. It made her decide she wouldn't be insulting or threatening the three sisters ever again

"I guess Sharon took pity on you after all," Becca said.

"Yeah, and from this moment forward, I'm leaving Sharon, Angela, and Bridget alone."

***

As soon as I arrived in my bedroom, my cell phone went off. Removing it from my purse, I checked the number. It was Julie.

"How was the trip to Blue Winter, Julie?"

Listening to my cousin's words, I felt pure anger.

"What do you mean, a pair of snobby girls humiliated you by filming you while taking a shower?" I asked. "Yes, I know you'd like to get revenge on them, and you should."

Continuing to listen to Julie rant about what had happened to her brought a wave of scorching anger rushing through me. She had not even been in Blue Winter for even a day, and already she had been recipient to having a pair of girls with a similar mindset as Tracy humiliate her. Well, I was damned if she was going to stand idly by and allow these girls to get away with it!

"Julie, I'm getting on a plane to Blue Winter to put a spell on these two girls that they'll never forget! Wait, what? You don't want me to? But they humiliated you! Yeah, sure, I'll calm down and not catch a flight out."

Listening further, I felt relief when Julie informed me that she and Aunt Katherine had just worked together to place a spell on the two girls. Amanda Hansen and Gillian Matthews were their names.

"Good going, Julie, the two bitches deserved it. You did the smart thing, convincing Aunt Katherine and Uncle Fred you need to get the heck out of that town pronto! Yeah, uh-huh, I'll be waiting when you get here."

Following Julie clicking off her cell phone, I brought my attention to the mirror where Trixie resided. I suspected she knew just how I was feeling when out of nowhere, she appeared in the mirror's glass.

"I can sense something's troubling you, Sharon. Tell me what's wrong?"

"It's my cousin Julie. A pair of mean-spirited girls named Amanda Hansen and Gillian Matthews humiliated her."

As she stood gazing at Sharon, Trixie couldn't help but feel tremendous sorrow for the girl who had heart and compassion enough to buy her. To allow her to come into her home, be a friend to her. No, she couldn't allow what had just happened to Sharon's cousin to go unpunished.

"Sharon, I'll make sure Amanda and Gillian suffer for what they did to Julie."

"No, it's all right. Trixie Julie told me she doesn't want my help. Besides, she's on the way back here even as we speak. I'm sure once she gets here, I'll be able to convince her to do otherwise."

Continuing to stare at Trixie, I was hit by a sudden want to have her come out of the mirror and join me on the bed.

"Hey Trixie, you think you can come on out and join me on the bed? I need you at my side right about now."

"That's what I'm here for, Sharon, to be a best friend for you," Trixie said, emerging from the mirror and doing just that.

"So, here we now sit, Trixie, a girl and her mirror demon," I said, bringing my head to rest on Trixie's shoulder. It didn't matter that it felt cold and clammy; what mattered was that we were best friends. Nothing would ever change that fact.

"And we will be best friends forever, Sharon."

When I informed Angela and Bridget about what had happened to Julie, they were mad as hell.

"I swear, Sharon, the three of us should get together and perform a spell. Make Amanda and Gillian seriously wish they were never born!" Angela yelled when I told her what happened.

"Angela's right," said Bridget. "They can't be allowed to get away with it."

"Now just relax and calm down, you two. Julie's on the way here, and when she arrives, then we'll figure out what to do about Amanda and Gillian."

"I'm in the mood for some ice cream, you up for that, Sharon?" Bridget asked.

***

"So, how's it going with your new mirror?" Angela asked, as Bridget and I strolled through Darkwoods, slowly licking chocolate chip ice cream cones.

"It's going great."

And it was, I realized. Then it dawned on me, I hadn't really introduced Trixie to my sisters yet.

"Angela, Bridget, how could you two have allowed me to not introduce you to Trixie?"

"Hey, don't worry about it, Sharon," Angela replied.

"Yeah, don't," Bridget said.

"Well, I'm not going to prevent you from meeting Trixie any longer. The moment we get home, I'm introducing you to her."

***

"Trixie, come on out!" I called out as Angela, Bridget, and I arrived in my bedroom.

"What's wrong, Sharon?"

"Nothing's wrong. Trixie, these two are my younger sisters, Angela and Bridget. I feel so utterly stupid that I didn't introduce you to them earlier."

"Hey, cut it out, Sharon," Angela warned.

"Yeah, Sharon, it was an honest mistake. Don't go beating yourself up over it," said Bridget.

"Well, anyway, like I said, Trixie, these are my two sisters."

"Are they natural witches like you, Sharon?" Trixie asked.

"One hundred percent."

***

A few days later, I watched from my second-floor bedroom window as Uncle Fred and Julie pulled up to the front of my house. Almost immediately, I felt tremendous excitement. My cousin was here. She was away from those spiteful two girls. As I watched Angela and Bridget rush out to greet her, I was filled with absolute bliss. Both my beloved cousin and my best friend, who resided in a mirror, were at my side. Things couldn't get any better for me at the moment.

"I can sense you're feeling happy, Sharon."

"Yeah, I sure am, Trixie."

FINAL ANSWER

by Dawn Colclasure

Miranda Morris picked a French fry up from her tray and looked around the loud cafeteria in her school as she popped it into her mouth and chewed. Her eyes scanned the group of teenagers scattered around the room, looking for anyone she knew or hated.

"So, what are you doing this weekend?" she heard her friend, Embery, ask, looking at her boyfriend, Gary, who sat next to her.

Miranda looked at the two of them sitting across from her as she listened.

Gary shrugged. "Nothing, really. Probably just driving around, listening to music." He smiled at her, inching closer. "Wanna come with?"

"That's boring," Miranda said, looking at the other French fry she had just removed from her tray. She dunked it into a small white container of ketchup, aware that her friends were looking at her, and smiled as she looked at them again. "Come to my house. I'm having a party."

They stared at her with confusion. Even Molly, Miranda noticed, who sat next to her, stared at her with likewise consternation.

"Since when?" Molly asked.

"Since now," Miranda answered, shaking her head at Molly. She turned her head to grin at Gary and Embery. "It's gonna be lit."

"And, what, pray tell, will make your party so lit?" Embery asked, looking at Miranda with annoyance.

Miranda smirked at her. She was probably upset because Miranda had just ruined her chances for an excuse to make out with her boyfriend in his car. "One word: Booze."

"I'm in!" Gary announced, sitting up straight and holding up his hand, as though he were in class.

Miranda smiled again, moving her gaze around the cafeteria. Her eyes landed on one person sitting alone and staring at her, and she flinched. Lyle Danvers was such a geek. She hated how he had such a lingering crush on her. She'd turned down his invitation to go with him to Homecoming, and she had hoped that had given him the hint that she wasn't interested in him. But he kept up with the stares, the stalking, and the notes in her locker.

And even if he wasn't a geek, she wasn't interested in dating a fifteen-year-old. That was two years younger than she was! He was just a sophomore and not a junior, like she and her friends. Anyway, she was more interested in guys who were into nice cars and fooling around, instead of reading books or tinkering with computers like he was always doing.

She frowned, looking at the cheeseburger she now held in her hands. Too bad she'd broken up with Chip. Otherwise, she'd have a guy sitting next to her and probably feeling her up under the table like Gary was doing with his girlfriend. Instead, it was her best friend since fifth grade, Molly, sitting at her side. Still, she wished she had a new boyfriend pawing all over her. Then she'd make it clear to Lyle that she was not available.

But Chip had cheated on her, so she got rid of him.

"What's up?"

Miranda turned her head to look at Molly. "What?"

"That face you made just now," Molly answered. "What's wrong?"

Miranda shrugged, removing a small pickle from her burger before taking a bite. "Lyle's staring at me," she answered as she chewed, looking down so he wouldn't see her answering. She didn't want him to know that it bothered her.

Molly scoffed. "What else is new?"

Miranda swallowed her food and chuckled. "If only I could kick his ass."

"Don't worry, you'll get him," Molly said, smiling. "And then he'll leave you alone for good."

"That's right, I will get him," Miranda agreed, nodding as she picked at the burger again. "But for now, I'm not going to let it ruin my plans for a party."

"So, you're really having a party?" Molly asked.

Miranda looked up, suddenly aware that her two other friends had grown mysteriously silent. She almost laughed when she noticed they were lost in a smooch fest.

She looked at Molly. "Yes, I'm really having a party," she repeated with sarcasm. Then she looked at her burger again. "Be at my house at five to help me decorate, okay?"

"Sure, I'll help you decorate for this party you suddenly decided to have," Molly replied with likewise sarcasm.

Miranda scoffed. "Whatever," she said, taking another bite of her burger.

***

The bus came to a stop, and Miranda disembarked. She walked the half block to her house, as she had done so many times before.

She finally reached her house, and she scowled as she noticed two kids from her school standing in front of a bush that was on one side of the stone steps of her front porch. "What are you doing?" she demanded, stomping across the grass of her front yard towards them.

They turned to look at her, and she realized they were the freshmen twins she'd been introduced to last month. Ken and Kelly both had brown hair and green eyes, but Kelly's hair went down to her shoulders. It was the only way to tell them apart, save that they didn't dress the same as most twins did.

"Don't be mad," Kelly pleaded.

"We were just looking at something," Ken added.

"What were you looking at?" Miranda asked, searching their faces.

"That," Ken replied, pointing.

Miranda looked at where he was pointing and yelped in alarm as she jumped back. A black cat lay dead on the ground in front of the bush, its middle cut open and maggots feeding on the organs within. Flies also buzzed over it. The carcass's lifeless stare was directed at the sky, and its tongue hung out of the side of its mouth.

"Oh, my God! That's horrible!" She turned to look at the twins again. "Did you put that there?"

"No!" Ken replied with alarm, his eyes widening.

"We were just looking at it," Kelly insisted.

Miranda straightened, regaining control of herself. "Well, that's enough looking. Beat it!"

The twins hurried away, and once Miranda was satisfied they were gone, she looked at the dead cat again and shuddered. No way was she going to dispose of it.

As she walked to the steps and ascended them to her porch, she pulled out her cell phone and dialed a number. She pulled her house key out of her pocket with her free hand as she used the other to hold her phone near her ear as she listened to the line ring. When someone answered, she smiled, unlocking the door. "Hey, it's me," she said. She frowned as she listened, entering the house and closing the door behind her. "Yeah. … Listen, can you please do me a favor? It's really important." She placed her key into her pocket and dropped her backpack on the floor as she listened. "I know. I'm sorry. I didn't mean all of that. Chip, please help me out. I'm having a party later, and I have an emergency." She listened again, then sighed. "Yeah. Sure, you can come to the party, as long as you help me out. Deal?" She listened again, then smiled.

***

Inviting Chip to the party had actually come in handy, Miranda realized hours later, watching as her ex-boyfriend deftly opened the keg of beer everybody else had struggled with. Once the first cup was poured from it, he stood, laughing as he looked around. "Cheers!" he announced, holding up his cup.

The rest of her friends crowded around the keg to fill their cups. Miranda smiled as she watched. It hadn't been easy to get the keg, but at least it had been worth it.

As the partygoers filed out to the rest of the house, she smiled at Chip. "My hero."

"Care to give your hero a kiss?" he asked, casting a flirtatious grin her way.

Miranda frowned. "Ugh. Drop dead." She turned and walked into the living room, lightly dancing to the music. As everyone danced, she took some time admiring the costumes and the décor she and Molly had hung up. Molly had brought along Embery when she showed up, with Embery volunteering to help out. Miranda had been happy to have extra help, and they decked out the house with balloons and streamers in record time.

She frowned when she noticed Molly was sitting in a chair, looking at a large hardcover book she had open on her lap. A couple of the other guests stood on either side of her, looking down at the pages.

Miranda walked over and looked down at the book. It had strange drawings of creatures and words written in different areas on the pages.

"What's that?" she asked, looking at Molly.

Molly looked up at her and grinned. "It's a book of spells. It's supposed to summon demons."

Miranda rolled her eyes. "Give me a break."

Molly shrugged. "It might work!"

"Or, not," Miranda muttered, turning to walk away. As she walked towards the kitchen, she hoped her little act got the others thinking she wasn't interested in that sort of thing. She was actually interested but preferred to keep her interest a secret. She and Molly had read many books on demonology, but Molly was the only one who unashamedly shared what she learned. Miranda, on the other hand, preferred to keep it quiet. If other people knew she was studying it, they might hit her up for black magic or something.

She waited until the party started to thin out. Finally, when a few hours had passed and a handful of her friends remained, she found Molly in the kitchen talking with Embery.

"I want to try it," she said, gripping Molly's arm.

Molly turned to look at her. "Try what?"

"Summoning a demon," Miranda answered.

Molly gasped, her eyes widening with excitement. "Here? Now?"

Miranda shrugged. "Why not? My parents won't be home until after two. We have time."

"Great!" Molly exclaimed. She turned to look at Embery. "Wanna join our circle?"

"What circle?" Embery asked, her face scrunching in confusion.

"A circle to summon a demon," Miranda answered. "You in or not?"

Embery smiled. "Let's do this."

"I'm in, too."

They turned to look at the source of the voice and Miranda cringed. Standing in the doorway of the kitchen was Lyle. Of course, Miranda hadn't known he was there; he had somehow been lost to her in the crowd of many teenagers partying and dancing throughout her house.

She swung around to face her friends. "Who invited him?"

"He sort of invited himself," Embery answered, shrugging. "He heard us talking about your party at our lockers."

She glared as she turned to face Lyle. "Fine. You can join us, just don't geek it up."

"I won't," Lyle promised.

They gathered in the living room and removed some furniture so that they could all sit on the floor in a circle. Embery had found a black candle they could burn, and Miranda watched the flame flicker as it remained lit in the center. She looked around at each one who was there: Molly, Embery, Chip, Lyle, and Gary. Now realizing that there were six of them, she smiled. Perhaps it had been luck that Lyle was there; six was a powerful number.

She carefully opened Molly's book and rifled through the pages. She finally came to the page she'd been searching for and looked down at the words. She and her friends held hands, and she recited the words.

After she finished, the flame of the candle went out.

They remained silent, sitting frozen in place as they waited for something to happen.

A powerful odor swept through the room. Miranda cringed as she covered her nose, looking around. The atmosphere in the room suddenly grew suffocating, as though heavy smoke infiltrated their lungs. "Who summons me?" a disembodied voice demanded from above them.

They looked at each other. Then Molly answered, "We do."

Molly's body exploded into pieces, blood, hair, and body parts flying around the room. They screamed at the sight of where Molly once sat, where only a large pool of blood and bits of skin remained.

"Holy shit!" Miranda screamed.

They got to their feet, looking around.

"What just happened!" Chip screamed, staring at them all in horror.

"Did a demon do that?" Embery asked, her voice calm as she looked at Miranda.

Miranda shuddered, trying not to see all the blood all over the walls and all over her friends. "I don't know."

None of them moved. They stood there as the reality of the disaster hit them.

"You want to know what happened?" Gary asked in a sarcastic tone as he looked at Chip. "I'll tell you what happened. As you can see, poor Molly just exploded."

They all looked at each other in shock. Then Lyle cleared his throat, and Miranda looked at him. "Well, it's a good thing I'm here," he said. "I know a thing or two about dealing with demons."

He must have noticed Miranda's surprised look because he shrugged. "What? I read about other stuff too. I know you're interested in demonology and stuff like that. I knew I had to be here with you. Ever since you told me that you love me, I knew I had to protect you."

Miranda gasped. "I never told you that I love you!"

His smile broadened, and he pretended to swoon. "She loves me."

"Kill Lyle now!" Miranda screamed, looking at him with an angry glare as she stormed towards him.

"Wait! We need him!" Chip said, stepping in front of Miranda to stop her.

"What do you mean, we need him?" she roared, angrily fixing her look of murder on Chip.

"He just said that he knows about demons," Chip reminded. "Maybe he can fix whatever happened."

"I seriously doubt there's a way to put Molly back together again!" she cried incredulously.

"I know, it's too late for Molly," Chip admitted. "But if there is a demon here, we need to get rid of it. Okay?"

Miranda bit her lip. "Fine." She angrily swung around, planning to get the book again, when Embery stepped in front of her. "Why did you say it like that?" she hissed.

"Say what?" Miranda asked.

Embery shot a look at Lyle, then replied, "The ILY thing."

Miranda sighed. "I don't know. It was stupid. But that doesn't matter right now. I mean, hello? Molly's dead! She just exploded right in front of our faces! What do we do?"

Embery shook her head. "I don't know." She looked around, rubbing her arms. "I don't know anything about this stuff."

"Well, I do," Miranda said, stiffening. At least by revealing this to Embery, she felt comfortable saying it. "Probably more than that creep does."

Embery nodded. "Okay, let's get the book."

Just as they turned to walk to another part of the room, the entire room disappeared, and they were enveloped in darkness.

"What's going on!" Chip exclaimed.

Light flooded through the room, revealing that the five teenagers now stood in a different room. This one was larger, with many other things in it that weren't normally found in a typical living room.

Such as a stage and towering red curtains that hung behind a lectern situated in the center of it.

Miranda gasped and reacted with surprise once she realized she was standing at a podium with a buzzer on it. To her right, she saw Chip in a cage with a large, thick brown snake coiled up at his feet. Embery was at a podium to her left. Next to Embery was another cage, this one with Gary in it. They both screeched in alarm when they saw a beehive hanging from the ceiling of the cage, over Gary's head.

"Oh, my God!" Embery cried, turning to look at Miranda. "Gary's allergic to bees!"

A roar of laughter sounded from behind the curtain, and the girls turned to see a towering demon wearing a white suit that somehow emphasized his red skin walk up to the lectern. Once he stood there, his laughter ended, and he smiled at them. "I know." Then he held his claws out at his side. "Welcome! Welcome, all, to another episode of Summoner!"

Cheers and applause sounded all around. Miranda and Embery tried to find the source of the cheering, but there was no sign of an audience or any people seated anywhere.

"Hey, wait a minute!" Miranda cried, looking around. Then she looked at the host. "Where's Lyle? He was with us, too!"

"We'll get to him," the host replied. Then he held up what looked like white index cards. "In this game show you lucky idiots get to be a part of, I will read to you a question from one of these cards. If you answer correctly, you are free. But if you're wrong, and I really hope you'll be wrong." He laughed with a grin of mirth on his face. "Then the person in the cage next to you will die! Isn't that wonderful, ladies and gentlemen?"

The invisible audience cheered and clapped.

"Now, it's time for Round One," the host announced. "Embery, you get to go first."

Excitable music played, and a spotlight shone from above onto Embery.

"Now, here is your question," the host began. "How many demons are there?"

Embery's face fell into a look of shock. She looked at Miranda, hoping for answers, but Miranda only shrugged.

She looked at the host again. "I don't know, like, a thousand?"

Laughter and jeers erupted from the audience. The host broke out into a hilarious giggle, slapping his leg as though laughing at a hilarious joke.

"That answer is incorrect, you mindless imbecile!" the host roared at Embery with rage. "And now you get to watch your boyfriend die!"

The girls watched in horror as the beehive above Gary split open from within. They screamed as the bees left the hive to cover his body with stings. Gary screamed and cried in agony as he was mercilessly stung by the bees, and then when his lifeless body fell, the entire cage was shrouded with a black covering.

"Oh, Gary! No!" Embery cried. She turned to look at the host. "You monster!"

The host grinned. "Why, thank you." He then held up his cards again as he looked at Miranda. "And now, Miranda, it is your turn!"

Miranda wiped the tears from her eyes and hardened her gaze. "Bring it!"

Excitable music played, and a spotlight shone from above onto Miranda.

"Now, Miranda, here is your question," the host announced in a serious tone. Reading from the card he held in front of him, he asked, "Name the demon who caused the Black Plague of 542 A.D."

Miranda's eyes widened. There was no way she could know this answer. And, anyway, the Black Plague didn't occur in 542 A.D. The demon was lying. But she only got one guess. She grabbed at a name she remembered reading in a book. "Ashtaroth."

"WRONG!" the host shouted, pointing at her. "Wrong! Wrong! Wrong!" Then he broke into fits of laughter, dancing around as he repeated the word "wrong" to a tune.

"Wait!" Miranda cried. "Aren't you going to tell us the answer?"

"Gee, let me think," the host said, pretending to be lost in thought for a moment. Then he smiled. "Nope! Now say goodbye to your good buddy, Chip!"

Miranda watched in horror as the snake at Chip's feet grew larger and then bit his face several times. Chip screamed, but he could not fight off the snake. The snake swallowed Chip in one huge bite, and then the cage was covered in black.

"Oh, no!" she cried, tears forming in her eyes. Breathing in large gulps of air, her body shook as she turned to look at Embery, who looked at her with likewise terror. "Embery, what are you going to do?"

"Oh, get over it!" the host demanded. "Serves you right, fooling around with something you had no business playing with in the first place. You play with fire, and all that! You, foolish humans, think you can control demons. Well, you sure don't know a whole lot about us!"

The girls slowly turned to look at their host.

"Please," Embery pleaded. "We're sorry we tried to summon a demon!"

The host waved it away. "Too late." He bowed. "Here I am! So now, you've got to deal with me, on my terms."

A drumroll sounded behind them. When it finished playing, the host grabbed the lapels of his coat and smiled. "Time for Round Two!"

Cheering and applause swept around the stage. When it settled down, the host smiled at the two girls. "Now, one of you will ask the other a question, and if the answer is wrong, then, whoosh! Off to Hell she will go! Let's get started!"

Miranda and Embery gasped as their podiums slowly turned to face each other. Miranda now saw a large screen appear on the wall behind Embery. She bit her lip, her heart beating in her chest as she stared at the question on the screen.

"Miranda, you will ask Embery the question you see on the screen," the host instructed. "Embery will have five seconds to answer. Once she answers the question, either a bell or a horn will sound to indicate if she is right or wrong. Begin!"

Miranda read the question on the screen: "What is the name of the angel who rebelled against God and was banned from Heaven?"

Embery smiled. "Lucifer."

A horn sounded from above.

"What?" Miranda cried, looking at the host. "It's the right answer!"

"Yeah, you might want to have a little talk with whoever wrote that book you guys like to read. Nobody wanted to write down or record the angel's *real* name. He actually goes by the name Lucihasnafromahgansyomghahafer. Sorry."

"No!" Miranda screamed, turning to watch Embery disappear within a wall of flames.

She turned to the host again. "You tricked us!"

The host shrugged. "Don't care." Then he slapped the lectern. "It's time for the bonus round!"

A cloud of smoke exploded where Embery once stood, revealing Lyle in her place.

"Oh my God, Lyle!" Miranda cried, wishing she could hug him. "Help me! Please!"

"Don't worry," Lyle assured. "I won't let him hurt you."

"If you two love birds have quite finished!" the host cried impatiently. "Let's get on with it, shall we?"

Excitable music played all around as the podiums turned again to face the host. Then it came to a sudden stop, and the host smiled, his red eyes flickering.

"Lyle and Miranda, you must answer my final question. You will have three seconds to talk among yourselves, then one of you will answer. If the answer is wrong, you die."

"And if it's correct?" Lyle asked.

The host shrugged. "You're free to go." He appeared serious again. "Now, then! Miranda! Here is your question: What is this holiday called where demons get to dress up as their favorite humans?"

Miranda and Lyle looked at each other. "We have no way of knowing that!" Miranda whispered.

"I don't think it's even a thing with demons," Lyle replied.

"I thought you read about them too?"

Lyle shrugged. "I only said that so you'd let me help."

"You mean you lied to me?" Miranda shrieked.

"COME ON!" the host whined. "You guys should know this, spending all that time reading about demons! Well, lay it on me!"

"Just say whatever pops into your head," Lyle whispered to Miranda, before they turned to face the host again.

Miranda gulped, her knees shaking. Finally, she spoke. "Davendium."

"What?" the host asked, holding a hand to his ear.

"The holiday," Miranda replied. "It's called Davendium."

"Hmm. Wrong!" the host replied. He pushed a button, and Miranda exploded into thousands of bits like confetti.

Lyle gasped as he turned to face the host. "Please! Stop!"

"Relax, Lyle," the host replied, grinning. "Because, guess what! I'm going to set you free!"

He smiled. "Really?"

The host held up a finger. "If! You answer my question correctly."

"But that's not fair! You keep asking us questions that nobody knows the answer to! You lied to us, and you tricked us!"

The host shrugged. "Well, duh! I'm a demon! That's what we do!" He chortled with glee. "Are you ready for your question?"

Lyle straightened, hardening his gaze. "Fine. Let's have it!"

The host grinned as he moved a question card up to his face. Several minutes passed as he stared at the question, then he moved the card down, casting a sinister grin in Lyle's direction.

"Lyle!" he cried. "What is the best way to banish a demon from a human?"

Lyle relaxed, grinning again. "An exorcism."

Several seconds passed. Then the host asked, "Is that your final answer?"

Lyle nodded, feeling more confident now. "Yes."

"You are correct! Congratulations!"

Lyle released a breath of relief. "Does that mean I get to go home?"

"It means you are free!" the host replied, holding out his hands. "Bye!" He snapped his fingers, and Lyle vanished from where he stood.

The next thing he knew, Lyle was floating in outer space. He tried to scream, but his lungs collapsed, and he couldn't breathe. Lack of sufficient oxygen caused him to fall into unconsciousness before his body crumpled upon itself and limply floated through space.

TALENT

by Maximiliano Guzmán

High-volume music.
Red, blue, yellow, green, and multicolored lights.
The heavy atmosphere of the room.
The scent of lemony perfume, death, and sweat.
She dances from one wall to another.
Her body moves to the rhythm of the music.
Her soul is young but…
Her hair is dirty, her skin decaying, and her tattered clothes still bear the memory of her tragedy.
A corpse in her infinite dance.
A corpse in her infinite dance…

Talent, passion, hard work, and eternity.

Her parents refused to watch her die in a hospital bed.

They saw in her the dream of a lifetime blossoming.

Amanda Kelly, since the age of eight, wanted to become a dancer. But not a ballet dancer—Amanda wanted to be part of Britney Spears' staff, dancing by her side.

Her parents promised her that if she studied, if she completed high school, she could fulfill her dream of dancing.

Young Amanda studied in the mornings, danced in front of the mirror at night with wild determination.

Britney Spears played on her headphones. Synchronized movements and skill, as "Baby One More Time" echoed in her mind.

Amanda moved from left to right, leaping, spinning, and rising onto her toes.

The music blared. Her parents in the kitchen pondered the savings they would spend on their daughter when she turned eighteen.

"We don't have the money."

"We can't tell her she won't be able to go to New York."

"There's a dance school in Memphis. It's less expensive."

"But Peter, her dream is the big stages."

Young Amanda didn't hear what her parents discussed, what plans they made for her future. To her, only Britney mattered—just Britney and her dance steps.

Amanda rested for a minute, observing her figure in the mirror.

Her body matured rapidly, her skin smooth, and her smile that of a dreamer. Amanda expressed her dream at every moment. In high school, all her classmates and friends called her "The Campus Dancer." Her nickname came from her constant dancing during breaks, lunchtime, and physical activities.

Sometimes she danced alone, sometimes accompanied by two friends, sometimes she danced for the entire high school and every resident of Pasadena during football tournaments.

She was a cheerleader, and her beauty set her apart from her peers. Her youth and enthusiasm made her popular. Amanda was the favorite among teenagers—the pretty girl of the high school.

"The Campus Dancer" continued her studies, preparing to secure her ticket to New York. On the internet, she found the McNamara Dance School. An ex-dancer from Britney Spears and Backstreet Boys taught there.

"I'll go there," she declared aloud.

In the photograph, Professor McNamara was a mental reflection of what Amanda dreamed of being at forty. Her eyes stared back from the computer screen.

Her parents are proud of her.

Her grades are excellent, and she has improved significantly in her training.

But "The Campus Dancer" has competitors.

A young girl named Michigan appeared at the high school on her first day of classes wearing a Christina Aguilera T-shirt and black sunglasses. Michigan is determined to steal popularity from anyone who dares to compete against her.

But Michigan is not just a dancer. That young girl can execute death-defying leaps and bend like a sheet of paper. Her techniques are foreign, inspired by Arabian and Oriental dances.

Michigan is strikingly beautiful, and her charisma dazzles.

Amanda knows her popularity is at stake.

What will McNamara in New York say if she sees Michigan dance?

Amanda can't even bear to think about it. She must refine her techniques, infuse her movements with meaning, develop her own style, and captivate her audience with sensual intensity. Dancing isn't merely about moving legs and hips or jumping like a kangaroo. It's about interpreting a melody or a song and expressing emotions to the audience. Dancing is about hypnotizing the crowd.

And Michigan is achieving just that!

On her first day at the high school, Michigan performed somersaults around the campus, drawing attention. Her movements exuded universal fervor.

"She's touched by a magical wand," Amanda's friends whispered.

"Michigan plays at dancing. I dance for real."

But Michigan was determined to dethrone her.

Each morning, her dances became more playful and extravagant.

The applause for Michigan overshadowed Amanda's popularity.

"Can you believe she can twist her head like the girl from *The Exorcist*?" a friend said to Amanda.

"That's impossible," Amanda replied.

"Watch," the friend demonstrated, slightly bending her neck. "But she spun her entire head around. She managed a full rotation while her body moved counterclockwise. She seemed possessed by a demon!"

"She's a fraud! And you're a liar!"

Amanda, after years of popularity, lost her grace and loyal followers.

Michigan graced the cover of Pasadena Now for her halftime performance during a local football game.

"She did it again. Head and body rotation."

Amanda's tearful solitude echoed across the campus.

The prolonged pain and her new competitor's fame turned Amanda into a gray shadow.

"Are you not dancing anymore?" her mother asked, concerned.

Amanda took a sip of Coca-Cola and burst into tears.

"What's wrong, dear? Haven't you tried dinner?" her father inquired.

Amanda didn't respond. She stood up and retreated to her room.

Michigan would be part of the selected group to participate in GOT TALENT.

That news was devastating for Amanda.

Her dream… Her dream…

But she wouldn't give up.

Michigan couldn't make it to the national program.

And Amanda was determined to shatter her classmate's dream.

More hard work, more enthusiasm, more talent, more sleepless nights. And then, a violent move that would alter the course of history completely.

"You're a demon!" Amanda shouted at Michigan during a training session on the campus.

"You're crazy, friend," Michigan replied, an unpleasant smile on her face.

"You're a demon, I know it!" Amanda declared.

From her pocket, she pulled out a crucifix and held it in front of Michigan's eyes. Their classmates watched with curiosity, laughing as Amanda mumbled strange words in terrible Latin while gripping the crucifix. Michigan burst into laughter, and her popularity compelled the other boys and girls on campus to join in.

"You're a fool, Amanda. A fool," shouted a friend—or perhaps a former friend—at Amanda. Furious, Amanda attacked Michigan. It was a sudden, clumsy, impulsive assault.

The crucifix struck Michigan's head, and she retaliated, lunging at Amanda. They tumbled to the grass, and Michigan scratched Amanda's face. Ugly scars marred her once-beautiful features, causing her head to throb and her fever to rise. The blows continued.

Amanda struck Michigan once more with the metal crucifix.

"You'll die, cursed demon!"

Michigan's gaze, distorted by bruises and blood, grew more intense with each precise blow.

"You're a demon. A damned demon. I know it, I know it! Show me your true face, damn you!" Amanda screamed.

The metal crucifix fell aside after Michigan's counterattack.

Amanda remained frozen, kneeling over Michigan's body.

For a moment, Michigan's blood-red face transformed into that of a thirsty animal. Her hands turned as black as night, and her fingers sprouted long, sharp claws.

One of those claws pierced Amanda's jugular.

The boys and girls on campus screamed, covering their eyes and turning away.

Amanda's blood flowed, and Michigan...

Seeing Amanda collapse onto the grass, Michigan wiped the blood away with her sweatshirt and fled toward the campus exit.

Amanda bled out, her terrified and silent classmates unable to comprehend what they had witnessed.

An acquaintance of Amanda's approached, using a towel to cover the wound.

A boy called an ambulance, but it arrived too late.

The high school administrators were informed by a group of boys about the incident.

When the ambulance finally arrived, the paramedics found Amanda's warm body drenched in blood. They kept the wound covered with the towel, placed her on a stretcher, and rushed her to the hospital.

"Notify her parents," an orderly told a crying girl on the campus.

Amanda remained in a coma for three days at Huntington Health Hospital. During her transfer, a nurse claimed to have seen an eerie fire in Amanda's eyes.

Concerned, Amanda's parents asked the police to locate Michigan and her family.

An investigation began, but Michigan and her family had already left the city.

The police traced the address provided for the Michigan family to an abandoned Walmart.

Inside, they discovered spoiled food and items related to Oriental and Voodoo witchcraft.

Amanda's high school classmates testified as witnesses in front of a state judge. They all agreed that young Michigan twisted her head and body like the girl in The Exorcist.

In the local newspapers, journalists wrote:

"WHO CONTROLS THE VIOLENCE OF OUR ADOLESCENTS?"
TEEN FIGHT ENDS IN DEATH ON CAMPUS
Pasadena now

JEALOUSY, ENVY, AND A SHATTERED DREAM
Pasadena Star-News

"THE CAMPUS DANCER" DIES DURING A DISCUSSION WITH A CLASSMATE.
Local News Pasadena

But Amanda's parents refused to watch her die. They refused to lose her forever.

They took her out of the hospital one minute after her death.

Her mother sensed that her daughter's body wouldn't rest in peace. She had been a victim of a demon—there was no doubt—and for that reason, her daughter wouldn't have the chance for paradise.

Amanda's body lay in her room for a week after her death until the day she opened her eyes, turned her head, and saw her father.

Her father, surprised and frightened, fell to his knees, sobbing at the sight of his daughter alive once more.

"She's not the same person," he said, "but she's my daughter."

"My daughter continues to dance. Her killer granted her eternity," Amanda's mother told *Pasadena Now.*

Her parents restructured the house where they lived with Amanda. They created a special room with three walls and one transparent wall to observe their daughter—the dancer.

They placed a music system playing Amanda's favorite songs. And in the front yard, a sign invited Pasadena neighbors to watch their daughter dance.

"THE MOST BEAUTIFUL DANCER IN THE WORLD"
Amanda Kelly.

Initially, the neighbors despised the idea of watching the deceased daughter of the Kellys dance.

"It's impossible; that girl should be buried," the neighbors said.

It's either a miracle or a curse," commented one of Amanda's high school classmates.

"She scares my children!" exclaimed an angry father upon seeing the sign.

Fear of this new presence in the neighborhood led Amanda's parents to fence their house.

Furious neighbors threw tomatoes, eggs, and excrement at the Kellys' home.

"They're condemning us all to hell!" shouted a neighbor as she hurled tomatoes at the Kellys' door.

"I can't stand the Dancer," said another girl, her brow furrowed.

But the Dancer Amanda Kelly is in her special room, moving from one side to the other, the loud music drowning out the young girl's grunts of horror and satisfaction.

She leaps from one wall to another, her hands in sync with each song.

"Peter, should we send the video to Britney?" Molly asks, holding a camcorder.

"Please, Molly. Just let her dance. We don't want more trouble with the neighbors or all of America."

"But it's our daughter's dream," Amanda's mother replies.

-No, Molly. ¡No!

"But Peter..."

Molly Kelly switches on the camera.

"Britney... My daughter always wanted to dance with you. Look at her there, dancing to your songs..."

And she films Amanda, caught in her broken, infinite dance. "Would you invite her to one of your shows?"

Peter Kelly, Amanda's father, steps out to the backyard to smoke. "You're crazy, Molly."

"Britney, pay no attention to this old curmudgeon," Molly says. "My daughter always dreamed of dancing with you. Do you like her?"

The room fills with colored lights—red, green, blue, yellow, violet—and Amanda Kelly dances... She dances.

"Britney, do you like her?" The camera zooms in on Amanda, who spins her head three hundred sixty degrees and smiles.

"Thank you, Mom," Amanda says.

Peter Kelly approaches the camera.

"I'm tired of this. Turn that thing off, Molly, please."

The recording fades to black.

WRONG NUMBER

by Mary jane Hill

It was late autumn, and I was sitting on my bed scrolling through TikTok when my phone lit up with a call from a number I didn't recognize. Normally, I decline random phone calls, but at this point, I was bored and decided to have some fun with a scam caller, so I picked it up. It wasn't what I expected.

"Hello, who is this?" I asked, annoyed, tossing my phone onto the bed after switching it to speakerphone.

"Is Alejandro there?" a voice answered. Instead of a spam caller asking about whatever scam they're trying to pull, I was met with the voice of a younger, genuine person, not someone who sounds like a spam caller at all.

"Uhm... no, there isn't any Alejandro here that I know of," I replied, sort of nervous. To me, he sounded my age and cute, even though I didn't know him, so I had no idea what he looked like.

"Oh, this must be the wrong number then. Sorry for that," he replied calmly, as if it had happened to him multiple times before.

"Oh, no worries. I have nothing better to do anyway," I replied, plopping back in my bed.

"Since we are already on call, why don't we get to know each other, eh?" he asked.

In the beginning, whenever I wanted to talk to complete strangers online, I had to sneak and do it. But I really didn't care. I am a social butterfly. I *need* to talk to people. Besides, in this day and age, all of us teens meet on Snapchat, Roblox, Discord, or wherever and just chit-chat. There's no harm. "That sounds like a great idea to me since I have nothing to do," I replied with an excited but nervous chuckle. I wanted to keep talking to him. I didn't want the call to end.

"By the way, my name is Aaron, and what's yours?" he asked.
"My name is Samantha."

***

I sat on my bed, smiling at my phone as a message from Aaron came through. We had been texting for a week, and I found out that Aaron and I have a mutual friend from Roblox. It turned out that our mutual friend was the one who gave him my phone number, and he used the "wrong number" as an excuse for him to talk to me. I didn't mind because I was always talking to people offline and giving out my number to people from the games we play together. Mostly Roblox and Minecraft, and occasionally I shared my number on Discord or Snapchat. My mother always threatened to ground me or to take my phone away if she caught me talking *again* to people offline or for giving out my numbers and how dangerous it is, blah blah blah, but they were my friends. I knew they wouldn't do anything to hurt me, right? They were not grown adults acting like children. I knew these people, FaceTimed them, and talked on calls with them. They were actual people my age, not some weirdo old man in his mom's basement being a pedo.

As another message came through from Aaron, I told him what was on my mind, since, you know, I'd decided to tell him I really liked him after I got to know him a bit better over the week. So I gathered up my courage after he replied that he enjoyed speaking with me throughout the week, too, and I asked him to be my boyfriend. Boys around here are stupid, always playing with the girls and cheating on them for no reason. I was recently in a relationship where this boy I was dating in person was always rude for no reason, had cheated on me multiple times, and was mentally abusive towards me, but not towards other girls. Plus, boys online were always so sweet and nice to me, and this would be my second online relationship. So, I had high hopes for Aaron and had prayed that he wasn't like the boys around me or one of those playboys. I waited for an answer as the minutes ticked by, fearing that he wouldn't like me back or wouldn't see me the same way I saw him. But it turned out he was a shy boy, and he hadn't really been in a real relationship. However, even being shy, his answer was yes.

***

As the months passed by with all the "I love you more" wars, kissy faces, sharing pictures with each other, having FaceTime calls, and all that, he turned out to be a really sweet boy. He would stick up for me when people were rude to me online; he was always there for me, always made me smile and feel comfortable when I was with him, and I did the same for him. He wasn't like my last boyfriend; he was sweeter, kinder, and nicer, and so many good things about him. My last boyfriend was the opposite of him. Aaron was absolutely perfect in every way imaginable. During our last conversation, he brought up something I wasn't sure I was comfortable with, but I was excited about the possibility of it happening.

"I have family up where you live, and my parents were planning on visiting my aunt. Would you like to see me while I was up there?" he asked.

I was so excited that he asked me if I would like to see him, but I maintained my composure and answered, "Yes, I would love to, but I have to ask my mom to see if it's okay. I'll let you know what she says."

"Oh, okay! Hopes she says yes because I have been dying to hug you," he replied.

I put my phone down and went to the kitchen to find my mom cooking sourdough bread. I stood beside her with a smile on my face until she stopped and paid attention to me.

"Mother," I began, "Aaron has family near where we live, and he asked if we could see each other. I told him I have to ask you first to see if it's okay with you. I *reallllly* want to meet him, so can I see him?"

"No," she answered quickly without looking up while she did her slap and folds on her dough.

"But whyyyyyyy?" I whined.

"Cause you're not meeting someone off the internet," she replied.

"Why? It's no different than me hanging out with Jessica?" I replied, crossing my arms and pouting.

"I know Jessica's mom," she answered, still not looking up from her dough.

"But you could meet his parents and get to know his parents thoughhhhh," I continued.

"I'm not a people person," she answered as she placed Saran Wrap over her bowl.

"You can meet them now. Sooner or later, you're gonna end up meeting them either way," I replied. As she was about to answer, my dad walked through the front door, and I got excited because he always sided with me.

"Daddy, Aaron's family is coming to visit his aunt who lives near us, and Mom won't let me see him," I whined.

He sighed. "Why won't you take her?" he asked.

"Because I don't know them," she answered, putting her hands on her hips. "You watch horror movies! You know the kind of people who are out and about in the world."

"You can't keep her imprisoned in here because you don't wanna meet new people or because you're afraid something from a horror movie is going to happen to her," he replied.

"Then why don't you take her?" she hissed, staring at me and glaring.

"Because I have work," he answered.

I smiled really big at my mother. "Please, please, it won't be that long. We can go to the agriculture far!" I offered.

The Agriculture Fair was a low-key fair we held in our main county park. It wasn't as large as the Salem Fair, but it had about five to ten rides and food vendors. There was a petting zoo, and so much other stuff to do. It would be fun for a first date.

She let out an exasperated sigh. "Fine," she huffed.

"YAY!" I exclaimed excitedly.

I ran back to my room to tell Aaron the good news of my mother agreeing to meet. I picked up my phone, sent him the good news, and waited for him to reply.

"Oh, really?! She really did agree?!" he asked enthusiastically.

"Yes, she really did agree," I answered excitedly.

"Oh, that's wonderful news to me. What time do you think we can meet next week?" he prodded.

"Uhm, probably Monday at the Agriculture Fair, if that's good to you?" I answered.

"Yes, all good to me since I'm coming this upcoming Sunday, so I'll ask my parents if I can," he said.

"Oh, okay. Well, see you then?" I asked.

"Of course," he replied.

***

It was Wednesday, and I was out and about in town with my mom. We went to Walmart to buy some groceries for dinner that night. She was making my favorite, lasagna. As we were shopping, a person came up behind me and suddenly hugged me out of nowhere. At first, it startled and scared me, but I kind of figured it was family. I was wrong. Instead of the expected family member, I found Aaron when I turned around. At first, I didn't believe it was him because he was supposed to come on Sunday, not Wednesday. But maybe his family changed plans.

"Aaron, I thought you weren't supposed to be here until Sunday?" I asked, narrowing my eyes at him.

"My family had made some changes to our plans, and I wanted to surprise you instead of telling you," he replied.

I looked around, but his parents weren't near or anything, and he was here alone. "Where are your parents?" I asked.

"Oh, they are just outside in the car. They sent me in here for some things to grab for lunch," he replied.

"Well, the fair doesn't start till Sunday, so for today, you wanna hang out if my mom lets me?" I looked over at my mom, hoping she would agree.

She was skeptical at first, but I showed her my doe eyes, and she caved.

"Sure, I guess," she replied.

***

On the ride home, I pulled out my phone as a notification came through. It was from Aaron. He had been messaging me while Mom and I walked around Walmart, but I didn't see it before we left.

"I miss you. Maybe you wanna call?" he asked.

I stared at my phone, wondering why he asked that. Maybe an hour later, after Mom and I got home and settled in, he and I were gonna spend the rest of the day together. I didn't question it and called him. As the hour passed, we chatted until my mom yelled for me, and I told him I had to go.

I giggled. "I assume you're here already. See you down there," I said. Before he could respond, I hung up, not bothered at all. So I walked through the house, excited to see him. The moment I saw him, I ran to hug him, and he hugged me back.

"Hiiiiii, you're finally here," I squealed.

"Yup, I'm here," he replied. I was so excited to do so many things with him this evening, but I was also a bit sad because I really wanted to show him the fair. Oh well, at least he was here right now.

"Hm, I don't know what to do, and I don't know where to start," I said.

"We can do whatever you wanna do," he replied.

I was looking over at my mom, who was putting up groceries, and she sort of looked and acted weird to me, as if she was on autopilot or something. I expected her to object, but she didn't. She wasn't acting herself, but honestly, I didn't really care. Besides, she was probably tired from working all night long. Who knew being a horror author was so hard?

"So, you wanna go out to do stuff, or do you wanna go up to my room?" I asked.

"I mean, it's already 5 pm, so it's getting kind of dark already. Maybe head up to your room?" he replied.

My mom didn't say anything, which was weird because I thought she would have said, "Keep the door open" or something, but she stayed quiet as we headed upstairs.

Aaron and I sat in my room, cuddling and watching a movie. He was talking to me about how he wanted a future with me, and I was nodding in agreement while half asleep. The drowsiness came out of nowhere, and I didn't know why.

I looked at my phone and saw a text from my mom asking, "Where are you?" and underneath her text was one from Aaron asking, "Who is with you, Samantha ...?!" It was the last thing I read before I passed out.

***

I woke up to a blinding, sharp pain in my right side. It was a blinding hot pain, and I struggled to breathe. I jolted awake, and to my horror, I couldn't move at all… like my body was numbed or paralyzed… I couldn't kick my feet or move my arms. I was looking around in my room, but it wasn't my room... I was in a different room in a place I wasn't familiar with. I saw a figure emerge from the darkness in the corner of the room, stand at the foot of my bed, and then move to the side of my bed. Confusion was finally starting to lift when I looked down toward the source of my pain, and jutting from my right lung was a knife. My eyes returned to the figure, still confused as it looked like Aaron, but it wasn't Aaron. I didn't know what it was, but every fiber of my being screamed "monster."

It took the knife out of my side, and as it slid through my torn skin, the pain was unbearable. I screamed and cried as loud as I could, hoping someone was there to help me or save me. His face was terrifying, with a huge, inhuman smile, sharp teeth, and an insidious look that covered his face. In one quick movement, he brought the knife down again and stabbed me in my left lung. I knew he wanted to kill me. He freed the knife and proceeded to stab me in my stomach, my legs, and then my arms. He was stabbing every part of me.

All I could do was lie there helplessly, watching him while crying and screaming, pleading with him to stop. I begged him to spare me. I was in so much pain. I could feel myself dying. I knew I was dying. With each thrust of his knife, his eyes would get redder, and the whites of his eyes and his eye sockets had gone black as if he had no eyes. Just red dots in the middle of an abyss. He was saying things as I drifted in and out of consciousness, hardly understanding at some points and then screaming loudly in my ears. "Never trust anyone, darling," and "You're so dumb for trusting me." He finally stabbed me in my throat, and I passed out as I gurgled on blood. The last thing I saw before my world drifted into an inky darkness was his sinister face and that smile too big for his face.

***

The darkness lifted to the sound of beeping, and I awoke in the hospital to that same face still hovering above me, still smiling with a mouth full of razor-sharp teeth. I screamed and thrashed in bed. Footsteps echoed in the room as someone came up to me, looking me over to see what was wrong. As my vision cleared, I could see it was my mom with someone behind her. As soon as my mom had stepped into the room, the thing above me on the ceiling went into a dark corner of the room, watching from a distance with crazed eyes and teeth exposed. My mom stepped aside, and Aaron stood behind her. I screamed as loud as I could and started crying.

"Get him the fuck away from me!" I hollered, trying to crawl out of the hospital bed.

He backed up, confused. "Samantha, it's me, Aaron..." he cooed.

"You tried to kill me; you played me and were stabbing me earlier!" I cried, still screaming in fear.

Everyone went silent and looked at me with fallen faces.

"It's been three weeks, Samantha... you have been in a coma," my mom said. As soon as the words left her lips, the figure in the corner disappeared.

"Samantha, when we were in that store, you ran off, and I couldn't find you for a week," my mom continued.

I lay there quietly, not knowing what to say, because I didn't just run off. I was with her the whole entire time... right? Or that's what I assumed. What was real and what wasn't real? As I looked over at the corner once more, I saw the figure emerge from the dark again, but this time there were two of them. The machines around me started beeping loudly, and I began to convulse. The room went dark, and red eyes were glowing above me. The glowing eyes started toward me, and just as they reached my face, they faded away. I looked around for my mom, but she was gone as well. Was she ever in that room with me? Was she another one of those figures? I struggled to form thoughts in my head as dizziness and a sense of euphoria swam through me. What happened to my mother? Where is she? As the thoughts raced through my mind, I felt something grab me as I faded off into nothing.

***

The newspaper articles would claim Samantha was found dead the next morning, and her mother would never be found. Samanth had indeed had her throat ripped out by the red-eyed monster, and she bled to death. But, of course, I would only know that since I was the one who killed her along with her mother. What can I say? Never trust anyone on the internet, am I right? They would believe her mother killed her and fled to some other state. Case closed. I walked away as the coroner team carried Samantha out of the house in a black body bag and loaded her into the coroner van. I looked back once more as they closed the doors behind themselves, licked my lips as I remembered her taste, and grinned, my eyes flashing red and returning to normal, satisfied with my handiwork. I turned and walked away, joined by my twin brother as we quietly walked down the sidewalk leading out of the suburbs undetected. Besides, who would be suspicious of two teenage boys in the area? No one had ever met us, and no one ever would.

IN IT TO WIN IT

by Trisha Ridinger McKee

Deni's fever was getting worse.

She wrapped herself in blankets, knowing sleep would be a futile endeavor at that point. The night was still early, and she had indulged in a nap after work, that feeling of illness lingering to the point that she knew it would not simply pass. She was going to be full-blown sick.

Full-blown miserable.

There was nothing on television that could hold her attention, so Deni grabbed her VR headset. Maybe some of her VR friends were on, and maybe they could get a game of Killer Chaos going.

Despite the dark overtones of the game, playing relaxed her. It would ease her into enough of an exhausted state to let her rest. Maybe.

Sometimes, the opposite happened, and she would spend the majority of the night playing with the time that should have been spent sleeping. The days following such indulgence were spent in a cloud of fatigue, like fighting through a mental fog.

And there were times, like tonight, that Deni felt a bit of apprehension putting on the headset. She was alone in her apartment, and not being able to see around her was a bit daunting. Her boyfriend, Shane, would not be over until the weekend, and while she usually had no trouble being alone, there was something about being in another world that left her feeling vulnerable in this one.

There were a few friends active, so Deni jumped right into the game, checking the daily challenges to see what goals she had to set. The object of the game was simple and based on the role you were given each round.

If you were innocent, you had to avoid the killers and gather keys to unlock the several locks on the front door. Once all the locks had been dealt with, the door would open and provide an escape.

If you were a killer, you had to kill as many innocents as possible.

The game itself was not too scary. It was a bunch of people running around a three-story home trying to fulfill their roles the best that they could. There was a lot of yelling, laughing, and cursing as people were stabbed or shot.

Deni had been playing the game long enough to know the good hiding spots, to know where keys were hidden, and how to outrun a killer. Truth be told, the thrill of the game was long gone, but it was the people who made it interesting.

Sara would be chasing you with an axe and still tell you about her day in excruciatingly boring detail. Ronnie was quiet until he was killed, and then you could hear him outside of the house cursing you out. There was also Pete, who could sweet-talk even the most experienced player into believing he was not the killer right up until the moment he shoved a knife through your avatar.

And SideBar82.

SideBar82 was the one person she was closest to in the virtual reality worlds they played in, and yet, he was the one person out of their group whose first name she still did not know. He was private. She knew he was older. She knew he had a job and lived somewhere along the East Coast.

And she knew he avoided the gaming drama, just as she did. They often would separate from the group and go play another game or explore another world until the arguments died down or the gossip faded away.

They were there for relaxation, a way to de-stress from a hectic day, a chaotic life. There was an unspoken rule between them that the chatter remained light and positive. They tried not to get too personal or too flirty.

Yet, they were linked by common intentions and a love for this fictional world. It was their escape, maybe more so than was healthy. Deni loved when the screen lit up, catapulting her into another reality. Everything was brighter in this world. Everything seemed easier when it was in cartoon mode.

Deni played a few rounds of Killer Chaos, and then Sara started fighting with another player, claiming he had been targeting her. Others got involved almost eagerly, and Deni knew any attempt to continue the game would be in vain.

"Wanna go check out the aquarium?" SideBar82 asked, and she found herself smiling, thankful she did not have the latest headset that recognized and mimicked facial expressions. He had a nice, low voice, although at times it was too low, and they would have to go into party mode so she could hear him better.

In the aquarium, Deni fed the fish and swam over to the sharks. Just as she felt exhaustion sweeping through her achy body, SideBar82 came over and said, "Are you okay, Deni?"

A jolt ran through her as she let herself fall to the bottom of the ocean. He followed. "I… um, I think I'm coming down with something. Don't tell me I look so bad, it's showing through my avatar?"

SideBar82 laughed. "No. But you aren't moving around as much. And you're quiet." She watched as his avatar seemed to watch her, and she tried to straighten, to somehow make her own avatar appear alert. "You okay?"

"Yes. A little tired and achy. That's all."

"Maybe call it an early night."

"No. I'm fine."

Just as she floated to the top, an avatar approached her. At first, the small, high voice of a child reached her. "Hi! Can you hear me?"

Deni nodded and turned, not willing to humor a child at this point. Just as she was about to ask SideBar82 why he hadn't chosen a private instance of this world, a chill ran through her, followed by a terror that froze her in place. She stared at SideBar82, wondering if it was a vibe he was giving off.

Just then, the child avatar jumped in front of her and, in a deep, menacing voice, shouted, "There's someone in your house! Get off VR!"

The intensity behind the tone and the words themselves caused Deni to whip off her headset and throw it to the side, jumping to her feet. She looked around the room and then ventured slowly into the kitchen, her senses on alert. Switching on every light as she passed, Deni moved to the front door, ensuring it was locked.

"I'm running a fever," she muttered. "Things are more dramatic when I'm sick."

That had to be it. The pure terror she had felt as the avatar warned her was not normal. It had to have been exaggerated and heightened by the fever. It made no sense for some random child to yell that. And to yell it in a completely different voice than was used moments earlier.

The idea of getting back into the game did not appeal to her. She did not want to chance another encounter or fever-induced hallucination. The only thing Deni desired at the moment was to fall into a deep slumber, hopefully sleeping away any illness.

But she merely fell into a fitful dream state with distorted images and repeated scenarios pushing her to wake up and try to sort reality from fiction. Was she really awake? Was she still dreaming?

Her aching head held a fog so heavy that Deni felt she was swimming through it to capture a thought. At one point in the confusion, she wondered if she was in party mode, and she softly said, "Hey, are you there?"

"I'm here."

The answer jolted her awake, and she realized she was sitting in her living room with the VR headset on. How had she gotten here? When had she put on the headset? How had she put on the headset? Her muscles screamed out in pain, and exhaustion swept through her.

"Deni?"

SideBar82 was in her ear, concern laced through his low tone. She looked around the brightly colored world and realized she was in *Home* mode. "Yeah. How long have I been on?"

"I don't know. I just jumped on. Are you okay?"

"Yeah. Running a fever but… wanna play a few rounds?"

Deni curled up in the corner of the couch and covered herself with blankets, but even her avatar was slower and less precise, causing her to lose almost every round. But this was better than writhing in bed with sweat-soaked, disturbing images. The previous encounter with the child avatar that had terrified her seemed more like a dream, and that was a theory Deni was more than willing to accept.

"Whoa, blondie, you're an easy target tonight. That's what you get for disappearing for a day," Peter teased after another lousy round.

But Deni grew still, his words taking a few moments to make sense. "I was on just a little bit ago. Earlier tonight."

"Blondie, you haven't been on since Monday."

The fog lingered, and she had to fight hard to remember. "No. Today is Monday."

The avatar in front of her laughed. "It's definitely Wednesday. I know because my wife is at her book club and not bugging me to get off this thing."

How did she lose days? Was she that sick? That exhausted? Trying to grasp onto a wisp of a thought, Deni moved to the side of the house to skip the next round and get some privacy. Because there had to be a logical explanation for this. Her fever was not that high, was it? And she knew she had not taken any medicine that might have contributed to long sleeps and incoherent thoughts.

"Deni? Where are you?"

"Hey, I'll be there in a minute. Adjusting my headset," she explained, debating on leaving the game altogether. But then what? She could not go to sleep again and risk losing more time. Her body aches prevented her from going anywhere, and watching television would just make her feel lonely.

She jumped back into the game, but as she rounded the hallways, she realized it was eerily quiet. The usual chatter and random screams were absent, and Deni slowed to a halt, looking around for someone, anyone to come out of a room and dart past her.

No one came.

But then she heard footsteps upstairs, slow and heavy. She breathed a sigh of relief until she remembered there had never been such a sound before. There was a stabbing sound when someone was killed, a creaking of floorboards every now and then, but the game did not use the sound of footsteps when someone walked.

"SideBar?" she asked softly, running into a nearby room and hiding behind a bookshelf.

There was no answer. Deni started to bring up her menu, but the footsteps got closer, and she grew still.

"Where are you?" It was a whisper, but it sounded like Sidebar.

Something held her back from answering. That chill of terror ran through her body, and she shivered, hoping she did not move her avatar too much. If she remained still, she might be completely hidden from whoever was in the house.

The lights in the mansion shut off, and she breathed a sigh of relief. The person was in the basement. She tried to remember how many locks had been unlocked, but nothing came to her. She would have little chance if she had to gather six locks, but she had even less chance by staying in one place and not even trying.

Not hearing footsteps, Deni peeked out and tried to look into the hallway. Glancing in the opposite direction, she spotted a key. She ran out and grabbed it, turning and checking the other usual spots for more keys.

In the hallway, she found a key hanging on the wall.

"Is that you, Deni? Come talk to me." It was SideBar82, and the menacing laugh that followed made her jump in fear. Taking a deep breath that hurt her chest, she realized the voice was coming from the floor above her. That propelled her enough to take the two keys and jump down the stairs to the first floor.

There were already two locks unlocked at the front door. Forcing herself to work quickly yet accurately, she reached up and unlocked two more locks.

Two more keys. She only needed two more keys, and she could escape.

"GOTCHA!"

Deni screamed and ran without looking behind her, but that long, taunting laugh followed. She managed to grab a key from a hallway table, and then she escaped into the basement, running to the other side to go up the stairs. She made it to the third floor and saw the last key in the bathroom on the side of the bathtub.

"Why are you running?" SideBar82 screamed from somewhere in the house. "You were never that good at this game. I'm going to find you, and when I do…"

Sliding behind the stairwell, she squeezed her eyes shut, trying to block that laugh from her mind. All Deni had to do was wait until he was at least a floor away and then -

"I see you, Deni. I seeee YOU!"

She opened her eyes and screamed, scrunching her shoulders and covering her face as if to hide even further. But she could hear his breath and knew he was right in front of her. All she could do was wait for the attack, the blow that was inevitable…

"Deni! What are you doing? Stop screaming. It's me. It's Shane!"

The scream died slowly, and Deni lifted her head, cowering against the wall. Everything was dark until there was a click, and light flooded in. The first thing she noticed was the dullness.

Deni usually hated ending a VR game and taking off her headset only to be met with the reality that appeared flat and dull compared to the brightness that had embraced her in the VR worlds. But this was one instance where she laughed with joy over being in reality. Relief made her weak, but then she jumped when her gaze landed on Shane.

Was that actually his voice she had heard? He had a well-known temper, and perhaps in her weakened state, Deni had imagined running the floors of the cartoon mansion. Imagined SideBar82 chasing her.

"What are you doing here?" she asked, once again flattening herself against the wall.

Only concern coated his stare. "Deni, I've tried texting and calling. I came here to check on you and found you in here... screaming. What's wrong?"

"No." She shook her head. "I heard you. You were chasing me."

"Chasing you? Deni, you look horrible. You're sick. Come here. Come here," he persisted in a firm voice that told her he meant business. She stepped out of the closet, trying to control the trembling. He pressed the back of his hand against her forehead. "You're warm. Why didn't you call me?"

"I... I don't know." Why hadn't she called him?

Within minutes, Shane had her tucked into bed. His demeanor was cold, almost resentful, and it did little to settle those nerves.

"Why did you leave the front door unlocked?"

The question caught her off guard, and she struggled to remember. "I didn't. I wouldn't." She always locked the door as soon as it was shut. Always.

"The door was unlocked. What's going on? You haven't answered any messages or calls. Your door is unlocked. You were in the closet screaming…"

"I'm sick. It's causing me to have these really vivid, scary dreams."

She remembered little after that, and soon she was tumbling into those ridiculous dreams once again. At one point, she was in a large room pushing large buttons over and over again until she reached out and poked a snake. Screaming, she jumped back.

"Didn't mean to scare you."

SideBar82 was in front of her, the colors vivid, and his avatar somehow conveying concern. She sputtered around until she was able to say, "That's okay. I - I was just startled."

"So, what happened yesterday?"

"Huh?"

"I mean, you came here and didn't acknowledge me once. I said hi. I waved. I was calling for you at one point inside the house. Then you were gone." His tone was unusually sharp, and she involuntarily took a step back. "I mean, good shit, right?"

"SideBar, no. I said hello. We were talking. Then you kind of scared me by laughing and saying you were going to find me."

"I mean, we always say we're going to find each other. That's the point of the game, Deni. But I'm telling you, we didn't talk. But that's fine. It can be that way-"

"What way? We were talking! I went to the side of the house for a minute, and then I returned to the game- and what does it matter? You won't even tell me your first name. I have to call you SideBar. Ridiculous." She tried to stand straight and stare right at him, but she felt her body trembling.

What was going on?

"You ran to the side of the house, and when I followed you, I heard someone screaming at you through your headset. I heard him."

That was what he called Shane. Him. They rarely discussed personal lives. It would break the fantasy world they were in.

"You heard him yelling, knew I was sick, and you're mad I wasn't as talkative?"

"No! I'm pissed you outright ignored me."

"But I didn't. At least not intentionally."

For a few moments, he did not respond. Then he moved closer. "Are you okay, Deni?"

"I don't know. Some weird shit's been happening, and I don't know if it's the fever or what."

"What's happening?"

She started to tell him, because he had been someone she had grown to trust over the last few months, between the late nights playing games and the messages they shared when they weren't on VR. But something stopped her. At this point, she was not sure she could trust anyone.

As if sensing her hesitation, SideBar82 said, "He was really yelling at you, Deni, and you said he does that often. Just tell me you're okay. It sounded bad."

Just like that, the trust that had been dwindling was restored, and she opened her mouth to tell him she was scared of Shane. She was ready to confess that Shane was somehow tormenting her while she was sick.

"What are you saying?"

The voice seemed to come from far away, but it grew closer until Deni opened her eyes.

Dull.

Real life.

Her eyes focused, and she saw Shane standing over her. "Shane, what's going on?"

"You were dreaming. Said SideBar. But I guess that's to be expected, right?"

"Huh?"

He tossed her phone onto the bed. "I read your messages."

Deni bolted upright, the sudden movement making her dizzy. "What the hell, Shane? Now, you're snooping through my things?"

"You're always on that damn game, Deni! You weren't answering my calls or texts, but you sure as hell kept messaging this guy. I mean, you told him everything. Your name, your town, and you even have your picture up. What the hell are you thinking? Forget that you're supposed to be in a relationship with me. Do you know how dangerous that is? Your door's been unlocked, you're out of it, and some guy knows where to find you."

"No, it isn't like that. He isn't creepy or -"

"You know what- not my business anymore. Stupid bitch. You can take care of yourself. Or have that loser come take care of you, if he isn't some psycho."

"Wait, Shane!"

"Shane?"

Deni looked around, wanting to cry when she saw the bright colors swirling around her. What the hell was happening?

"I was just fighting with Shane." She stared helplessly up at SideBar82, hoping he could somehow make sense of everything.

He nodded. "He's been getting worse. More… aggressive. You need to get away from him."

"He left."

"That's good, Deni. I promise it's for the best. Want to go somewhere else?"

But before she could agree, they were inside the house, and she was running. And instinctively, she knew she was running from something… someone.

There was that maniacal laugh, and she grew cold with fear.

And as her name was whispered through the house, Deni struggled to pay attention. Was that Shane? Was he tormenting her because of the messages he had found? Had this been an act of revenge all along?

All she knew was that she had to keep running and hiding, because she knew if she got caught, something horrible would happen. Something…

An avatar ran past her, and for a moment, she felt relief. This was just a normal game with other players. But then she noticed it was the same avatar from before. The child…

Stopping suddenly, the avatar turned back to Deni. "There's someone in your house," the child-like voice said.

Deni was rooted to the spot with fear, and the avatar lunged toward her and repeated in a much deeper, angrier voice, "There is someone in your house! GET OUT!"

Deni ripped the headset off and bolted to her feet, positive she heard footsteps on her second floor. She forced herself to be still, to silence the heavy gasps for air. Just when it was silent for a few moments, she heard her name being whispered.

Shane.

Turning, she realized someone was sitting in the chair across from her with a VR headset on.

"Shane?" she whispered as the footsteps slammed down above her head, near the staircase. "Shane, someone's here."

She tiptoed over to him, still uncertain as to whom she could trust. As she gasped out his name one last time, she poked him in the shoulder, only for his body to slump sideways, the headset sliding enough to show open, lifeless eyes.

"NO! Shane! Holy shit, Shane, wake up. Please," she pleaded in between choking sobs.

"He's not going to wake up, Deni. I solved a really big problem for you. You're welcome."

Deni forced herself to turn around, to face the person, even though she knew by the voice who it was.

SideBar82.

"What are you doing here? Why are you here?"

"To save you. That's what you wanted, right? All those nights complaining about his temper, his lack of attention… I took care of it. And I can promise you, I will never leave you alone long enough to feel ignored again. It's what you wanted. You practically begged me-"

"No!" She shook her head frantically as sobs burst from her. "No, I never asked for this."

"You did. So, let's make this easy, and sit down where you were. Where you usually play VR. Come on, be a good little avatar. That's it. Put the headset on."

There was nothing to do but let him lead her to the chair. He tied first her legs to the chair and then her upper arms, leaving her enough mobility to work the hand controls.

"Let's get on and play some Killer Chaos, Deni. Let's celebrate how we first met. Through the mutual love of killing."

She wanted to argue, but she knew words would do no good. Not now. It was too late. So, she settled in, hoping to escape this situation through another world, at least.

There was the groaning of the couch that told her he was settling in within inches of her. "By the way," he added with a maniacal laugh. "The name's Mike."

BLOOD AND INK

by DW Milton

I absolutely hated it. The inkwork was beautiful, but it looked so dumb on her arm. Bridgette almost drove into oncoming traffic trying to wrangle her T-shirt sleeve to show off the tattoo.

"Are you sure I am old enough?" Christy piped up from the back of the Jeep.

"No one cares, Christy, as long as you can pay," I rolled my eyes.

"How much are we talking about?" She leaned forward.

I had saved six months for this. Sold multiple term papers and did a crapload of sitting for the Polansky pets. My first foray into rock and roll rebellion, and here I was driving to the city with my so-called friends: Bridgette, a bully socialite wannabe, and Christy, an anorexic, whiny tart.

Christy hung out with Bridgette because Bridgette's parents were never home. Christy hated home because her folks were always home. Bridgette hated home too, but because no one was ever home. Her parents were always on the islands, gambling at some exclusive resort, but never taking her with them. Bridgette, like the Polansky pets, was more of an accessory than loved.

I just wanted the ink, and to get it, I put up with a lot like these two idiots, their leech friends, home, school. I followed the rules and never gave anyone a moment's trouble. Everyone thought I was an angel.

Bridgette and Christy discussed the artist's rate. Ten dollars extra if you wanted the ink anywhere but your arm. Fifty bucks an hour for original work. Tip was always twenty percent. Christy thumbed through her wallet, lamenting that she wouldn't have enough.

"Been dancing again?" I laughed as she fingered multiple greasy ones. She gave me a look. Bridgette snickered.

"No," she was emphatic, "Trey finally paid me."

Trey was Christy's shitty on again off again boyfriend mooch. Christy lightly dabbled in dealing. Mostly pot but sometimes a little harder, which is why Bridgette (and Trey) kept her around.

Drugs were not my thing.

"What about the special arrangement?" Christy asked Bridgette.

Bridgette shut Christy down, "That's not up for discussion."

Christy bit her lip. Apparently, that was not up for discussion in my presence, whatever the *special arrangement* was. I had heard that sometimes artists would take sex as payment for ink, but in our case, that would be illegal. None of us was of age.

Bridgette swung a left, almost tipping the Jeep over into a dirty parking lot; then she nearly hit a dumpster while attempting to park.

"Blood and Ink?" I read the glowing neon sign surrounded by innumerable patterns covering the storefront windows. Tribal, cartoon, sugar skulls, flowers, Betty Boop. You name it –there was a pattern.

Christy whined, "I still don't know what to get. How about a flower? Or an Earth for Earth Day?" Trapped in the backseat, she squealed, "There's Bugs Bunny!" Then, "Oh, how cute, Strawberry Shortcake! I used to love her!"

The door chimed as we entered. Templates of characters and artwork covered the walls. It was overwhelming. I might have sympathized with Christy if I didn't have my design. Without it, I would have sounded like a dumbass, too.

The dude behind the counter was massive and genuine. Ancient eyes clocked us for what we were. Posers; it did not matter that we wore the torn swag, flannel, and *Doc Martens*.

Bridgette stammered; her voice raised an octave with uncertainty, "Is, um, Brian here today? We, uh, have an appointment."

The dude growled, "In the can."

She mumbled, "Thanks," and rejoined us.

"Friend of yours?" I raised an eyebrow.

"Not personally," she shrugged me off.

"Charming."

Christy ran over. "I have found it! It's perfect." She pushed both of us over to a panel and cooed over a daisy chain. "I'm going to have him make it an anklet!"

I almost vomited.

***

Brian came out of the bathroom, and Bridgette ran over for hellos. They discussed his work. She wanted two dolphins swimming in a yin-yang configuration. Christy sauntered over and smiled at Brian. It was obvious why. Despite the *Call of Cuthulu* tat on the side of his shaved head, he was drop-dead gorgeous. Christy demanded that Brian do her first. Bridgette and Christy argued, but Brian smoothed them over. Christy then Bridgette. Christy's was a pattern-15 minutes tops. Both joined him behind the counter to prep.

Inhumanly tall, the other artist seemed to have grown in the last minutes. He eyed me as I wandered the shop, studying the walls, trying to be innocuous.

"What about you?" he growled. I could not place the accent.

On his inner left forearm was delicately inked dragon, consuming his own tail; he leaned on the counter taking me in. Since I was not much to look at, I ignored his stare.

"Do you do ink original work?" I asked.

"What do you think?" he raised a thick eyebrow. Bending, he brought up and slapped down a large photo album. He turned it around for me to see. I paged through, slowly drinking in the images. His work was exquisite, fantastically beautiful with robust colors and fine details.

The more I saw, the more I itched to bolt. This man was an artist. I was obviously unworthy. I looked at the door.

"You have something drawn." It was not a question.

He held out a hand with impossibly long fingers tipped by blackened nails. Reluctantly, I surrendered my sketch. I expected him to laugh; instead, "You like to dabble on the dark side, do you, little girl?"

"Uh, no, it's just a symbol."

"No, it isn't, little girl." He dug a sharpened nail into the paper, "That is dangerous. Pick something cute and cuddly off the wall like your little friends." He slid my drawing back at me and then shut his book, returning it underneath the counter.

I folded my sketch and shoved it back into my back pocket. Emboldened, I tilted my head, as if sizing *him* up.

He glared. "Look, little girl, you don't know the forces you are messing with." The man's irises boiled scarlet in their bloodshot sclera. He was irritated with my bravado. Waving his bizarre hand as if swatting away a mosquito, he said in his thick accent, "Pick something off the wall or leave."

Christy bounced over clueless, interrupting, "Lookie see!" She giggled, lifting her leg, "Brian did strawberries in my anklet for me!"

I turned and walked out of the store.

***

"What is wrong with you, Becs? We all agreed we were all going to get ink today. You totally fobbed it off!" Bridgette scolded as if I were four years old. I hate when anyone calls me Becs.

"Chicken," echoed Christy, now sitting shotgun. "Your arm looks so good with those dolphins in that Korean thing," she cooed in Bridgett's ear. "Are we going back to your house? I told Trey and his friends to meet us there."

Bridgette glared at me in the rearview. I needed to set her straight.

"I didn't fob off, and I am not poultry. Stupid jerk wouldn't ink my design. So, I left."

"Well, what did you want?" Bridgette accused. "The Periodic Table?"

Christy shrieked with laughter.

"Close," I had to admit, "By the way, the yin-yang is Chinese."

"You have to buy the beer since you were too lame to get your ink," Bridgette declared.

***

I did not have a fake ID, which meant I was going to have to sweet-talk some guy into buying it for me. Rumor was that Christy blew for beer in the parking lot, but I knew that to be bogus. Christy was easy, but not that easy; besides, she was the one with a fake ID. The second reason Bridgette hung with her.

Bridgette nearly clipped another car as she bounced the Jeep into the brightly lit convenience store parking lot and pulled into a space.

"Go!" she commanded. Neither of them shoved, so I could get out of the backseat via a door like a normal person. Instead, I had to climb out the back.

The door chimed as I swung it in, almost whacking Trey.

"Hey slut, watch where you are…" Then he recognized me. "Hey Becs, you with Christy?" He looked around me towards Bridgette's Jeep. He had two cases, one in each hand.

"Oh, good, you got the beer."

"No way, freak." He shoved me aside, "This is for me. Get your own."

Trey was a creep, and I had easily clocked him for what he was, little rich boy, too cool for school, but also too dumb for it. On the other hand, I was so smart it scared the shit out of him. Without my academic abilities, Trey would have been out of our exclusive religious academy and shunned in public school. Not to mention out of his father's good graces and cash flow.

It sickened me how Trey and Bridgette believed that they had worries, had a shitty deal with their parents, their lives. They knew nothing of trouble or hardship. As long as I kept them on the honor roll, in their parents' good graces and, ultimately, their parents' bank accounts. I kept their lives worry-free. Deep down, I hated every one of them. Moreover, I hated myself for envying them.

"What a dick," a voice behind me. He was one of Trey's friends. I didn't know his name, but he had nice eyes. "Here," he handed me another case. "Carry it out of here, and it's yours."

"I am eternally grateful," I replied.

He smiled, "Josh."

"Rebecca. Thanks again."

"See you at the party?"

"Sure," I nodded as I lugged the beer back to the Jeep.

***

The house was already jam-packed with people. Some she knew, most she did not. As long as everyone knew it was her party, she did not care. Aloof, I sat with my half-drunk beer, legs hanging over the dock.

That was where Josh found me. Not being much of a conversationalist, I floundered, "How did you buy the beer?"

He smiled. It was a nice smile. "What, don't I look 21?" He almost burst holding in his lie. Finally laughing, he confessed, "I stole my brother's ID before he went back to college."

I nodded, lost for additional conversation.

Unaffected, he leaned in so close I could smell the beer and something coppery on his breath. "I heard you ladies went to get ink today? Can I see?"

Grimacing, I gestured to the house. "Yeah, they did. I did not."

"Chicken?" He flapped his wings and cackled.

"Yup, you said it." Triple annoyed, I leaned back to swing my legs over to dry land and tried to stand, but he grabbed my arm, almost knocking me into the water.

"Hey, asshole!" Ripping my arm away, "What the hell!"

"Sorry, sorry, I'm sorry, ok? I was just joking."

"Creep," Pouting, I rubbed my arm.

"Naw, don't take it like that. You're just not committed."

"What the hell is that supposed to mean?"

"All I am saying is cold feet before a tat is cool. It happens. I waited for my first, too. Want to see?" He slid up his shirt sleeve.

"Who told you that?" But I knew who, "Never mind." I stood to go.

"Wait, wait, it's just what that chick Trey digs said. Sorry."

For the second time tonight, I had to set the record straight. "The guy wouldn't give me the tattoo I wanted, so I left. Is that cool with you?"

Surprised, "Really? I asked him about you personally. No questions asked. In fact, that's how Trey got him to ink that skinny chick, Christy." Josh paused.

"What are you talking about?" Yet, I was too irritated to care. "Well, whatever. Apparently, I am not good enough for that tattooed creep's ink."

I snorted and walked toward the house. My beer was flat. He followed me. Inside, he grabbed two new beers from the fridge, handing me one. He kicked his open and took a swig. Trey was bouncing around the kitchen. He stopped at the closest couple. I saw him offer two white squares of blotter paper.

"What is Trey doing?"

"Trippin," Josh laughed. "You should. Might loosen you up a bit.'

I did a double-take. "Has everyone here dropped?"

"Pretty much," Josh nodded.

I watched Trey dose the crowd. Each willingly took the small square and placed it under his or her tongue. A few traded squares with a French kiss. I was despondent. This was just another party that was going to deteriorate into a mindless bore.

***

"What did you want?" Josh tried to coax me back into the bleak reality of the kitchen.

"What?" It was noisy inside. The music pulsed like a heartbeat.

He leaned in close to me so I could smell the beer on his breath. "Your tat? What did you want?"

"Never mind," I repeated. I took my unopened beer and walked away. Again, he followed.

"Seriously, Becs. What did you want?"

"First, never call me Becs!" A few partygoers nearby turned and stared, but it was nobody I knew. "And second, forget it."

Ugh, what a drag. I huffed back outside, kind of hoping he would follow.

He shadowed me back outside. "I could draw it for you."

That got my attention.

"I am a pretty good artist, and my ex-girlfriend, before she got her ink, used to have me draw it on her first just to see about placing and ...." He went on for another minute or two about a girlfriend, but he had me at *draw it for you.*

"With what?" I was excited and hopeful for the first time in a while.

"Uh, well, she always wanted me to use a Sharpie so it would last for a few days."

"Go get one."

Josh hopped up and sprinted back to the house.

While he was gone, I took out my sketch and carefully unfolded it and smoother it over the deck. I looked around; I guessed the light was good enough out here. There was installed lighting for docking the boat at night in addition to the full moon. I took off my shirt and shivered. Maybe we should go inside, but it would probably interest spectators. I wrapped my shirt around my shoulders and waited.

Josh returned with a black Sharpie. He did a double-take as I was sitting in my bra.

"Perfect."

"Uh, yeah, where do you want it?"

"My back," I indicated the sketch next to me.

He examined the symbol. Turning his head sideways and then back. "That's it?" He flipped it right-side up. "I like it better this way."

"No, this way." I reinverted the symbol. "It must be between my shoulder blades, the circle in the middle, the body, here this," I pointed to the sketch, "along my spine. Can you make it the same size?"

Josh measured with his thumb and forefinger. "Sure. No problem. Are these horns?"

"It's the moon," I corrected.

Mumbling under his breath, "Ok if you say so, still looks like horns to me." He took another swig of beer before popping the cap off the marker. I felt the cool tip against my skin.

"Hold still," he cautioned. I steadied. Halfway through, he took off his flannel shirt and gave it to me to cover my front. The night air had gotten colder.

He chewed the cap while he drew. Inside, the party raged. Music pumped near peak decibels; funny thing, the neighbors never complained.

"Done." Josh sat back, comparing the sketch to his work. "Damn, I am good! I should get a job at that place. Try out your tattoo before you get your tattoo!" Now completely tripping, Josh's pupils were saucers.

"Go see!" He was excited.

Throwing his flannel on for modesty, I hightailed it to the bathroom.

***

Skirting past a couple making out, I shut and locked the bathroom door before the girl could slur, "Hey, I was next!"

Under the sink, I found a mirror. In the balanced images, I saw my new ink. Josh did a good job. The wings were a bit off-center, but he had drawn them over bone.

It was exactly what I wanted. The girl outside pounded on the door, saying something about going to burst, but I ignored her. Who knows why that brute wouldn't ink it? I thought it was pretty cool myself. As I stood admiring Josh's work, humming to the music, the screaming began.

A pounding on the door. A panicked turning of the knob; something crashed against the door. A large crack erupted down the center of the pressed wood.

A low growl, guttural, then sniffing like an animal.

I backed away, trapped.

The music pulsed, slowing like a dying heartbeat. The heartbeat stopped.

***

Inside the closet-like space, alone and afraid, I waited. I became the little girl I was back when my father died, and the never-ending shit show began, so I crawled in the back corner of the closet-like space, pulled up my knees, and cried.

Tears spent, my curiosity finally eclipsed fear, so I peeked out the bent door. Puddles of blood-streaked, horrid skid marks down the hallway to the front door. I slowly stepped out of the bathroom, moving down the terrible passage. I turned the corner, and then I saw the walls. Initially, there were a few spatters of blood here and there until I reached the kitchen, where I nearly fainted from the gore. Blood dripped from the cabinets and coagulated on the floor.

Josh popped out from behind the refrigerator and grabbed me.

"Hey Becs, where have you been? You gotta come." His eyes glistened. His lips pulled back, revealing two massive fangs barred in an inhuman smile.

Every remaining sane fiber in my being screamed *RUN!*

I twisted in his hand, needing to get out of the house. Bridgette's Jeep was just outside in the driveway. Josh squeezed my arm tighter and tighter. I felt nauseous from the metallic smell of the blood. It lingered in my nose and throat.

Josh wrenched my arm up behind my back.

"Let me go!" I hollered. "You are breaking my arm."

He laughed.

Josh dragged me towards the living room. "You are coming to see," his eyes wild, drooling like a ravenous animal. We struggled.

"No! Let me go!" I bucked and kicked. Then an overwhelming force pinned me from behind. All I saw was this massive shadow.

"I got her!" Josh grumbled. "She is mine!"

There was no response except for some grunting and a deep throat growl, not unlike what I heard outside the bathroom door. I tried to move, but Josh was kneeling on my back, high, where he had drawn my mark not an hour ago.

Whatever it was slinked away. Josh lifted and then carried me into the living room.

***

"It can't be," I whispered in horror.

"Oh, but it is," sneered Josh.

He dropped me on the lush carpeting. Bending down, he hissed into my ear, "His blood is the ink which gives us eternal life."

"I like you, Becs. I wanted you to join us, but I guess He found you not worthy." Tongue tripping over his obscene teeth, his eyes burned at the taste of his own flesh. Now a predator, Josh sniffed me then slipped over to the mound of fading bodies to feed.

The beige carpet was stained red. A massive pile of half-dead friends and classmates twitched and whimpered. In the dim light, I saw a fleshy arm rip back a head; veins, tendons, a windpipe cracked. Twin geysers of scarlet liquid ran in arches, a human fountain into a gaping thirst-driven mouth. Above the elbow, a familiar tattoo glowed and swam in its skin. It was a set of dolphins, in a circular nose-to-tail configuration.

Choking on my own breath, I realized it was Bridgette!

She grunted and snorted, enjoying the meal. Raising her head, I saw her eyes were stones of obsidian. She grinned, her face split, revealing a red hole of rows and rows of triangular teeth.

Something crawled over the top of the bodies. A thin form with beady but empty eyes and the broad mouth, packed tight with needled teeth, had bits of fresh flesh clinging as it sucked the marrow from a ragged bone. Emanating in a sickly glow from its leg was a ring of fruit dancing and floating in the night.

Strawberries, my mind screamed. Christy looked right through me with her vacant eyes.

Trey came up behind me. He had grown to a massive size, jiggling and blob-like and full of blood. A low warning growl emanated from what was his mouth, now a set of hooked suckers like the parasite I always knew him to be.

My so-called friends watched me.

Josh continued to feed on a junior from my Spanish class.

I shifted in their stares. *What were they waiting for?*

I decided I did not want to find out, so on a shot of adrenaline and pure fear, I sprinted out the front door and into the night.

***

I ran down the street, breath burning in my lungs. Chills seizing my muscles. At the end of the street, I stopped dead in my tracks.

Where was I going to go?

Tears welled back up in my eyes. Life at home was never perfect, but now I stayed away as much as possible. Since my father died, to be there with my alcoholic mother and her crap string of boyfriends, each one worse than the next, for a single night, riddled me with anxiety with dreams of escape.

I wrote term papers, took SATS, scammed the rich kids to pay the electric bill, groceries, and the rent. If I had not been on scholarship to that elitist school, I would have had to deal drugs or sell myself to cover tuition.

Even if I could, there was no one to call. Everyone I knew was already here, and my mother either was with one of her boyfriends or passed out on the couch.

There I stood in the shadow of the night, more lost and alone than ever. Looking back down the street to that house of horrors, I decided what to do and where to go, but first, I needed to find a set of car keys.

I turned and walked back. Inside, unhindered and unharmed, I walked down the back hall to Bridgette's room, where I found the keys to her Jeep in the ceramic sugar skull she kept on her dresser.

***

It was after midnight when I pulled into that crappy parking lot. Colored characters stared down at me. Cartoon eyes with their black pupils mocked me. White-toothed mouths smiled. The neon sign glowed. I opened the storefront door to hear the chime. Behind the counter, He stood with His arms folded across his chest, waiting for me.

I hesitated, knowing what I looked like-a junkie coming off a bender, crackhead looking for a fix, sorority girl on a walk of shame. I knew what I wanted, but I was uncertain how to ask.

"You are back."

"What did you do to my friends?"

"Why? Are you interested?"

"Is that *the special arrangement*?"

He laughed deeply. I shivered.

"You could say that." He smiled. Lips pulled back, revealing twin fangs of incredible sharpness.

Terrified but committed, I played my last card. "One of them said it has something to do with the tattoo ink."

The fiend stroked a cultivated goatee the same color as His back nails. "What else did he tell you?"

Had he had that before? I wondered. The room shifted. My resolve weakened, so instead, I focused on a pattern of Bugs Bunny eating a carrot. My mind replayed an episode of Looney Tunes where Bugs drank Dr. Jekyll's potion and transformed into a monstrous rabbit version of Hyde.

Immediately, I understood. That was that me. I was a Hyde parading around like Dr. Jekyll. All my hustling, bravado, and lame efforts to escape my family, my home, my life were ridiculous attempts to hide who I really wanted to be. Laughing, tears sprang to my eyes. I doubled over and laughed so hard my stomach ached. I cried with unadulterated realization and relief.

"Nothing," I giggled, "He didn't say anything because he was too busy drinking the blood of a girl in my Spanish class." Sighing, I wiped my tearing eyes.

I was so busy rambling on about the atrocities I witnessed that I did not notice Him move out from behind the counter.

"I don't know why, but I took Bridgette's car and drove here."

He stood in front of me in full glory, an absolute cliché without the Hollywood cloak. Beautiful. Seductive. The Dark Lord.

Beyond terror, I dared, "What the fuck did you do to them?"

His red eyes mocked me, "Do you really want to know?"

"Yes," I heard myself beg.

"Then pick something off the wall," He commanded.

Who knew that Dracula was also a tattoo artist?

***

Over the buzz of the needle, he instructed, "By taking in my blood, you are pledging yourself to an ancient and sacred covenant. I will care for you, and you will never want for anything again."

He smiled, those beautiful fangs bared. "I will be the father you have always longed for, my daughter."

Not that it mattered, but I asked anyway, "What do you want from me in return?"

My Dark Lord raised a thick eyebrow, His blood already flowing through my veins, "your eternal soul, of course."

"Ok," I agreed. "That seems fair."

***

The following Monday morning, I drove Bridgette's Jeep to school, parking it in her usual spot. I sat for a moment, radio on, music blaring. My new tattoo itched, but Father said it might. Tilting the rearview, I lifted my T-shirt and turned to see. Despite the thin red halo that was my skin adjusting, the ink was black as night and just as beautiful. My Dark Lord did not trace Josh's crude strokes; He gave life to the ancient symbols. I sat mesmerized as they hovered in my flesh. His ink, his blood, and mine. It was the darkest magic, and it was our secret.

Letting the back of my shirt drop, I slid up my right sleeve to view my other tattoo, Bugs Bunny eating a carrot. I smiled.

A large thump broke the spell. Looking up, I saw Trey, his fist lifted, ready to wallop the Jeep's hood for a second time. Before he could make contact, Bridgette screamed.

"Hit my Jeep again, Trey, and I'll make you eat your balls, dick first!"

Trey snickered.

Bridgette stepped up alongside the open passenger side window. "I see you were the one who stole my Jeep."

Christy bounced up beside Bridgette and announced, "I told you that you should have called the cops, Bridge."

"We can't call the cops, idiot. *Remember*."

A look passed between the two girls, much like the look they shared only two nights ago regarding the *special arrangement*.

I grinned. In fact, that *special arrangement* was what brought me to school this morning. My Father instructed me to gather my friends and bring them to Him.

I leaned over and opened the passenger door. "Get in," I commanded. "He wants to talk to you."

Bridgette stood, her favorite *Doc Marten's* set. "What the hell are you talking about, Becs?"

"Maybe *she* went to the cops." Christy's face paled.

"She wouldn't dare." Trey hung an arm around Christy's narrow shoulders. "She's chicken shit."

"Get in," I repeated. "Where is Josh? We need to bring him as well."

Leaning forward, I triggered the passenger seat to lift. As I did, my sleeve shifted.

"Holy shit!" Trey exclaimed. "Is that a tattoo?"

A momentary cloud hid the sun. A chill slipped in and around the Jeep.

Bridgette shoved Christy out of the way to get a better look at the ink on my right bicep. Her face crinkled, and then she laughed.

"That's so fucking fake. Where did you get it? Chuck E. Cheese?"

Christy giggled nervously.

"We should not keep Him waiting."

"Who's waiting?" Christy's voice cracked.

Impatient, I disengaged the parking brake and dropped the gear into reverse.

Trey and Christy climbed into the back. Although I drove, it was still Bridgette's Jeep, so she rode shotgun.

***

We picked Josh up from his house. By the time we hit the highway, Christy was balling, and Bridgette had chewed through her hot pink lip gloss. Josh growled at me from the backseat.

Trey said, "fuck it" and lit up a joint.

Neither the shitty parking lot nor the creepy characters in the storefront window looked any better in the daylight. I led the group to the shop. Trey practically had to carry Christy.

A familiar chime announced our arrival. I held the door open, allowing my friends to enter. As each of them passed me, I drank in their fear and feasted on their hate. Once all of them were inside, I stepped in and let the door close, locking it behind me.

I watched as Our Dark Lord reprimanded my friends for their carelessness, their gluttony, and their disregard for the terms of the *special arrangement*.

The party, he called, *Indulgent*.

The mass murder and resulting pile of bodies, sloppy, was all he said.

The risk of exposure that my four friends caused him by their behaviors. Reckless, He snorted.

My new father then pointed one of his impossibly long fingers, tipped by a blackened nail, and each of them caught fire as if drenched in lighter fluid and caught with the tip of a lit match.

In seconds, my so-called friends had been reduced to ash.

No one screamed. There was no time.

I stood silent, frozen, frightened beyond belief. There was no reason for him not to strike me down as well.

With the same terrible finger, he gingerly scratched the snout of the dragon gracing his forearm. His red eyes then turned on me, but he smiled.

"Do me a favor, my daughter, will you get this retched mess out of my shop. The broom and the dustpan are in the back. Hurry now, there is much to learn."

21 YEARS LOST

by Alex Foster

University is a camp story, small talk between old timers reminiscing over better days before the world ended.

My only university experience came today while standing in RMITS' overgrown lobby. The sun peeked through brown, shattered glass, dirty, rigged teeth, letting light scrape across anguished skeletons.

Arms stretched, legs spread, jaws wide, permanently screaming as moss sprouted from their empty eye sockets. 25/10 victims, sixteen of them, are permanently stuck in time. Science Fiction movies scavenged from search parties detailed such a world. In Terminator, the apocalypse was brought by nuclear warfare from rogue machines.

That occurred in 1998.

What really ended the world happened on October 25th, 2003.

And it wasn't machines. Scientists never figured it out before being slaughtered by their insane colleagues. All we know is that one day, the world was one big teenage movie with cars, glittery pink outfits, and *people*. By the 26th, Melbourne was burning, twisted flames capturing silhouettes of *Crackheads* torturing, pillaging, and murdering everyone.

It's 2024 now.

More specifically, it's late 2024, twenty-one years after 25/10.

The infection left its marks, but they are covered in an ocean of green, burying the past so we can focus on our future.

We say at camp, mankind briefly went extinct. Either lost to the infection or by people who swallowed their humanity, doing anything to survive. Twenty-one years forward, we are scraping together the mentality lost after 25/10. Putting broken humanity together, building a new world based on values like having *fun, parties, charities, drinking, kindness, not killing someone for tinned food.* What humans should be doing, like in the movies (minus Terminator).

My journey started two weeks ago when we ventured from our fortified settlement at Yea, Victoria, through bush-turned-suburbs towards the NGV. The NGV is where eight settlements, stretched around Victoria, are gonna hold a party, in an art gallery secured deep in what was the "red zone," long before Crackheads started dying off.

My parents' generation survived 25/10. Now it's my generation rebuilding Earth in the image of a pre-outbreak world. Putting together the lost puzzle with little parties and fun activities, uniting what's left of humanity.

"Stop Bush, stop the war," McKenzie said, reading out loud a faded poster peeling from the wall. Mackenzie is 18, young, handsome, and energetic.

I'm the only kid born in 2003 left in Melbourne, if not Victoria. We had one other kid my age, but he died back in 2017 from smallpox.

"Didn't Iraq have illegal nukes or something?" Alannah said, peering down a dark, dank elevator shaft. "We probably would've been nuked anyway if 25/10 didn't happen."

"Thankfully, the world ended before Saddam could destroy it," I said, moving towards the door. A mountain built of mossy debris and twisted, rusting metal beams blocked the wooden door with "exit" written in faded pond green.

"Oi McKenzie, help me move this bitch."

We tackled the debris for an hour before a sly smile crept across Mackenzie's face.

"Didn't want Alannah helping you?"

"You're never gonna let me off for that, aren't you?"

"Oh, after you nearly fucked my only friend group by being a sleazy cunt? Yeah, nah. Couldn't you have tried, I don't know, going for someone who wasn't a close friend? Like that Eliza chick? She was pretty fly, wasn't she?"

"She's 13, dude…"

After liberating the door, we shoved it open, accompanied by a loud crack and plaster flakes fluttering down. Sunlight blasted our eyes, illuminating crashed cars, crumbling vine-covered skyscrapers, and skeletons spread every inch of the sidewalk. Everything was blanketed with sprouting greenery, a mask hiding 25/10 devastation.

"Regardless, it's over now. Isn't that right, Alannah?"

"Huh?" she yelled, head snapping out of the elevator hole.

"We're just friends, aren't we?"

"Yep," she said, opening a crumpled, browning map dated *June 2001*. "Lost friends. Know where we are? There's too many fucking stains on my map."

"We're on a fucked up street, in a fucked up world, Alanna," I said. It's an old proverb our parents whispered to each other, hiding from crackheads prowling the streets, driving cars, shooting guns, screaming, howling, *hunting survivors*.

Now the roads are empty mass graves, their street signs covered in overgrown moss.

We passed the Victorian Library, a crumbling Classical Greek-styled building stranded above an ocean of grass, when I heard them. Feet crunching on moss-covered bones, the quick taps swerving past rusted cars clogging down Swanston Street, getting louder.

At first, we thought they were naked humans. Pale faces slightly puffy, looking sick with the flu rather than what ended civilisation.

Dad almost made that mistake during the first day's post 25/10. My family (including a four-month-old me) was returning from a camping trip in the Grampians when the car radio burst with news of infections, Melbourne burning, and John Howard allegedly dead.

When the radio died, Dad stopped at a farmhouse, hoping someone knew what had happened. He ventured forward with us behind in the car, keys ready to go. Through filtered wire windows, Dad saw a man in the kitchen. Singlet slumped over his big belly, shorts tightly wrapped around fat legs, smiling, cooking smoke rich with pork chop fumes.

Dad's friendly, greeting smile was short-lived when he saw two teenagers and a woman lying dead, heads smashed in, skulls leaking rivers of blood down tiled floors just beyond the kitchen.

The man turned and smiled at Dad. He was cooking slices of them.

We left quickly after that.

Crackheads are unpredictable. Some facts are universal, like freshly turned Crackheads are most violent, killing anyone on sight. Hormones mingled with the virus, sending waves of anger and hatred bursting through their veins.

That's one solid fact in an ocean of blur.

After the initial infection period, some Crackheads will leave you alone, screaming, crying, shuffling down the ravaged streets, throwing bottles against shattered windows. Others might slash you, attacking with knives before bolting away. Worst is when they hunt, the virus feeding off an urge to torture, rape, kill us, and when our numbers plummet too hard, each other.

These Crackheads bolt past us, they're hideous screams woven with odd words like *"emcoming,"* and *"ampid!"*

We blink, ballooned eyes staring at each other.

25/10 came as a bushfire. The Crackheads swept across Earth, destroying everything in their path. Mankind hid in the shadows while infected hordes played in burning cities and scavenged bushlands looking for us.

But all fires burn themselves out. With shopping malls worldwide picked clean, and Crackheads more interested in murdering than farming, their population rapidly plummeted. By the mid-noughties, only small pockets of crackheads existed, those smart enough to shelter and repopulate, but most perished.

I remember Crackheads as a blur in a kaleidoscope of childhood memories. Dad hugging me as we hid from an approaching horde is one of my earliest. But growing up, we noughties babies rarely saw Crackheads, let alone talk about them. Those dark apocalyptic days post-25/10 were taboo, bringing thousand-yard stares from survivors or nasty glares. Memories of '03 are too fresh. Everyone is now focused on justifying the horror humanity went through by building a new, fair world.

"Where they… they…. They?" Mackenzie stumbled before I responded with one simple word.

"Crackheads".

"This is wrong," Alannah said with a hint of fear. "They shouldn't be out here. Gill said there weren't any nests left till South Australia."

"Yeah, well, fuck Gill, I'm more scared of what they were running from," I said. "Did you hear they were screaming something?"

"Yeah, that's what fucking Crackheads do, man, they scream random shit," said McKenzie.

"No, I mean they were screaming something like 'ampid' or some shit like that, I don't know," I said. "Just sounded like they were trying to get away from something."

"Get away from what? Melbourne hasn't been a red zone for, like, over a decade now?" Mackenzie said. "There's nothing left here."

Like the infected, we hear it before seeing it. The ground started rumbling, noises drowned by dozens of chirping birds flying out from abandoned, rusted cars. Paper ads swirled in the air, calling for the Livid Festival in October 2003, an anti-Iraq War rally, Steve Irwin sponsoring a new Honda, all dancing with the pounding ground.

It was a stampede of massive grey elephants, their feet squishing squealing cars, crushing moss-covered bones. Trunks swinging like grandfather clocks, wrecking trees and trams in one swoop. Escapees from the Zoo, where most of the exotic wildlife is from. Probably Werribee.

"Run, fucking run!" I screamed, and my legs bolted across the road towards Melbourne Central.

I don't even check behind me as I feel the elephants charge down the streets.

Melbourne Central is a construction site permanently stuck in time. An old bullet tower covered in dangling vines is drowned in tanned light from the giant, dirt-covered glass rooftop above. Built around the tower are three empty floors filled with slouching scaffolding, cones, and tools glued into the ground by moss.

"No, wait, fucking hold on," Alanna said, patting herself down. "The map, I think I fucking dropped it."

"You're shitting me?" I spoke.

"Nah, I'm not, man. I fucking dropped it."

"Shit… shit!" Mackenzie's hands lay on his head like a prisoner of war, wandering back and forth. "We should go back and look for it."

"Nah, man, if we dropped it in the grass, we'll never find it. You saw how long that shit was. And I don't want to be out there with the Crackheads loose."

"Fuck man, fuck!"

I looked around, wondering what Melbourne Central would look like if they completed construction.

Maybe it would be a movie theatre. Three stories of seats with popcorn, hot dogs, and 3D glasses: watching a projector play *Kill*

Bill Vol 2 on the bullet tower. Sitting between girls, noses stuffed with smells of fried food as the speakers boom across filled seats. A world with more than 4 girls from my generation! Just pick and choose your future wife from the seats around you!

So many potential girlfriends got smothered in 2003.

It's not like I have never watched films before. On Fridays after a week of farming against the blazing Australian sun, our settlement held movie nights. Nothing spectacular, just Gill's projector playing Disney movies in a barn house with mosquitoes casting black shadows across the dimly lit screen. It always felt fake, artificial — a poor mimic of the blaring, flashy movie theatres buried with the old world.

"Ah, ain't the end of the world," Alannah said, ironically. "There's probably, like, another map around here somewhere. We just gotta keep on looking."

So, we headed deeper into the building.

The sky tunnel "connecting" Melbourne Central to Myer shopping mall collapsed halfway, with metal poles and rigged, teeth-like, concrete patterns curving down into the open, chill air. Moss bulked along the single strip of rusted metal uniting both buildings, left after two decades of exposure.

I crossed over it first, extending my hand out to Alanna, who crawled across the metal beam like a koala.

Below, a main road clogged with cars made for a hard landing.

25/10, according to everyone alive back then, happened at the prime "traffic hour". Roads clogged with vehicles became massacre grounds as crackheads dragged people out of their cars and slaughtered them. I've seen shaky VHS footage of one highway strip blazing minutes after the outbreak. A snaking line of flames danced on burning cars and people who became torches with legs, screaming.

That's why McKenzie dipped. If falling on rusted cars didn't kill you, the tetanus would. He tried finding an alternative route to Myers that didn't involve going outside for long periods. The elephants, the Crackheads, although brief, scared us shitless enough to stay indoors.

A small creek peeped from the beam before transforming into a symphony of cranking metal. Alanna's face drained of colour leaving a white canvas dotted with terrified eyes and trembling teeth.

"Jump."

"I can't!"

"You got to. I'll catch you, promise!"

"Oh fuck, fuck, fuck, fuck, fuck, fuck, fuck!"

The metal spasmed; little concrete flakes burst from the tinting beam.

"Just jump!"

My hand wrapped around a rusted metal pole twisted out from the concrete. The other hand stretched out, fingers grasping at Alanna as she stood up.

"Come on! Come on!" I scream. *"Fucking JUMP!"*

Alanna sent the metal beam crashing down as she leapt. A thick metallic clank echoed down empty streets, then thicker thuds as it rolled down the pavement. Alanna lay next to me as stars flew above my pounding head. She must've hit my forehead while jumping.

"Fuck, you alright?" Alanna said, resting her head on the ripped flares she wore.

"Yeah… I'm fucking great," I said, but my attention was drawn to her face. Amber hair curled with the grit that smeared her light, tanned skin. Round brown eyes, light pink lips, creeping open, revealing slightly yellowing teeth. In that second, everything dialed down, leaving me, her face, and this moment alone in a warm, happy void.

"Here, let me get you up."

"Yeah, sure."

We pushed through the turned tables, broken chairs, and anguished skeletons of what was a cafeteria. Colourless signs coated in a layer of light moss told of souvlakis, curries, sushis, foods reduced to only pictures and our imagination. My food experience was one grey slump of vegetables and fish, maybe game if we were lucky. I always wanted to try exotic dishes like pasta and kebabs.

Maybe when we dragged humanity out of this apocalyptic hell, I'll sit old, eating the sweet, corny taste of Pizza alongside Kebabs wrapped in rye bread filled with thick, chewy slices of meat.

The food court opened to another shopping centre. Flapping pigeon wings echoed down three stories of abandoned shops, bouncing off tipped mannequins dressed in fading flared jeans held up with glittery belts.

"Woah look," Alanna said, one hand shaking me, the other pointing at a pile of skeletons bunched up around an escalator. A small hill built of anguished bones, decorated with faded clothes and metal spikes sprouting out from their backs.

The skeleton's collective tanned brown shade was brought out by an ocean of dried blood splattered underneath this mountain of death.

"I've never seen anything like this," Alanna said.

"Yeah, that's fucking grizzly," I said. "Poor fucks. Probably were trying to escape the initial outbreak and clogged up the escalator."

"... Making the perfect massacre ground," Alanna continued, bending over to free a pink sparkly purse from the clutches of a tight bone hand.

"Airs dry. Could be stuff still intact here."

Scavenging through the purse, she tossed out a greying driver's license, and I picked it up.

A blond chick stared back at me as I read her ID.

Lia Slauder. Born 13th May 1983.

20 years old when she died. Nearly my age.

"Oh, that's fucking awesome, look at this shit." Alanna grabbed a bright pink flip phone dotted with silver sparkles from the bag. She flipped it open, pressing the phone against her ear while twirling thick clumps of brown hair.

"Hey, is this KFC? Yeah, I'd like to make a reservation for two. Yeah, that's right, my friend over here and me," Alanna pointed one of her slim, weathered fingers at me, grinning.

"Oh, you're taking me out?" I said through sly, flirty teeth, "Like a little date?"

"Aye, don't count your lucky stars. It's a friend date." But her face suggested otherwise.

"Okay, well, you can get me a Big Mac, sugar mummy."

"Double cheese?"

"Triple it."

We stared, smiling at each other. Her soft brown eyes were inviting, complemented by radiating warm pink lips as she made motions similar to brushing a cobweb out of the way.

She didn't look it, but behind Alanna's lily-pale features was the most exotic girl I'd ever met.

In another world, Alanna grew up far away in Sydney's outer suburbs. A smart girl like her probably would've made it to Sydney University, Slim figure strolling across campus blasting Christina Agurila from an iPod.

But 2003 had other plans.

Her Dad worked the weekend shift in downtown Sydney on 25/10, his flip phone never picking up as Alanna's (then) unknowingly pregnant Mum crouched through blood-soaked streets to escape into the countryside.

Barely anyone survived the city or inner suburbs that day.

Months later, Alanna was born in a rat-infested basement deep in the outback. The nine survivors with Alanna's Mum raised worried eyebrows at her newborn, seeing just another mouth to feed against waning supplies.

Most secretly left that night – sneaking out with all the food, fearing a crying baby might draw attention to roaming Crackhead packs hunting down survivors.

Yet sixteen years later, when we first met, only Alanna would still be alive from that group.

By then, she was a scrawny refugee, young face creased with fine lines of soot and eyes bulging from withered sockets.

She barely had escaped the vicious 2019-2020 wildfires raging across Australia that killed her mother, rapid flames pushing Alanna's settlement of thirty from rural New South Wales into Victoria.

With no family left, McKenzie and I absorbed her into our duo. My generation are orphans of the noughties. All our parents perished, leaving us to swiftly form siblings out of friends. Otherwise, we'd have no family.

It was the three of us until a bug knocked McKenzie sick in his bed for vomit-filled months.

Then it was just the two of us.

On one humid summer night filled with frog croaks and the sound of Dido's *White Flag* blasting from my boombox, we lay side by side in a field just outside Yea's fortified walls. Our eyes were locked, smiles filtered in sleek silver from the full moon, and hands moist in each other's palms.

"I like you," Alanna finally said.

"I, too, have warm feelings for you."

"No, I'm serious, I actually really like you. Everyone I ever loved died. But since I've arrived, you've always been there for me and… you're really like the only other person *I feel* something with."

"Not McKenzie?"

"I mean McKenzie too, but, you know, differently."

"What you mean differently?"

"Let me show you."

My hand tightened around her as our lips met.

Our love thrived alone. But in the tight-knit settlement of two hundred people thirsty for cheap gossip decades after reality TV last aired, we always came under the spotlight. Each step we took became town talk, before being bombarded with complaints about McKenzie looking alone as we two trotted hand in hand.

It flamed roaring arguments between us. Alanna wanted to wind down our relationship to avoid the public eye and integrate McKenzie back into our lives, but I wanted to keep the status quo.

"Fuck 'em all. Why the fuck should we care what they think of us?"

"It's not about what they think," she yelled back in the stuffy renovated house we lived in behind the settlement's wooden walls. "It's about being a good fucking friend. McKenzie was always there for us, and we've been ditching him for what? Some cheap teenage romance? Fucking listen to yourself."

Not only did I not listen, but I also failed to find a compromise.

Between my parents' death and meeting Alanna, I grew up not feeling loved as part of a greater generational trauma. Campfire talks between Gen Zers always revolved around craving human touch. Finding a partner became romanticised in the hope it'd fill the lack of parental affection.

That's how I got greedy. The *love* radiating off Alanna after years spent dry made me want to fully embrace her.

But she wanted space, and space is what she got.

We broke up soon after — friends once again.

"Guys!" McKenzie's voice echoed from the first floor, bouncing off musty windows and into our ears. "You've got to come see this."

McKenzie stood hands on his waist, staring down a giant black hole when we saw him. The ground must've given in, rubble sloping into the black depth that smelt dank and wet.

"Fuck," Alanna said.

"Fuck indeed," said McKenzie. "I think this must've been part of the subway system."

"Like the food chain?" I said.

"No like... You remember that story Gill told us?"

"Which one?"

"Where she was on 25/10."

"With the trains, right?"

"Yeah, well, back before 25/10 trains used to run underneath the city. People back then called them subway systems or the Metro. Or at least that's what Gill called it."

When I said no one survived the cities on 25/10, only Gill is an exception.

Gill, a sweet, plump, white-haired woman who runs our settlement, isn't the image of an only survivor, but on outbreak day, she had been waiting at Melbourne's underground station. Seeing hordes of people screaming down the escalator, some covered in blood, she squeezed underneath a parked train, thinking it was a terrorist attack.

"But I knew it wasn't a terrorist attack when *the Crackheads* came," she told me once while setting up the projector for movie night. "Course I didn't know what crackheads were back then, but they didn't sound like terrorists. I didn't hear any gunfire over the screaming and crying. Just crunching noises and ripping noises, like someone stepping on bones over and over and over again."

A sea of blood, covering splattered organs, torn limbs, and dead bodies, greeted her as she crawled out three days later.

Crimson, red-soaked walls and ceilings were filtered grey with smoke pouring from the outside, making it unbreathable.

"I remember staring at a pair of eyeballs. Just eyeballs, floating in a puddle of blood," she said. "It was a scene out of hell. Hate underground spaces now."

"Oh, hell nah I ain't going down there." McKenzie backed away from the hole. He threw his hands up as if to surrender, revealing wrapped cotton creased with thick dirt covering both palms. "That's fucking wack."

"Oh, come the fuck on, McKenzie," I said. "It'll be something new for all of us."

"Yeah, that's the fucking problem. *It's new.* We've never been underground. None of us has. How the hell are we gonna navigate down there?"

"I don't know, maybe call Gill, she'll know," Alanna said, slipping the pink phone out of her pocket and chucking it to McKenzie. He caught it, sparkly flakes flittering down like silver snowflakes.

"Thanks," McKenzie said sarcastically.

"No problem. You guys got your torches, right?" Kneeling, Alanna swung her backpack to the ground and shuffled through the compartments.

"Yeah," I say doing the same.

"You guys aren't serious." McKenzie's eyebrows open wide, trembling creased lips revealing teeth, biting down nervously. "After everything Gill told us."

"Gill told us each station had a sign telling what suburb you are in." Alaana pulled out a thick, handled torch. "The railways are a straight shot. We follow them till we get to Flinder Station. Then it's like a 5-minute walk to the NGV."

"You guys are fucking nuts," McKenzie said. "Why don't we just… I don't know, find another fucking map?"

"You wanna go outside again? Really? With the elephants and the crackheads? A paper map wouldn't survive 21 years outside, McKenzie. We'll just get lost searching for nothing. The tunnels, at least, will take us directly from one station to another." With one hand wrapped around a thick metal pole, Alaana supported herself as she descended into the darkness. I listened to water dripping from the black hole, the occasional whirr of wind echoing down there.

"You'll be fine. Promise."

"Fuck." McKenzie's face screwed, watching me follow Alaana down into the hole.

My torch ripped through the pitch blackness, revealing snippets of grey, rusting railway and junk mushed by water exposure.

It was the darkest place I have ever explored, which I guess is what we were looking for.

Something new.

The coolest buildings we saw growing up were squat town halls or two-storied shops.

The city wasn't like that. Colossal skyscrapers surrounding us lived up to the stories we heard growing up of *the red zones,* cities filled with Crackheads. But the Crackheads died out, leaving us an alien world to explore.

The elephants and the Crackhead family only justified a reason to spend time exploring these massive structures. It fulfilled our curiosity about experiencing an urban world rather than aiding our safety. We could've used the street signs to navigate outside – but adolescent curiosity and arrogance towards the dangers underground made us want to explore new environments.

We walked until we reached a platform.

"Hear that?" McKenzie said, his torch jumping to a small rustle hidden between knocked rubbish bins and bones across the platform.

"My parents used to take the metro for work back in Sydney," Alanna said. She climbed over the gap and onto the station. "Mum told me you could see rats running across the railways. Beedy little fucks. They're probably everywhere now."

The platform floor was covered in mud. A layer of scummy film covered dotted pieces of junk and…

My eyebrows raised as my torchlight screwed itself onto the glittery silver fur of a dead possum. A swirling trail of intestines lay floating in a thick blood stew from its torn guts. This was fresh, its black, marbly eyes fixated on the skewed expression creeping across my face.

Something *really* didn't feel right.

"What the fuck is that?" Alanna said.

"A possum. A very fucking dead possum. Something ripped its stomach open. A… dingo maybe?"

"We don't have dingos this far south," Alanna said.

"Oh, fuck me cunt!" McKenzie's trembling torchlight illuminated one dead possum after another. All were ripped apart, bloody bits swirling in the damp mud.

Butterfly wings began to flutter in my stomach.

"There must be… over a fucking dozen possums here. Fuck!" I said, feeling tremor in each word.

"This is '03. This is fucking '03 as fucking shit, man," McKenzie said through jittery teeth. "We shouldn't be down here. Fuck! What the fuck is this shit?!"

Cockroaches scuttled blindly through the mud, pouring into our torchlight and charging past us. It looked like they were running from something, living on rotted leaves and residue from the street before getting scared off.

The crackle of bones quickly drew our light to the escalators suited behind large algae-covered columns decorated with fading street maps. We stayed dead silent. My ears hurt from listening so hard to the cold quietness, and my breath began rapidly accelerating. I felt my body shaking violently and my heart leaping from my chest.

After watching horror movies, we ransacked from abounded Video Stores in my youth – I'm pretty damn sure what happened next could be considered a *jump scare.*

My beam snapped onto a white pale face peaking from behind the escalator. His white hair grew widely from a slim, withered face, leaving drooping eyelids and colourless hollow cheeks. Drolling spit morphed with possum blood around his mouth, trailing from pink weathered lips and dripping onto the man's malnourished body. He was extremely skinny – reminding me of the refugees in our camp who fled the post-Crackhead famines that came with Y2Ks closing.

There probably were more visual descriptions, but I didn't look long enough before bolting.

That's something I noticed was missing from the pre-03 horror movies. After the main jump scare, *there was no fight or flight response.* The main character just stood like a deer caught in headlights as the monster sprang towards them.

To give slack, no one pre-03 probably knew what it was like surviving in *flight or fight* mode for your entire life. Humans weren't hunted back then, which made their survival movies feel corny 21 years later.

A naked family slithered from behind the escalator and into our torchlight. Five beady, wide-eyed children clutched human bones in their skinny hands, nails overgrown, toned down to a light brown from years of uncleanliness. Both parents had pale faces sunk around the bones, lines creasing under black eye bags, cracked blue lips, and foreheads covered in sprouting wild white hair.

They're *Tassies* – crackhead inbred nests, the last danger left from Y2K's devastation.

Crackheads often kill and eat their newborns, a nod to their already plummeting population, encouraged by disregard for self-preservation and lust for murder.

The second win for humanity is Crackheads can't infect. Only 25/10 victims and their descendants are Crackheads. Which makes most of them either old — or young and feeble today.

Sometimes, though — very rarely — Crackheads form isolated nests, sexing each other repeatedly to create inbred hives.

We call them *Tassies*. I've never encountered them personally — but travelling merchants bring stories of nests attacking lone wanders, stalking prey for days before ripping them apart.

I used to think Tassies were bogeymen, stories to keep kids from exploring outside our settlement's walls after dark. But today I learnt they are, in fact, very much real.

The Crackheads charged, spiralling towards us like feral white ghosts waving human femurs. The parents, noughties veterans, screamed raspy insults:

"Cunthole!! Stab ya!!! Piss shit cunnttt!!! Come here and fuck good!"

And the children howled unintelligible sounds.

We bolted like frightened gazelles, our boots letting off thick metallic taps echoing down the tunnels, softening as I followed Alanna's light (and fanatic yelling) into the train's ripped-open door with McKenzie close behind.

Slashing torch beams madly lit up bones, suffocating the train's walkway, its angle slightly tilted towards us from the crash.

Pure adrenaline tinted everything – while thoughts became crystal clear, my body movements were erratically primal. I remember thinking, *"damn, I'd never move this fast, I must be having an adrenaline rush," while on all fours, my arms worked grappling chairs independently,* swinging myself up against gravity.

Another robotic-sounding thought was *"I'm gonna get a disease from touching shit"* as my fingers, sparked by someone's small hand wrapping around my foot, automatically reached for the closest bone.

A Crackhead — a twelve-year-old male, maybe — growled just below the torchlight, insane quivering eyes locked onto me as its fingers hardened around my boot. Its brown hair rested in wild clumps stuck together with the same grime that simultaneously creased his face with dirt.

One ear was missing, a little pinkish stub — and its gums had gaps intertwined between crooked yellow teeth. Droll drizzled down onto the crackhead's chest, vertebrae bones lining thin pale skin – likely from decades of malnourishment.

I thrust a skull onto its forehead, making the Crackhead flinch but not much else. My hands slipped as the skull bounced off its forehead after the third strike, tumbling down the train. Adult voices echoed below me. Raspy swearwords bounce madly off broken windows, swerving between McKenzie screaming and mingling with my rapid breaths. Rigged nails pierced into my pants. The Crackhead was crawling up my leg, dragging me down across sharp spiking bones that ripped into my shirt like a cheese grater. A burning sensation like acid exploded across my gullet. My hands clutched back its forehead as wild, snarling teeth bit towards me.

If the adults and other children hadn't been occupied by something underneath me, I'd be dead.

Instead, I shoved the Crackhead beside me, dust exploding underneath its impact from crackling skeletons.

I flailed onto a femur still attached to a shoe and shoved its pointy end into the Crackhead's neck. A waterfall of blood burst out, draining the Crackhead's skin, pale, ballooned eyes accompanying insane grinding teeth as I pushed harder down.

It was my first kill – and I felt nothing.

Like clockwork, my adrenaline-gripped body threw me, crawling, crazily up the carriage. Hatred filled the vortex left when my adrenaline withered out. Decades of running, cowering in the dark, and surviving off quick decisions made killing it feel like a long time coming.

In the hours before dusk, running out from Parliament Station east of Melbourne Central, we realised McKenzie wasn't with us.

"He wasn't behind you?"

"It was fucking dark and… fuck!" I said.

I felt guilt sinking in my stomach. Or maybe it wasn't guilt, *but shame.* Disappointed faces from our settlement flickered through my mind like a zoopraxiscope. Blurred features morphed into one giant judging monster nodding their heads disapproving at us. *Things like this weren't meant to happen anymore.* We were the new generation. Our parents sacrificed themselves – and others – to swipe away the ripples of Y2K: starvation, selfishness, and survivalism for civilization.

Mateship.

Alanna and I acted in the Metro like it was still 2003. *Every man for himself.* Abandoning our friend for self-preservation.

"I still remember what my Mum told me. How it felt like when everyone abandoned her when she had me," Alanna said as the orange light scraped across the horizon. Black silhouettes of buildings stood like jagged teeth, silent, minus birds echoing through the ruins.

"She felt betrayed, but unsurprised. Her group had done worse. A few weeks before I was born, a Crackhead horde was trailing them. Food was low, and everyone was tired. Then they caught someone in the group stealing from the rations. You know what they did to him?"

She looked at me. Dried tears rested on hollow, black eye bags drooping her sockets to look permanently sad. "They cut his Achilles tendon so he couldn't walk. The logic was… it'd be one less person to feed, but also that the Crackheads would find him first and that'd give the group some extra time to run while they tortured him for shit and giggles."

Alanna looked down, staring at the ground as I took hold of her hand. I could feel the seconds flying, turning into the minutes we should've been using to run further from the Crackheads. But I could also feel the spirit in her pulse under my fingers. And I could also see her eyes. It wasn't panic. But resilience hidden behind a veil of sadness.

"I feel like we did that to McKenzie. We left him behind for *them*. So, we could fucking run. It feels like something our parents would've done. Not us. Fuck. 2003 never really ended, did it?"

Silence filled the air.

"My family hid to survive," I said. "After 25/10, locals from around the farms formed protective groups. We had to run and hide when all the Crackheads in the city spilled into the countryside. And you know what's fucking ironic? It wasn't even them that killed my dad. But other humans.

"It was over Dad's backpack during the Y2K famines. Mum and I watched as a group of survivors literally beat the shit out of him right in front of us. We couldn't even bury him; we were so weak from hunger. Mum died later in 2017 from an outbreak in the settlement. And as fucked as it sounds – *I'm glad she died when she died.* The world wasn't as fucked up like when Dad died. Mum died when we lived in settlements, and we could afford to bury our dead."

I looked into Alanna's eyes.

"We shouldn't leave McKenzie behind."

"What if he's dead?"

I paused. We couldn't bury him. Hauling McKenzie's body from the Metro with Crackheads breathing down our necks would be impossible. Another pang of guilt hit me. McKenzie shouldn't be left rotting outside – or become Crackhead food. He should be buried underneath a tree with a gravestone. Even if it's just a small belonging of his.

"We bury one of his belongings back home," I said.

"Like what?"

"I don't know. But it's better than nothing."

The pitch-black Parliament station entrance stared back at me. The staircase leading into the underground was buried under a grassy hill with little marble steps peeking out occasionally.

A skeleton lay flat just outside the staircase. The skull's jaw was locked wide-open with a kitchen knife lodged into its back spine.

"Well, if we're going down there," I said, walking over and pulling the knife out. "We should get prepared."

We clamoured down the unmoving escalators, trying to avoid echoing our footsteps. My torchlight bounced wildly off torn, musty posters for Craig David's Melbourne tour, The coming *Matrix Revolution* movie (which was going to be released two days after 25/10. Bugger), a new rotating flip phone held by a chick in white flares, and other throwback ads of an extinct world.

It was a mess at the bottom. Fallen bricks, yellow wires dangling in puddles of water, and skeletons littered every corner. Our feet softly crunching on bone let off a chain reaction of squeaks, as small black shapes darted zigzagging across the ruins.

"Well, no going back now," I said, my words slicing through the tense, quiet atmosphere.
"We might never get back, *full stop*," Alanna said coldly. "Let's just be careful. I don't want to be here any longer than we need to."

A whirlpool of tense emotions tugged down on my stomach. The only thing to ease it would be seeing McKenzie alive again. This is one reason out of many I went into the Metro again. Going underground was scary — but it'd be even worse living with the *what-if* of McKenzie's current circumstance.

I needed confirmation of whatever the truth.

We reached the train, still wedged into the curving tunnel, when I saw a faint light. Little shimmers of warm orange fixed themselves onto the train's glass windows, illuminating them with a withered brown colour.

Fire?

We turned off our torches. It was flickering all right.

"They must've made a campfire," I whispered.

"You think they saw our torches?"

"I don't know. They could be waiting to jump us."

"Fuck!"

The thought of an ambush sent shivers bolting down my legs, an invisible force tugging them the other way. My throat clogged up with fear.

"Fuck this shit, cunt," I grunted, swallowing my anxiety and forcing each step forward.

I figured staying squeezed against the slim space wedged in between the train and the tunnel wall would be our best bet. Bone-filled carriages acted as a natural alarm system, each crack ringing like a dinner bell.

I was right.

Tinted a tanned brown through shattered windows, the Tassies, sitting cross-legged on withered grey passenger seats, gnawed juicy chunks of possum meat. Orange light danced from a distant burning fire, splashing warm colour on feeble-looking children, little more than stick people. No wonder they looked half-dead. If they kept breathing in fumes and eating possums, it'd kill them.

How did they even survive this long? I thought.

I felt a finger jabbing into me.

"Platform, look."

Alanna's whisper was full of tremors, holding back tears, and my stomach dropped a thousand flights when I understood why.

Just by where passengers got off to get on the platform, a pile of rubbish was burning. Next to it, the Crackhead's mother cut into McKenzie's dead arm with a sharpened bone. A red, smouldering blob dotted with cracked white bone stood for half his head. The other half had one eye dangling from its red socket and a semi-torn mouth permanently locked in fear. The Crackheads had ripped off his clothes – revealing what they had done to him. Violent red lines streaked across his paling, dead body, legs torn brutally open, revealing savage bone rising from a crimson mess.

Nausea hit me rock hard, sending my vision spiralling madly. My throat swelled up, and my stomach dragged against the floor. Vomit etched at the back of my throat when a singular thought flew through my head.

"It reminds me of what the Crackheads did on 25/10."

The first hellish hours after 25/10, when Crackheads killed everything on sight before their rage-filled hormones crashed in. Stuff '03 survivors told me. Seeing entire streets coated crimson red with bodies splattered across the ground. Howling Crackheads who minutes before had been normal upstanding citizens, beating people to death with their fists.

How quickly it all happened. This must've been what 25/10 felt like. One moment, humanity was king of the world, strolling through Melbourne, acting as if everything belonged to us. Next, our friend lay dead, and we were hiding in the shadows.

This shouldn't be happening anymore. *Not in 2024.*

I forced a gush of vomit back down, stomach acid biting into my swelled throat.

"Hey, hey!" A hand shook me back to reality.

"Huh?"

"Shhhh, not so loudly." The black silhouette of Alanna's finger rested on her mouth. "Take out your knife."

I felt my fingers shaking violently against the knife's plastic handle, trying not to drop it. I could only fear how loud dropping it would be.

"You know how I survived the fires?" Alanna whispered.

I shook my head.

"I could run. Really fucking fast. You had to. The fire was on our ass."

She stared at me. Tears rolled down her face.

"I'm gonna run back to Parliament Station screaming," Alanna continued. "They will chase after me, but they are weak. I'll be faster than them. Hopefully, it'll give you time to crawl underneath the train and grab something of McKenzies."

"Nooo" the "ooos" wobbling between my stumbling, terrified lips. "No… we shouldn't do this… It's stupid."

"No. No, it's not." I felt Alanna's hand gripping my bicep. "It's like you said. This isn't for us, it's for everyone back home, for our parents who died. The 2000s are over. We've already taken back this world from *them*. Now we need to take back what makes us human. Humanity can't be animals anymore. We need to start burying our dead… we need to start acting like humans again!"

Her words blurred in my ears, juggled up with fear before forming in my head as unconnected sounds.

Then her lips were on mine. Quivering lip muscles rubbed against mine, and I felt Alanna's tears dropping down her cheeks as I grabbed her tightly.

"When you get McKenzie's shit, run straight up the escalator," she said, pulling back, both hands holding my biceps.

"I saw some street maps of Melbourne on the columns when we looked around before. Make sure you find the NGV on the map and run towards it. We will meet there," Alanna said. "If the map's correct, the NGV is not too far away. Just across the Yarra River."

"I love you," I blurted out.

"I love you, too," Alanna said, her hand guiding my back as I crawled underneath the train. The damp smell intensified below the carriages, and gushes of cold air mingled with my tears as I slowly clawed forward.

The platform was reachable when I heard Alanna's voice boom around me:

"HEY FUCKERS! OVER HERE!"

A choir of insane shrieking drowned her voice. Rapid footsteps clunked down the train, and I watched as dirty feet jumped on the ground, chasing after Alanna's dwindling voice.

Thick heartbeats exploded across my tensed body – not just for me but now for Alanna.

What if they catch her?

I physically controlled each breath, as my skin crawled red with stress. For a while, I lay fidgeting with rocks between the tracks crying. Tears strolled down my cheeks while everything became numb.

Curiosity killed the cat. Curiosity killed my friend. We didn't *need to be here.* Tracking long-abandoned tunnels, hoping each station leads directly towards Flinders Station, was stupid. But that wasn't the reason we were here. We were here because we felt *humanity retook the world.*

No dangers were left after Y2K's destructive wake – everything was our playground to explore.

Ripe for taking.

Boy, were we wrong.

I hated everyone when I rose later from below the train and climbed onto the platform. I hated our settlement for letting us venture into an unknown environment, I hated Alanna for convincing us to be down here, I hated the party for being hosted in a city under the pretext that it'd be safe, and I hated our parents for dying before telling us the dangers beyond the settlement's walls.

I hated everyone but myself. Now thinking — I was avoiding taking the blame. If I knew I even *partially* bore blame for McKenzie's death, I'd go crazy with guilt.

Tightness gripped my throat, and a wave of numbness flooded my brain when I stood above McKenzie. Vomit etched in my throat while everything became blurry.

Next to McKenzie's mangled corpse lay his clothes. A scattered gallery of bloodied cloth, torn and drenched across the damp ground. Mud mingled blood stains homogenised McKenzie's clothes as an amber-brown clump of fabric.

Until a silver twinkle caught my eyes.

The bright pink phone dotted with sparkles shimmered among McKenzie's ruins. It lay on the tiled ground, wedged between two thick brown leather boots, laces floating in a puddle.

I picked it up. Something poetic rang about this like the phone saw two time periods plagued with death – one during 25/10 and another in its recovery. But my brain flooded any further thoughts about this in a sea of anxiety and stress.

I barely stuffed it in my pocket when I heard a low growl rumble behind me.

A tingle ran down my spine like Chinese firecrackers as I swirled around. Dread gripped my chest as the Crackhead mother lurked behind me.

I tightened my grip on the knife.

The mother stood there, withered arms and legs standing wide apart, skinny stick fingers clawing rhythmically to its twitching pink lips as spit flickered out. The mother was naked and aged.

Its skin, ghastly pale and malnourished, acted like a canvas showing 21 years of brown scars running across its tormented body as if the creature were some twisted modern art piece.

"Awww, Awww, fawrk! Yoor the one zhat kilt lil' Shittosser! Cunt fuwker dick nah!" Its voice croaked a thick, raspy accent, tuning each word almost unintelligible. *"Rekkun ammha jack on shawur dwead bwody arn weiner farg yoor mouth ashter I kil' ya like yoor farkface fweind!"*

With a speed that matched its frantic twitching, the mother lashed out, clutched the knife's blade, and snatched it from my hands.

Blood streamed from its palms as I backed away, stunned by the thing's strength. The mother examined the knife, grinning, then swung it around, slashing in my direction.

"Lil' fwakcunt!! Ooon zhe dai iss' oll append twinny'-sowmting yars' argo, I kilt mmiii two kiddies arnd hussby witz ar fawrking 'nife!" The mother made stabbing motions in the air, deranged eyes still locked on me.

"It fwelt sho gooooood!!! Mi Shildrawn wos' so smorl, but 'sere wheres milles' of zere guts yinside 'em!"

The mother pointed the knife at me and smiled an evil smile.

"I woon-der 'ow mooch guts 'ar yinside ya, dickface!"

It advanced towards me, waving the knife madly.

The anxiety flushed out, and filling its vortex was a burst of adrenaline enhancing my senses. I dashed behind the column, feet bouncing in rhythm to the mother who was preparing to pounce.

"Fuck you! Let me outta here!" I remembered screaming.

The mother hissed again, bubbly spit flickering like raindrops.

A singular thought shot through the pounding primal adrenaline. Rehearsing the whole moment in my head, *it probably was a bad idea.* Anxiety clogged up any counterargument and threw the idea into action. *Flight or fight mode.*

The pink phone crashed into its eyes with a thick, heavy thud that sent the mother stumbling back. One weak hand covered its eye as the mother snarled, sagging body hunched over.

Anxiety tried tugging me back as I hurled myself at it, screaming war cries. I grabbed the creature's knife-bearing hand tightly as we grappled each other. Weakened by old age and fear, its arms quivered.

Ancestral anger mingled with the adrenaline ignited into a bizarre superiority complex over the Crackhead. After cowardly surprising us on 25/10 and tearing humanity's achievements into smouldering ruins, physically overwhelming the mother felt like showing it a *human renaissance* was coming. The mother–Tassies were echoes of a near-extinct *pestilence,* a bump in humanity's domination over Earth.

They once killed us, stalked us, and forced us into hiding, but in the end, humanity would bury Crackheads alongside the sabre-tooth tiger and other long-gone hunters of mankind.

It was mankind's turn to shine again.

"GET THE FUCK OUT OF MY CITY!" I screamed.

An arrow drilled through its neck. The crackhead's head slapped against the wet concrete with a sickening crunch.

Two young men wearing outdoor gear decorated with utility belts stood mouth wide open, eyes locked on the dead mother. One stood with his feet divided between the train door and the platform, knees bent, face creased with dirt that ran like little crumbs through his thin brown mustache. His gut-soaked army knife shimmered against the flames, orange reflection mingling with fresh crimson blood drolling down.

The other man — a lanky, wide-eyed Native, shocked face toned by shadows cast by his wide-brimmed military bucket — held a crude crossbow, its string taut, pointed straight at where the creature stood.

The Indian man's face twisted up suddenly, bearing white teeth as his eyes drew to mine.

"Whoa," he said. "You alright?"

"YOU'RE ALIVE!" Alanna rocketed down the carriage, swinging herself through the train door and into my arms.

"What the fuck happened?" I sputtered out, confused.

"I got lucky," Alanna spoke in a weary, relieved voice as if the worst had already passed. Head buried in my chest, her words mingled with the hyper-intense booming of my heart trying to break outta my chest.

"I ran out of the station... and these guys were on patrol from the NGV."

"Heard her screaming," the Native said slowly. He swung his crossbow over his shoulder and trudged towards me. "Like she said. We had night shift. City is dead quiet around now, so she gave us quite the jump when her voice bounced off the fucking buildings."

The other man stood bent motionlessly, heavy dirt-etched hands resting on his knee. He looked like a marathon runner after the big race.

"Tassies, man," the other guy eventually said, "Gave me a PTSD attack. Haven't seen Crackheads in fucking years... and then suddenly there were like 10 of them chasing your girl over here. She basically ran right into us."

"Yeah, not the first time I had to run for my life," Alanna said, pulling out of my arms. McKenzie's mangled body drained our brief excitement as Alanna stared glumly at his remains.

"Oh hell, I'm sorry," the Native said softly. "I don't even fucking know if we can even bury him here. He's too..."

"Ripped apart," the other man said before the Indians gave him a nasty look.

"No... no it's okay." A pulse began to throb in Alanna's voice as she stared into my eyes sadly. "You... you got something of McKenzies, right? Something to take home and bury?"

I stepped over the dead mother, its marble eyes staring blankly at the ceiling underneath a pool of blood where the phone sat. Its silvery sparkles either had fallen off on impact or were coated in red gore when I picked it up. Long, crimson blood streaks ran down my shirt when I wiped it clean.

"This, this will be buried." The phone rested on my trembling hands. "This was the last thing we gave McKenzie."

Both patrolmen guided us to the NGV that stood like a lighthouse – campfires inside illuminating its boxed silhouette against towering skyscrapers turned obsidian black from midnight darkness.,

Smoke lazily danced from pit fires in iron bins, scraping against the gallery's high ceilings as we walked in. People zig-zagged like tightropers around tent stalls fuming with spits rotating brown crispy game. Slint-eyed guards wearing mismatched military and civilian gear toned a homogeneous dirt colour from grime, nodded at our patrolmen as they filtered back into the crowd. Alcohol bottles littered the ground alongside nibbled animal bones, crunching underneath heavy booted feet from people swarming us with questions.

"Where you from?"

"You guys walk or drive here."

"You're from Yea, right? Think our blokes traded with your blokes for wool last year."

"You should come to the coastline. We got so much fish, and some of our cooks were chiefs before 25/10. The food is really good back home."

When our newbie card expired, and everyone's interests turned back to partying, Alanna and I sat watching the event above from an indoor balcony. Drunk teenagers or armed guards passed us, venturing into long, snaking exhibit rooms, but other than them, it was just us.

I felt worse than being in the sewers.

In the sewers, we shoved remorse deep in the back of our heads, focusing purely on survival. The second we were safe, the floodgates opened, and rage, grief, and loss exploded through our heads, clouding us with guilt for McKenzie's death. Hugging each other tight, we sat drowning in thought, replaying what happened over and over again in our tormented heads.

"It's weird," I finally said, breaking the silence. "I don't remember mourning my dad like this."

"Yeah, same," Alanna said softly. "When Mum died, we just kept running."

I pulled out the flip phone from my pocket, fingers tracing its hard, cold metal exterior.

"You think we're gonna get any closure from this?" I said.

"I have no idea how grief works. I don't even really think I've ever mourned before. Everyone just dies… and I guess at one point I just got used to it."

"Huh. Guess this is some sort of fucked up luxury." Hands cushioning my head, I lay down, eyes locked on the creaking grey roof. "To be safe enough to grieve."

"To be safe enough to be human again." Alanna's arms and feet wrapped around me, head buried in my chest, sore with stress. Her wet tears soaked my shirt, creating moist spots tingling my skin.

We lay there for a long time.

THE DEADLY SEVENTEEN

by Andrew Buckner

The night before her eighteenth birthday, March 18th, 2026, Morgan Rodchester took one look in the vanity mirror in her bedroom, saw a graying old woman staring back at her, and clawed at her face until there was nothing left but bone.

As if to confirm that these wounds were self-inflicted, the local authorities quickly took note of and documented the chunks of flesh still stuck under her fingernails.

What was just as strange as this tragic and horrific incident was the fact that two other Lion's Paw High School Seniors had also died in the past three weeks. Both of whom were, like Morgan, dangerously close to their eighteenth birthday.

What made matters even more bizarre was that the first victim, Liam Johnson, was decapitated shortly after vaping marijuana on Wednesday, February 26th, 2026.

This was punctuated by Liam's corpse missing a head, a vape pen found several feet from where his body was found in his bedroom at 1366 Woodlawn Way, and a picture found on his iPhone of a cloud of smoke rising from his headless shoulders.

Though Liam's iPhone 17 was seized by local authorities and examined for fingerprints, no telltale evidence was found.

The second victim of these fateful strings of incidents occurred ten days later on Saturday, March 7th, 2026.

The murder happened when Ava Lansworth was alone by herself in her bedroom at 1449 Rosemarker Drive. She was singing "Happy Birthday to You" to herself while streaming her favorite slasher movie from the 1980s, *Slash and Slash Again!* on SlashTube, which had been her Birthday Eve tradition since she was thirteen.

On that night, Ava felt a sharp sting in the back of her neck every time she got to the word "you" in "Happy Birthday to You."

It wasn't until she had completed the brief song that she reflected upon the pain she had felt while singing. This made her instinctively touch the part of her neck where the pain had exploded several times during her solo performance.

After touching the area where the pain had repeatedly arisen, she brought her hand to her face and saw blood.

Before she could get up to look in a mirror and see what was going on with her neck, she smelled smoke.

It was then that her body went up in flames.

When Ava was found in what remained of her home, which had caught fire shortly after her lifeless body hit the ground, what stuck out to the local authorities was that ten still-burning candles were sticking out from the front of her neck. Eight more were found crammed down her throat.

By the time that these two murders had happened, most of Lion's Paw, Ohio, had gotten out of the small town and had moved to places unknown to the rest of the populace.

"If teen horror movies have taught us anything," seventeen-year-old Emma Grey mentioned as she was actively driving out of town with her mother, Patty, and father, Darren, towards a cabin they owned in Pennsylvania, "it's that staying in the area where the murders were happening is a recipe for death."

"It also makes you look guilty as hell," Darren mused to himself, but knew better than to say aloud.

Twenty-four hours later, after settling down for her first night outside of Ohio in her life, Emma's dark red hair twisted itself into a knot and strangled the young woman, who was a month away from her eighteenth birthday, in her sleep.

When authorities arrived on the scene, they found no other signs of foul play and quickly ruled the incident a suicide.

Patty and Darren were interrogated for the next several days, and the cabin was meticulously searched, but nothing suggested that Emma's parents had strangled their daughter.

As the next few months went on and twelve more students of Lion's Paw High School's Class of 2026 were found dead shortly before their eighteenth birthday in various ways that involved trauma to the neck and head, those who fled Lion's Paw after the first two murders and those who stayed in the area both soon learned that whoever or whatever was causing these deaths was going to get these teenagers regardless of their location.

It was on graduation day, Saturday, May 16th, 2026, that Lion's Paw High School's Class of 2026 Valedictorian, Willow Dusk, decided to take action against whatever unknown entity or entities were slowly robbing her classmates of their eighteenth birthday.

In order to do such a thing, Willow planned a post-graduation "celebration" for the seventeen remaining students of the Class of 2026 who had decided to stay in Lion's Paw after the first two deaths at her two-story home on 1631 Placeholder Drive.

When the remaining graduates had all assembled at 8:07 p.m., Willow made her intentions clear.

"The person, people, supernatural beast, or whatever villain we have at the heart of this unfolding horror tale," she began by shouting to the remaining graduates, who had all assembled in her living room and were frantically complaining about a lack of beer and weed on the premises, "will be rooted out and overtaken tonight!

Whether I have no idea how to do this, I have a feeling that we have come to the third act of this movie we are living, and what better night for this to happen than graduation Night!"

A few rowdy cheers and random boos exploded from her gathered classmates, who were fondling each other, making out, and pushing each other off the expensive leather sofas Willow's parents had bought for each other the previous Valentine's Day.

"Yes, this is our version of the big Randy Meeks speech moment about the rules of surviving a slasher movie in the original *Scream,*" Willow continued and added to the effect by pulling a beer from behind her back and waving it in front of everyone, who all cheered in unison. "Okay. So, what I have ascertained from the sixteen victims, God rest their souls, who have fallen victim to whatever masked slasher or digital ghost or whoever is killing our fellow classmates off in this particular horror tale is that they were all alone at the time. So, don't do what people in horror movies do and separate from one another.

Another thing I noticed is that, though none of the victims have died in the same way yet, neck and face trauma have all been a pivotal part of the demise of the victims.

So, cover that shit up somehow."

"How?" the eternally acne-scarred Aiden Masdow squeaked, then adjusted his designer frames from the middle of Willow's parents' expensive sofa.

"That's on you," Willow stated with a dismissive wave of the hand. "Maybe we all, and this is especially directed to you, Aiden, should put on masks.

Or maybe we shouldn't because then if the villain in this tale is a human slasher, that will just make this climactic act even more difficult."

"I thought you had answers," point guard for Lion's Paw's Basketballers, Kamden Russell, exploded with a turn of his head towards Willow and then a quick return to having his back turned to her to look for the beer and weed he had expected to find at this so-called "party."

"I only have observations," Willow shot back and then addressed the rest of her classmates. "If you'd like to enlighten us, you can gladly stand up here, Kamden."

After waiting awhile and getting only a slight headshake from the still-distracted Kamden, Willow went on with her speech.

"All of us have our eighteenth birthdays coming up by the end of this year. Therefore, we are all in danger. That is why I organized this gathering.

"So, if we've learned anything from all the teen slasher movies we've ingested throughout our lives, we know that we cannot engage in fornication."

"Fornication?" Aiden asked while everyone else from the Class of 2026 besides Willow booed.

"Fucking. Sex," Willow stated to the dunce master himself. "But I guess that won't be an issue for you."

The crowd around Aiden exploded with laughter and applause.

"Daaammmnnn," they all wildly blared at Willow's response to Aiden. "She scorched you, bro!"

That is when a loud moan, like that heard between two individuals involved in the current topic at hand, silenced the laughter and applause.

It was coming from somewhere near the upstairs living room, where everyone was gathered at that time.

Willow cocked her head to the sound while Kamden, his cheerleader girlfriend, Ilsa Thorne, and several of Kamden's teammates all started to wolf whistle at the sound.

After a few steps towards the unexpected din, the power went out quickly.

When it came on, everyone except Willow was wearing bloodstained masks that matched the wide blue eyes, always pig-tailed blonde hair, and rosy cheeks of their host for the evening.

"What is this?" Willow screamed with terrified tears glistening in both her eyes.

Willow's body became rigid and alert at the sight of the masks everyone around her was wearing.

"You can't escape your past," they all chanted in a singsong manner in unison as they stepped uniformly, mechanically towards Willow. "You can't escape your future either. Time is our master. For your blood being spilled tonight will make you the seventeenth victim of our pact with the great, unholy goat Razmus. Seventeen is both the lucky and unluckiest number of them all."

After these words were chanted by the group, the lights went out again.

Willow wanted to run.

Instead, she quickly stopped when she noticed that her classmates, the people she believed were on her side just a few minutes ago, were all around her.

They were all near enough to her that she could smell their unmistakably coppery scent, which made Willow think of blood.

Hoping the lights would turn back on, Willow saw that all seventeen members of her class had identical butcher knives, all of which were in their right hands, pulled out and waiting to stab and cut her.

She deliberated about what she had uttered about protecting her face and neck and tried to do so with her hands.

This caused all seventeen of the Willow masks that were surrounding Willow to glow.

Then, all the masks began to radiate in unison, like a phone screen.

On the masks played the videos that Willow's parents were planning on playing for her own graduation party tomorrow.

At first, we saw Willow being born on the night of July 4th, 2008, while fireworks exploded all around her.

The mask screens then showcased Willow's brother, Aaron, who was born two years later on September 4th, 2010.

The mask screens then turned into a video of the moment. Willow, after eating at McDonald's with her grandmother, Eve, first met her brother shortly after he was born.

Then, the mask screens quickly flashed pictures of her first days of school.

They showcased the picture of an irritated Willow, which was taken by her father shortly after Willow got her driver's license, right after she had turned sixteen.

Willow believed this picture was "obnoxious" because it was taken by her father right before her first shift at her first job at the local ItAllCostsaDollarandYourSoul Dollar Store.

Despite all the high strangeness that was going on around her, this and the picture of Willow meeting her brother for the first time temporarily quelled the anxiety that was twisting her innards and making her so scared she felt like she would vomit at any moment.

Then, things got really horrifying.

The mask screens then flashed Willow's obituary.

The headlines stated that Willow was the seventeenth and final slaying from the Cult of Razmus, whose identity still remains unknown.

Before Willow could grasp what she was seeing, the Cult of Razmus, or "The Deadly Seventeen" as they called one another in private, closed in on her further.

Willow couldn't move.

Everywhere she looked, she saw the knives of the cults waiting to be stained with her blood.

"Why?" was all Willow could utter.

Then, as if collectively answering her question, the mask screens all showcased an online article that stated, "Eighteen is the most wicked number. Eighteen is the first step onto the doorway of adulthood. Turning eighteen means that joy is ending and all that awaits you is bills and work and politics and voting and worshipping at the altar of material gain."

"We can't fight time," Willow screamed. "We can't be young forever."

"You can," the mask screens all read and then collectively made an ear-splitting buzzing sound. "This is our graduation gift to you. You will not have to follow the pre-set path that *they* have carved for you."

After these words flashed on the masks, the cult moved closer to Willow.

She tried to fight off the seventeen bodies that were locking her into the middle of her living room floor, but she couldn't move at all.

Pressure was squeezing on her shoulders, then on her neck.

"Their going to take it off," she contemplated but couldn't cry out. *"They are going to take off my head! That is what this pressure is!"*

"Mom! Dad," Willow screamed at the top of her lungs.

That is when pictures of Willow's mother and father flashed on the mask screens.

They were headless and lying in bed together.

"The sound we all heard earlier," Willow pondered to herself as she tried to figure out what was happening, *"that was them. But how? Why? They knew company was coming over."*

That is when the mask screens zoomed into the date on the watch of Willow's dad. It read, "March 17th, 11:58 p.m."

"Last night," Willow realized. *"But who did I talk to this morning?"*

That is when the six-horned, six-legged, and six-eyed demonic goat Razmus's features exploded on the mask screens.

"Our leader is clever," the cult chanted. "He takes many shapes. He may even be us right now. He could be you. He could be this building in which we are all standing."

"Why?" Willow blurted out in as timid a tone as ever had escaped her lips.

That is when the walls in Willow's home began peeling themselves away.

Vengeful goat horns poked through the floor where Willow was standing.

The lights flashed on once, then went back to darkness.

In that instant, Willow saw that even the lamps that contained light bulbs had Razmus' scowling, angry face.

The lamps then grew teeth and jumped to the ground.

Willow then envisioned a seventeen-year-old jumping off a bridge.

This made her think of her older brother, Jeffrey, who had jumped off Lion's Paw Bridge and drowned in Lion's Paw Waters two years ago to this date.

"He never got to see his eighteenth birthday either," Willow sorrowfully whispered to herself, and, for a moment, she forgot the nightmarish situation that was unfolding before her.

A clop-clop-clop sound was then heard.

Everything went silent.

Razmus himself then appeared in the entryway to the living room of Willow's home.

The goat-like fiend, who was walking on two feet instead of four, then put his hands together and pulled them apart.

The entirety of The Cult of Razmus then moved over to the right and left sides of the living room.

"What are they gaining from this?" Willow shrieked at Razmus and then spat in his face.

"They will never see eighteen," Razmus hissed in a voice so mighty that it made the ground under her feet split open. "They will remain seventeen and, therefore, not have to pass into adulthood. These lucky souls will continue to bring me seventeen new seventeen-year-olds from each new Senior class every year in exchange for their eternal youth.

If they fail, then they will be forced to go through the endless stresses and woes of adulthood for lifetimes on end.

When I finally come to take over Earth in the year 3000, I will then take them down to my layer of Hell and make them my slaves, my tools for my murderous desires."

"Just like you are doing now?" Willow announced and spat at him again.

Wiping her saliva from three of his six eyes, Razmus laughed hysterically at Willow's reaction.

"Fulfill your pact," Razmus then commanded his cult. "Make daddy happy and ensure that you never turn eighteen this year."

This caused Willow to run towards the front door of her home.

Razmus stood and smiled as he watched the situation.

It wasn't until Willow threw open the front door to her home and began to run outside that she noticed that all the masks had disappeared from her living room.

When she opened the door, her Jeffrey and her parents' bloated bodies were on the other side of the doorway.

"Come," the trio said as they popped up in front of Willow and smiled sinisterly at her with maggots dripping from their heads and worms writhing around and eating their empty eye sockets. "Join us. Four is a party!"

Then, the trio tried to grab Willow with their skeletal hands.

Somehow, Willow escaped.

Willow's front yard then turned into a bridge. It was just like the one her brother had jumped off two years ago.

As she saw her feet begin to teeter over the edge, seventeen masks began illuminating around her.

They pushed her gently, gently, then violently.

"Geek," they all chanted in the voices of the people who had bullied her throughout her childhood. "Nerd. Bookworm. Brother killer. Lesbian."

The mask screens then reflected the time during her sixteenth birthday when Willow tried to kiss her then best friend, Aurelia Meyers, during one of their more personal conversations, and the embarrassment she felt when she realized that she was misreading Aurelia's silent signals.

"Just jump," the mask screens chanted. "Make it all better. Nothing awaits you on the other side of eighteen."

"No," she screamed, then backed up away from the edge of the bridge.

It wasn't until she felt a tightness in the middle of her throat a few seconds later that Willow realized that it was a knife causing the aforementioned pain.

A second later, she realized sixteen more blades were whittling away at the other sides of her neck.

The first of the last two things Willow noted as her head fell off her body, went down into the murky, blood red waters just beneath the bridge, and heard a splash as the rest of her frame was thrown into the ocean that now surrounded her, was a vision from one of the mask screens of the cult succeeding in killing seventeen new Lion's Paw High School Senior classmates year after year until Razmus' anticipated return in 3000 A.D.

The second thing she noted was that her own face had a mask.

It was one that was flashing the seventeen faces of the cult members who had now helped decapitate her body and throw her overboard.

From somewhere beneath her feet, Razmus' unmistakable hiss exploded.

Soon, an offer for vengeance was made.

GATEWAY DRUG

by Lindsey Beth Goddard

Danny Thornton hated everybody in his high school. *One more year until I can drop out,* he reminded himself before pushing the gymnasium doors open, just wide enough to peek through. The lights were off. The room was empty, aside from the basketball hoops towering above him at each end. Sunlight poured through the high-set windows, shedding its beams across the tiled floor. Danny slipped through the doors and pulled them shut.

There was no P.E. during sixth hour on Friday, and Danny knew it. He also knew there was an exit door behind the coach's office. It was an emergency exit off the short hallway leading to the sports equipment closet. The door had an automatic lock, making it impossible to get in from the outside, but from the inside it opened with ease.

Danny crept through the shadows between the patches of sunlight, the roots of his unkempt hair damp with sweat. His heartbeat thudded in his ears as he glanced back at the gymnasium doors to make sure he was still alone. He was. He wiped the sheen of perspiration from his forehead and told himself he wasn't scared of getting caught. *Scared* wasn't the right word. He was on edge because getting caught would ruin his afternoon.

He passed center court, his footsteps quiet and quick. He

couldn't wait to leave, to be free of this place. Sixth hour was the absolute worst. It was Mrs. Prichett's class, and if the subject matter—algebra—wasn't bad enough, the teacher was a real bitch, too. Yesterday, she'd forced Danny to take a pop quiz out loud while the entire class listened. It was punishment for nodding off during her lesson. Everyone laughed at Danny when he got several answers wrong, and his face turned a deep shade of pink.

Mrs. Prichett, with her tightly wound bun and thin-framed glasses, looked as if she wanted to look the part of a *strict school teacher*. Danny clenched his fists at his sides, the memory of his chuckling classmates replaying in his mind, a never-ending loop.

He inched past the window of the coach's darkened office. He could see the hallway up ahead. *Almost there.*

Danny jumped back, surprised by his reflection in the dark office window. He quickly recognized his own shaggy brown hair and dark eyes staring back at him. He let out a short, nervous laugh.

No one was around. He'd be outside soon. Away from these assholes.

There were only two people in Danny's life he considered "friends". One of them sold weed; the other worked at the video game store down the street from his house. Danny socialized with them on a regular basis, but it was only out of necessity. The dealer let him buy whatever small amount of weed his allowance would provide for that week, and the game store clerk hooked him up with coupons and discounts. Sometimes they would shoot the shit for ten or fifteen minutes, but even those guys weren't close to Danny, not really. He didn't have any real friends, and he liked it that way. At least, that's what he told himself. The truth was, his acne-covered face and long, dorky nose, combined with his quiet demeanor, made Danny easy prey for the hungry predators that walked the halls of his school.

He rounded the corner of the hallway and hurried to the exit. He reached out, hesitantly, with his fingers above the push bar. He knew from experience that there wasn't an alarm on this door. Yet he always felt like there *should* be. Like it was too easy. He held his breath and pushed it open anyway.

He stepped into the sunlight and peered around. He didn't see anyone other than a woman up ahead, jogging, her back turned to Danny. Coast clear.

He angled his face towards the sun and let it warm him. He closed his eyes and listened to the birds chirping, to the cars rolling down the street. Sweet freedom.

He adjusted the book bag on his shoulders and headed for a nearby alley. It was one of his favorite spots—quiet and shady—between a vacant hardware store and a run-down Chinese restaurant. If he came home early and his parents were there, they would start asking questions. So, Danny found ways to kill time.

It was a short walk. He arrived at his private alley in less than a few minutes. The air was ripe with the smell of rotting Chinese food from the dumpster, but Danny didn't mind. It would help mask the odor of his smoke.

He shrugged the backpack from his shoulders and leaned against the brick wall. He unzipped the front pocket, reached inside, and retrieved a small plastic bag. The smell of its leafy green contents caused the corner of his mouth to curl into a half-smirk. He dug around in the canvas pocket again until he found his one-hitter and lighter. Danny packed himself a hit. He held a flame to the end of it, took a pull, and let his head fall back against the dirty brick wall as his lungs absorbed the smoke. Mrs. Prichett and the anger she caused him would be gone in 3,2,1...

"You like to get high, do ya'?" Danny jumped. He almost dropped the one-hitter. There appeared a tall man in a black fedora leaning against the dumpster to his right. The hat matched his outfit, which was black from head to toe. He wore a vest beneath his fancy jacket, but no tie. Danny stuffed the paraphernalia into his back pocket, confusion wrinkling his brow. He was certain he'd been alone mere seconds ago.

"Now, now," said the man with a wave of his hand. "No need to hide what you've got. I'm cool with it, *dude*." The word "dude" sounded wrong coming from this man. Even standing in the shadow of the vacant warehouse, he looked old to Danny. *Ancient*. Long, white hair fell from beneath his fedora hat, in sharp contrast to his dark attire.

"What do you want?" Danny eyed the man cautiously as he stepped into the sunlight, drawing near. His skin was so pale that Danny could see the veins in his hands, face, and neck; so dark beneath his alabaster flesh that they resembled cracks in a porcelain figure. Danny shivered.

"I want to offer you a new kind of high." The man flashed a smile full of yellow teeth that were too sharp. *Cat-like,* thought Danny.

The man inched closer, and a stench filled the air. It overpowered the dumpster full of old Chinese food, as well as the pot smoke lingering in the breeze. The man was only a few feet away now. He stopped, holding Danny with his stare. Danny's nostrils flared. He tried not to show how the smell made his eyes water and his throat start to gag. It was awful, like sulfur or rotten eggs.

"I'm not interested." Danny lifted his backpack from the ground. "And I don't have any money." He tried to move away from his unwelcome intruder, creeping sideways with his ass sliding against the wall, one hand gripping his book bag.

"Oh, but I think you are." Again, he smiled, with a mouth full of what seemed like monstrous fangs, which sent a tremor through Danny's limbs. The old man fixed Danny in a chilling stare. His eyes, which had appeared brown from a distance, now glimmered with a deep shade of red. "That low-grade garbage you're smoking is terrible for your lungs. It costs too much money, and the effects wear off too quickly. *Am I right*?"

Danny nodded.

"I've got something way better. A different kind of drug. It will take care of anything that's troubling you. Your problems will bother you no more. In fact, this stuff is so good, the first hit is free. Because I know you'll come back for more."

Danny gulped. "I don't mess around with the hard stuff, man. I'm not a junkie."

The stranger chuckled. "No need to worry about that. This is a non-addictive experience, like acid or 'shrooms, only nobody *ever* has a bad trip." He stared at Danny and repeated the word, "*Ever.*" The man's eyes no longer held any traces of brown, instead shimmering a vibrant shade of crimson.

"If I take this free sample, will you leave me alone?" Danny's voice was desperate, an octave too high. He wanted to run, but his legs were planted to the ground as if they had grown roots right through the cement.

The man stepped closer, bringing a new wave of the sulfur-like stench with him. Danny felt sick to his stomach. The man reached into the breast pocket of his black dress suit. His spindly white fingers emerged, holding something dark and small between his withered fingertips.

"Hold out your hand," he instructed. Danny did as he was told. A small, dark blob plopped against his palm. It resembled tar at first, but a wave ran through it that made the substance look a lot like black Jell-O. Danny wasn't sure if it was supposed to be smoked or taken orally, but either way, it didn't matter. He wasn't going to take it.

"Now, let me explain how to take it." The man said, as if reading Danny's thoughts. He slid his hand beneath Danny's upturned palm. The stranger's skin was surprisingly hot, and he wanted to recoil, but didn't. Partly because he was hoping his cooperation would end this encounter very soon, and partly because his body felt frozen in place.

The man held a finger over the small, circular blob, and before Danny could attempt to pull away, he smashed the substance down, grinding it into his skin. Danny regained control of his body, fresh fear overriding whatever spell he'd been under. He pulled his arm away, screaming, "What the hell, man?"

"That's how you take it," said the man through his rotten grin. Danny raised his hand just in time to see the dark substance disappearing into his pores. He *felt* it seeping into him. It was as cold as the stranger was hot.

The man turned and walked away, and with his back turned to Danny, he uttered, "When you need me, you'll know where to find me."

Danny didn't know how long it would take for the effects of the drug to kick in. He opted to hightail it home and hide in his room until he figured out exactly what he'd taken. His parents might be home and question his early arrival, but it was worth the risk.

When he got there, sweaty and still a little panicked, Danny saw that neither car was parked out front. His parents were at work, or maybe even driving home. Either way, the coast was clear for now. He breathed a sigh of relief and ran up the stairs. Locking the door of his bedroom, he popped in a CD and attempted to drown out his thoughts.

Nobody ever has a bad trip. Your problems will bother you no more. The stranger's words echoed through his mind, but he didn't believe any of it. If anybody was going to have a bad trip, it was Danny Thornton. He had dubbed himself The King of Shitty Luck.

Danny waited and waited, but he didn't have a bad trip. In fact, he didn't trip at all. After three hours of hiding in his bedroom, Danny decided that the stranger was nothing more than some old creep who got his jollies off harassing young boys. He ate his microwaved dinner, shoveling large spoonfuls into his mouth. He was tired, unusually tired for this hour.

He went back up to his room, lay down on his bed, and soon Danny Thornton fell fast asleep.

In his dreams, Danny stood in front of a house that looked familiar, but he didn't know why. It was a split-level home of moderate size. The second story was done in white siding, the bottom level in decorative brick. Black shutters framed the windows. Only one light was on, illuminating the upstairs window like a rectangular star against the dark, moonless night.

A single tree stood in the yard. Its limbs were so twisted it appeared as though the branches grew in knots. The tree was the only interesting thing about the yard, with its freshly mowed grass and pruned shrubs lining the porch.

Danny yawned. A thought occurred to him. *Why am I yawning in a dream? Hey! How do I know that I'm dreaming?*

Unlike other dreams, which felt real until he woke up, Danny was somehow *aware* that he was asleep in his bed, that his mind had conjured this entire thing up. He frowned. Of all the sexy scenarios his hormone-driven mind could have whipped up, of all the girls he pictured naked in the hallways of school, why was he standing in front of a plain-looking house on an average suburban street?

He shrugged. There was only one way to find out. For some reason, his unconscious mind had brought him here—to this house. He didn't know how to wake himself up, so he might as well get on with it and do something. He crossed the lawn and stepped onto the concrete patio. Danny tried the door knob, but the door was locked.

A strange voice filled his mind. *"Try the back door,"* it suggested. He smelled the sulfur stench before he saw the man in black standing on the lawn. A fedora hat atop his long, thinning white hair; the man extended a spindly finger, pointing the way. He spoke in a hushed tone that was somehow crystal clear in Danny's ears. "*She forgot to lock the back door.*"

Danny stood on the porch and considered his options. Maybe the drug was finally taking effect on his brain. Maybe he was tripping in his dreams. This certainly didn't feel like any dream he'd ever had. It felt different, more like an alternate reality—one where Danny was *aware* of his dreaming.

To make sure it *was* a dream, Danny concentrated all his thoughts on one idea: a two-headed squirrel. Soon enough, a furry little two-headed squirrel scampered across the grass. It stopped, its four beady eyes staring in different directions. It raised an acorn to both of its mouths, allowing each one a turn to nibble. *Okay, now I know I'm dreaming,* he thought. He looked up to where the ghastly man had been standing, but there was nothing there but an empty lawn.

Danny was growing bored with this dream, or trip—whichever it was—and he was eager to get on with some action. Besides, what could possibly go wrong? This wasn't real.

He headed around the side of the house, dropping down low when he came to a large window. He crawled past it and stood. Walking quickly, he stuck to the shadows and avoided the light of the street lamps. Even in this dream world, he knew that a nosy neighbor could easily spoil his mission. Of course, he had no idea what that mission actually was, but it didn't matter. Danny felt compelled to continue.

A chorus of crickets serenaded him as he crept through the dark like a burglar. He came to the back door and tried the knob, a little shocked to discover that the creepy old man had been right. It was unlocked and swung soundlessly open.

Beyond the door lay a dining room with hardwood floors and posh furniture. The room had a modern, stylish look, even in the darkness. His eyes had adjusted well enough to see clearly. Or maybe that was the drug heightening his senses. Danny couldn't stop thinking about the tar-like substance and how it had seeped into his pores. This dream felt so vivid, so *real;* he was certain he was tripping in his sleep.

He tiptoed through the house. All was quiet, except for the white noise of the air conditioner and the heavy drumming of Danny's heart. *Why am I here?* he wondered.

Artwork decorated the walls. Nothing special. Just the generic stuff you could find at K-Mart or Target. He passed a hanging mirror opposite the decorated wall.

Then stopped.

He gasped and spun around to face the glass. Nothing was reflected in the mirror. That is, *he* was not reflected. The wall behind him was there, along with the ugly artwork. But no Danny.

He lifted an arm and waved his hand, the way he'd seen countless movie characters do while confronting an empty mirror. Nothing changed. *I'm invisible. Holy shit! I'm invisible!*

Adrenaline coursed through Danny's veins, bringing a newfound confidence. To think he had been sneaking through the yard, so afraid of getting caught, and all along he had this unknown special power. Yes, *power.* That's exactly what it was, because Danny felt very powerful indeed. *I can do anything,* he thought.

Looking around the room, he noticed a framed photograph hanging a few feet from where he stood. He stepped closer. All at once, he knew why the house had looked so familiar. A middle-aged couple smiled at him from the photo. They stood in front of the house with its white siding on the top, brick on the lower level, and black shutters flanking the windows. The tree with twisted branches stuck out of the ground just behind them. It was a young, wispy tree in the picture.

He knew this photo. It was the same one Mrs. Prichett kept on her desk. Danny had glanced over at it many times, as he was forced to stand in front of the class for some form of humiliation or another. It was hard not to notice the large 8 X 10 picture towering over everything else on her desk.

In the photo, Mrs. Prichett and her late husband beamed. He held her close, his muscular hand wrapped around her waist. Danny suspected that her husband's sudden passing was the reason why Mrs. Prichett was such a bitch, but it didn't matter. All that mattered was how she made him feel. And she inspired him with only one feeling: a cold hatred that burned through his veins as if his blood had been spiked with dry ice.

"Just think of what she's done to you," the voice whispered in his head. Danny glanced around the room, expecting to see the man in black standing there, thin white hair and alabaster skin glowing in the shadows. But no one was there. Only the voice in his head saying, *"She let them all laugh at you."*

Danny's hands trembled with rage. He balled them into fists. His adrenaline surged. An intense fury blossomed in the core of his being, growing larger by the second, filling him with such hatred until only one thought remained: *revenge.*

Danny approached the French door near the dining room table. He peered through. The kitchen lay just ahead.

He hurried to the counter and opened a drawer. Nothing but dish towels and sponges. He slammed it shut, then opened another—*slam,* then another. *Slam.* He found pencils. *No.* Scissors. *Maybe.* Silverware. *Definitely not.* He needed something sharp. Something with a good grip, because his hands were shaking faster than a trading card on the spokes of a bicycle wheel.

Otherwise, he felt good—somehow confident, ready to release the pent-up emotion that rattled him from spine to fingers. He continued rifling through the kitchen. After half a dozen drawers were slammed, a shaky voice called from the other room, "Hello? Who is there? I am on the phone with 9-1-1, so whoever you are, you better leave!"

Shit. Danny hadn't considered that being invisible didn't mean Mrs. Prichett couldn't *hear* him. He'd been making a racket in the kitchen, alerting her to his presence. Now he wouldn't be able to sneak up on her in bed, like he'd been hoping to do.

He stopped moving for a moment. He stood very still, biting his lip. And that's when he saw a wooden block sitting atop the island counter. The handles of a dozen knives jutted out from its surface, calling his name. *Danny...Danny, come play with us.* So, he did. He selected the largest one, squeezing it so tight that all traces of blood left his knuckles.

He bolted through the French door and scanned the area. A doorway across the room led to a small foyer. He hurried to it and glanced to his left, where a staircase led to the second floor. A panicked Mrs. Prichett sat halfway up the stairs with the phone pressed against her worried face. She locked eyes with the knife, but not with Danny. No, she couldn't see Danny at all. A maniacal laugh erupted from his throat, and for a moment, he wondered—Could she hear his laughter? Could she hear him taunting her? He hoped so.

"Oh my god," she breathed, no doubt wondering why a butcher knife from her kitchen was floating in the air, angled and shaking as if it were held by an invisible madman. And it was. Danny grinned.

He charged up the stairs. The woman shrieked and was almost to her feet when he jumped her. The side of her face hit the corner of a step. There was a crunching noise as the bones in her cranium fractured. Danny liked it. He wondered what other noises she might make when the real punishment began.

He raised the knife and brought it down onto her back, purposely avoiding the spine. He wanted her to feel this, all of it. She screamed and wheezed as the blade punctured her lung. He smiled and yanked the knife from her back.

Danny brought it down again, plunging deep into the muscles just below her shoulder. She shrieked and pleaded as she bucked wildly, like a bull at the rodeo.

She managed to thrust her elbow backward and connect with

Danny's chin. It hurt a lot, but the pain gave him a second wind. He wanted to see her face. He wanted to watch the light fade from her eyes.

He couldn't flip her over with the butcher knife clutched in his hand. So he dropped it. Why did he need it, anyway? The bitch couldn't even *see* him!

He gripped her roughly by the arm and turned her over. She was crying. Her glasses sat crooked on her face. They were bent into an odd position on the side of her head that had slammed into the step. A greenish bruise was already forming there.

Her eyes pleaded with the empty air, looking not at Danny, but past him. Nothing new. Things had always been this way between them. She never really saw Danny Thornton, no; she merely gazed through him as if he were a nobody.

He wrapped his hands around her throat and squeezed as tight as he could manage. Her eyes grew wide behind her broken glasses. She tried to jerk her head from side to side but managed a barely noticeable shake. Her arms flailed as she threw punches at random, unable to see her attacker and too frenzied to aim, even if she could.

She made no sound at all. She couldn't. Her windpipe was pinched by Danny's thumbs. The blows softened as her arms lost muscle power. Her eyes stared blankly. She was barely fighting at all now. An eerie shade of lavender had washed over her face. Her lips were deathly pale, trying to form some semblance of her final words. Mrs. Prichett and the anger she caused Danny to feel would be gone in 3,2,1...

Danny woke up and stretched. He couldn't remember what he had dreamed about last night, but he knew it had been good, because he *felt* good. In fact, he felt like he'd been asleep for days and had awakened to a brand-new life. He knew that wasn't the case. For one, it was impossible, and secondly, his cell phone told him the time and date. He'd been asleep for nine hours. Still, he felt somehow different this morning. Better.

The sun was shining, and Danny had time to spare, so he decided to walk to school. He didn't want to snap out of his good mood. The jerks on the bus would make sure that he did. They would see him smiling, or walking with a bounce in his step, and they'd take that good mood away from him. Simply because they could.

Danny didn't head straight to the school. He decided to savor this rare feeling of happiness before it was inevitably crushed. He walked with no particular direction in mind, unconsciously letting his legs lead the way. He passed a flower garden, a small dog yapping behind a wooden fence, and a little girl riding a pink tricycle. In the distance, a lawn mower grunted and came to life. Danny took it all in as he walked on and on, simply enjoying himself. He turned down whichever street appealed to him most, thinking, *so what if I'm late for school?*

He came upon a house with white siding on the top, brick deco walls on the bottom, and black shutters framing the windows. A police car sat empty at the end of the driveway; another one was parked at the curb. The cement porch was lined with yellow plastic strips that read "CRIME SCENE" in bold, black font. A figure in blue passed the open threshold of the house.

Danny's blood ran cold. A slide show of violent images flashed through his mind as he stared blankly at the yellow tape dancing in the wind. He saw the knife plunge into Mrs. Prichett's back, blood shining on the blade as he removed it. He saw it slice into her shoulder, saw her flesh rip open, her clothes becoming sticky and red. He saw his hands around her neck. The woman's eyes pleaded behind broken glasses. The lifeless, glassy eyes looked through him.

But—it had all been a dream, right? Just a dream? Danny smiled. It was a dream. He was certain of that. But it was also something *more*. Those things he had done—they had really *happened* somehow.

Danny turned and headed back. He knew, now, why his feet had carried him here. His senses were heightened. Foreign chemicals still lingered in the tissue of his brain, the vestiges of a strange, black substance. As he quickened his pace, taking the streets that would lead him to school, he thought maybe—just maybe—his good mood might last.

Danny arrived at school one hour late. He got a tardy pass from the office and made his way to his locker. The halls were abuzz with gossip. The news of Mrs. Prichett's death was being whispered from ear to ear. A few students even talked right out loud. "Stabbed *and* choked," he overheard them say.

His ego grew a little larger as he realized *everyone* was talking about the murder. Students gathered around the drinking fountain or traded one book for another at their lockers, pondering the gruesome crime scene, wondering how gory it had been. Some were sad, some indifferent, and some actually looked relieved. Danny guessed that the recently widowed Mrs. Prichett had been hard on more students than just him.

He was filled with a smug satisfaction as he spun the combination on his locker and yanked it open. *He* had done that. Danny Thornton. *He* had killed mean Mrs. Prichett and silenced her bitchy tongue forever.

His ego swelled, and Danny decided to try the impossible today. He decided to talk to a girl. He spotted Lisa Hargraves coming down the hall. She wasn't the prettiest girl in school, but even Danny's burgeoning self-esteem didn't trick him into thinking he stood a chance with the popular girls. Lisa was somewhere in between, and, even better, she was alone. It was easier to approach girls when they were outside of their herd. Not that Danny had ever tried before.

He closed his locker and swooped in beside the girl. "Hey,

Lisa," he said. She had light blue eyes, brown hair, and a plain face with lots of freckles, but she was cute enough that Danny had caught himself looking at her a few times. "Can I walk you to class?"

Lisa stopped and turned to him, crinkling her nose in disgust. She rolled her eyes. "Yeah, right, Danny, in your dreams." She started to walk again, but Danny stayed behind. Blood rushed to his face and neck, and he knew he was turning pink. But he didn't care. All he cared about was the sudden ache in his chest. Lisa's words had pierced right through his heart. Her rejection of him hurt more than any bully in the past. It stung so badly, he could only think of one response.

"You know what?" he said. "That's a deal, Lisa. I'll see you in my dreams!"

Danny laughed. A few classmates shot him a scrutinizing sneer. The warning bell rang, shattering the silence that had formed all around him. Everyone had seen Lisa take him down a peg and heard his crazy reply.

Fuck them, he thought. *Fuck them all!* Danny Thornton hated everyone in his school. He would see them in his dreams, tonight and the next night, just as soon as he found the man in black.

"When you need me, you'll know where to find me," he had said. And Danny *did* know where to find him, and he wanted more of that strange, black substance. No matter what the cost.

ABOUT THE AUTHORS

Andrew Buckner

Andrew Buckner is a multi-award-winning poet, filmmaker, and screenwriter from Ohio. His short dark comedy/horror script "Dead Air!" won Best Original Screenwriter at the fourth edition of The Hitchcock Awards. His recent volume of verse, The Burden of All the Beautiful Things, was a finalist in the Poetry - General section of the 2024 American Writing Awards. Buckner also received second place in the Literary - Coming of Age category of the Spring 2025 Bookfest Book Awards competition for his novella Exitus Marquee. A two-time semifinalist in Alien Buddha Press' annual Horror Showdown, Buckner's book, The God in Me Will Emerge: Poems, recently received third place in the Poetry - Contemporary category of the Fall 2025 Bookfest Book Awards. Also a noted critic, actor, and experimental musician, Buckner runs and writes for the review site AWordofDreams.com.

Bill Camp

With a last name like Camp and a hometown like Erie, Pennsylvania, I was born to write horror. I currently live near the Great Dismal Swamp in Suffolk, Virginia, with my family, which includes my wife, child, four cats, and two dogs. My short stories have appeared in the anthology Rebels, Creepy Podcast, Madame Gray's Poe-Pourri of Terror, Teach. Write., Page and Spine, and parABnormal Digest. I have also published poetry in Alternative Deathiness, Teach.Write., Lite Lit One, and New Author's Journal. I am also a current member of the Horror Writers Association.

Dawn Colclasure

Dawn Colclasure is a Deaf writer in Eugene, Oregon. She's a freelance writer, book reviewer, and columnist. She is the author and co-author of several books. Her poetry, articles, essays, and short stories have appeared in magazines, newspapers, websites, and anthologies. She publishes the SPARREW Newsletter online each month. Her websites are https://dawnsbooks.com/ and https://www.dmcwriter.com/. She's on Facebook, Bluesky @dmcwriter.bsky.social, on TikTok at: https://www.tiktok.com/@dawncolclasurewilson and Instagram @dawn10325.

H.L. Dowless

H. L. Dowless is the kind of writer who doesn't just craft stories—he inhabits them. A veteran of more than three decades in the literary trenches, he has built a career defined by relentless curiosity, fearless adventure, and an unshakable devotion to the written word.

A Writer Forged by Experience

Dowless's work is steeped in the grit and color of a life fully lived. He has traveled widely, taught both stateside and abroad, and embraced a lifestyle that blurs the line between author and adventurer. Whether trekking through foreign landscapes or immersing himself in off-the-grid living, he channels every experience into his writing with raw authenticity.

A Prolific Voice Across Genres

His bibliography spans poetry, fiction, how-to nonfiction, and sweeping speculative works. With hundreds of traditionally published pieces to his name, Dowless has appeared in journals, magazines, and publishing houses ranging from Leaves of Ink to

The Scarlet Leaf Publishing Company and DLG Publishing Partners.

His poems—often reflective, unvarnished, and deeply human—capture the rhythms of rural life, the ache of memory, and the thrill of wandering far from home. His fiction, meanwhile, blends the mythic with the visceral, offering readers worlds that feel both fantastical and lived-in.

A Life of Adventure and Connection

Beyond the page, Dowless is a teacher, traveler, and outdoorsman—equally at home on a cruise ship, deep in the wilderness, or at a bustling literary event. He embraces life with the same intensity he brings to his writing, meeting readers wherever his journeys take him.

A Literary Presence That Endures

Now living a "true literary lifestyle" in Ecuador, Dowless continues to chronicle his experiences, insights, and philosophies with the same fire that has fueled his career for decades. His blog, Rowdy Living Press, offers a window into the mind of a writer who refuses to live quietly or write timidly.

Thomas Folske

Thomas Folske lives in Minnesota, USA, with his wife, five kids, and three black cats. He holds a BA in Creative Writing, an AA in Liberal Arts, an AS in Education, and a certificate in Creative Writing. He has had over 80 short stories published by various publishers over the last ten years, most in the last five years. See more at:
https://tfolske1987.wixsite.com/mysite and
https://www.amazon.com/-/e/B00UKTWZ6I

Alex Foster

Alex Foster is an Australian horror writer.

Lindsey Goddard

Lindsey Beth Goddard is a tortured poet and dark fiction author, living in Missouri, whose short stories have been published in e-zines such as Gamut Magazine and Carnage House, as well as in anthologies such as Error Code and The Asylum of Terror (1 and 2). Her work has been performed on popular podcasts like Creepy Podcast and Chilling Tales for Dark Nights. She is the author of four short story collections, two poetry books, and a novel. For more information, visit: LindseyBethGoddard.com

Megan Guilliams

Megan Guilliams is an Independent Fiction author who specializes in Urban Fantasy, Horror and Dark Romance. She is a Franklin County native who lives in Virginia with her husband and two children. When she's not writing Young Adult and New Adult Fiction, she enjoys painting. Filling the walls of her home with colorful lowbrow art and Pop art, Megan enjoys bringing her book's characters to life. As a young child, Megan dabbled in short stories, often entertaining her peers. While Megan doesn't hold any specialized degrees that led her to her writing passion, she currently has over thirty novels published on Amazon and Kindle. You can find more of her work in the year to come, as well as read her story "Kroak" in Nature Triumphs: A Charity Anthology of Dark Speculative Fiction, "Love, Lies and Bleeding" in The Devil's Playground: A Horror Charity Anthology for Drug Addiction, "The Christmas Wraith" in Last Christmas: A Holiday Horror Anthology, "She Bitch" in Piece by Piece: An Anti-Valentine's Day Collection of Short Stories, Poetry and Prose. "A Taste of Heaven" in Beauty in Darkness, a Literary Tribute to TS Woolard, and "The Lights" in Confessions from the Think Tank, Volume 1. A Kid's

Space Camp Charity Anthology. Concept by Editor Rob Tannahill. All Published by Dark Moon Rising Publications. You can also find her poem "Leon" in Sleeve of Hearts, Poems, edited by Lindsey Goddard, and brought to you by the Weird Wide Web. Other published shorts by Megan Guilliams include: "Over Easy" in Dark Harvest an Ecohorror Anthology, Published by Twisted Dreams Press, "House of Shadows" in The Stranger at my Window, Published by Baynam Books Press, and "But... I Jest" in Tales From the Lark Side A Horror Comedy Anthology, Published by Weird Wide Web and Edited by Lindsey Goddard.
https://www.amazon.com/stores/Megan-Guilliams/author/B0CTP2D7XD

Maximiliano Guzmán

Maximiliano Guzmán (b. 1991, Recreo, Catamarca, Argentina) is the author of the novella Hamacas (Zona Borde Editorial) He serves as an editor for the digital magazine La Tuerca Andante (Argentina) and has published short fiction across magazines in Argentina, Chile, Ecuador, Peru, Mexico, Uruguay, Cuba, Croatia and the United States

Van Haney

After being a child actor and growing up in the film industry, Van Haney craved the bizarre, horrific, and macabre. She also has a thriving TikTok where she tells ghost stories and has previously been published in An Anthology of Young Poets and recognized in the Books of Horror Short Smack. Van also has three books on Amazon, as well as a short story.

Kasey Hill

Kasey Hill is a critically acclaimed, versatile writer from Franklin County, VA, known for her work in several genres, including urban

fantasy, horror, thriller, paranormal romance, and metaphysical/New Age topics. She has
authored both fiction and non-fiction, with a particular interest in Wicca.

Her fiction often dives into the supernatural and the macabre, blending mythological elements with modern storytelling. She has published multiple novels, poetry collections, and short stories. Notable works include her Guardians of Light series in the mythology fantasy genre and her poetry, which has received recognition for its depth and emotional resonance. As she grows in the horror genre, she has a particular penchant for Southern Gothic/Appalachian Gothic storytelling, such as her Adult Horror novel Devil's Claw and her Young Adult horror series, The Whispering Spirits, featuring The Haunting at Foxwood Village and Dark Coven. She has several Horror short stories circulating for anthologies and Ezines, featuring her unique style of worldbuilding.
www.kaseyhillauthor.com
www.facebook.com/kaseyhillauthor
www.instagram.com/kaseyhillauthor
www.tiktok.com/kaseyhillauthor
www.amazon.com/stores/Kasey-Hill/author/B00O2WT210

Maryjane Hill
Maryjane Hill is a fifteen-year-old aspiring writer from Virginia. She has one children's story book out called Bella the Vampire. This is her first short story publication.

Toshiya Kamei
Toshiya Kamei (she/her) is a queer Asian writer who takes inspiration from fairy tales, folklore, and mythology.

Basile Lebret

While he's French and lives south of Paris, Basile Lebret writes in English. Since it first sprouted in 2022, his work has now spread to over twenty publications in the US, the UK, France or Canada. The most recent include The Perfect Day by WATG Press, Life, Death, and Transmutations by Dark Moon Rising Publications, Lowell & Benson's The Dichotomy of Love and Squirm Books' Skin Deep. Soon in The Anthropocene Epic by Beyond the Stars Press. His first collection Welcome to Valenton has just come out courtesy of Carnage House. Find him on any network: @evoripclaw

Kevin LeCompte

Kevin LeCompte is a high school English teacher who loves stories of all genres, though he tends to lean towards horror because he grew up in the 80's and was sneaking out of bed to watch scary movies way before he should have been. He loves to read obsessively and learn from writers who are currently doing it best.

Mark Mackey

Mark Mackey is a long-time resident of Chicago, Illinois, with no plans to relocate elsewhere, either city or state. Has written tales included in various anthologies and co-written the Soulless, a harrowing horror novel commencing on an ocean liner and concluding on a mysterious island.
https://www.amazon.com/stores/Mark-Mackey/author/B0054EB7PY

Trisha Ridinger McKee

Trisha Ridinger McKee is the author of 16 books and over 100 published works. Her work has appeared in publications including: Chicken Soup for the Soul, Travel Magazine, Night to Dawn, Deep Fried Horror, Crab Fat Literary, and many more. She lives in a small town with her family, including her bulldog and mastiff.

DW Milton

DW Milton is a pen name. The author has a day job but would rather be writing speculative fiction.

Michael Errol Swaim

Michael Errol Swaim is a horror and fantasy author. His first horror publication can be found in issue three of the e-zine Carnage House, and his stories and poems also appear in The Horror Zine, Flash Phantoms, Mocking Owl Roost, the Weird Wide Web podcast, and multiple anthologies by publishers such as Hellbound Books, Dark Moon Rising Publications, and Wicked Shadow Press. He is a member of the Cherokee Nation and lives in Northeast Oklahoma with his wife Mandy, his kids, and his cat, Wolfgirl. His first extreme horror novella, Absorbed By Excrement, is available from Amazon.

www.ingramcontent.com/pod-product-compliance
Lightning Source LLC
LaVergne TN
LVHW091116080826
845145LV00008B/1936

* 9 7 8 1 9 7 2 5 9 6 0 3 6 *